100 Reasons to Celebrate

We invite you to join us in celebrating Mills & Boon's centenary. Gerald Mills and Charles Boon founded Mills & Boon Limited in 1908 and opened offices in London's Covent Garden. Since then, Mills & Boon has become a hallmark for romantic fiction, recognised around the world.

We're proud of our 100 years of publishing excellence, which wouldn't have been achieved without the loyalty and enthusiasm of our authors and readers.

Thank you!

Each month throughout the year there will be something new and exciting to mark the centenary, so watch for your favourite authors, captivating new stories, special limited edition collections...and more!

Dear Reader

Hi, there. Would you believe I have been writing romances for twenty-five years? Amazing! Not that I was published all that time. My first book didn't appear till 1990. You have no idea how excited I was to finally become an author for Mills & Boon. They are great publishers, who are currently celebrating their one-hundred-year anniversary. That's an even more amazing achievement! My congratulations go to them, and to their wonderful editors, who continue to deliver quality romances for you to read.

I hope you enjoy my latest story, THE GUARDIAN'S FORBIDDEN MISTRESS, which is mostly set in Sydney. My hero is an ex-bad boy—a popular theme of mine. And my heroine is a darling. This fast-paced, very sexy story has a deeply emotional core and a highly dramatic ending on a tropical island. May it leave you breathless!

Miranda Lee

THE GUARDIAN'S FORBIDDEN MISTRESS

AND

THE MAGNATE'S MISTRESS

Miranda Lee

MILLS & BOON®

Pure reading pleasure

First published in Great Britain 2008
Harlequin Mills & Boon Limited,
Eton House, 18-24 Paradise Road, Richmond, Surrey TW9 1SR

© Harlequin Books S.A. 2008

The publisher acknowledges the copyright holder of the individual works as follows:

THE GUARDIAN'S FORBIDDEN MISTRESS © Miranda Lee 2008
THE MAGNATE'S MISTRESS © Miranda Lee 2004

ISBN: 978 0 263 86417 5

Set in Times Roman 10½ on 13 pt.
02-0408-82295

Printed and bound in Spain
by Litografia Rosés S.A., Barcelona

CONTENTS

Miranda Lee is Australian, living near Sydney. Born and raised in the bush, she was boarding-school-educated and briefly pursued a career in classical music, before moving to Sydney and embracing the world of computers. Happily married, with three daughters, she began writing when family commitments kept her at home. She likes to create stories that are believable, modern, fast-paced and sexy. Her interests include meaty sagas, doing word puzzles, gambling and going to the movies.

Recent books by this author:

BLACKMAILED INTO THE ITALIAN'S BED
THE RUTHLESS MARRIAGE PROPOSAL
PLEASURED IN THE BILLIONAIRE'S BED

THE GUARDIAN'S
FORBIDDEN
MISTRESS

PROLOGUE

'MORE coffee?'

Nick shook his head before casting a speculative glance at his one-time boss and long-time best friend.

They were sitting on the back terrace of Ray's magnificent Point Piper mansion, enjoying a leisurely lunch together as they always did whenever Nick returned to Sydney.

Ray had asked all the right questions about Nick's island resort project, and had seemed genuinely thrilled when Nick told him it was going to be huge success. He'd promised to fly up and see the place in the near future.

But Nick had a nose for trouble. Always had, right from his childhood days.

'Is there something wrong, Ray?' he asked quietly.

Ray turned his head towards Nick, his grey eyes clouding over.

'Nothing I can put my finger on,' came his guarded reply. 'But I have this gut feeling that I'm not long for this world.'

Nick was totally taken aback. 'Have you been to see a doctor?'

'I had a full check-up not long back.'

'And?'

Ray shrugged. 'I was advised to lose a few pounds. And to drink a little less.'

'But there's nothing seriously wrong with you?'

'Not that they could see without more invasive tests.'

'Have you been feeling unwell?'

'No. Not really. But you can't live for ever, Nick.'

'You're not old, Ray.'

'I'm sixty-one this year.'

So that's it, Nick thought. Ray was finally going through the mid-life crisis which most men went through at forty or fifty.

'I've decided to redo my will,' Ray announced. 'I should have done it after Jess died. But I just couldn't seem to get round to it.'

'You're not going to go leaving *me* anything, I hope,' Nick warned. 'You've already done enough for me, Ray.'

Hell, Ray had been responsible for giving him his chance in life—making sure he got an education, then giving him a job when no one else would. And that was just for starters. Ray had taught him everything he needed to know to succeed in the entrepreneurial and the entertainment world. To top it off, he'd given Nick the unique opportunity to invest in a movie which had been Australia's most successful to date.

Outback Bride had been one of those films which no one had wanted to back beforehand but which everybody wished they had afterwards. It had made Ray a massive fortune up to date, with Nick's meager five percent investment raking in over twenty million so far.

'I thought you might like the Rolls,' Ray said. 'It still runs like a charm. I do realise you prefer sports cars these days, but there's nothing to touch a Rolls-Royce.'

Nick smiled. 'Okay. You can leave me the Rolls.' Man, but he loved that car. He'd spent countless hours in his youth washing and polishing it, feeling like a prince every time he'd sat behind the wheel. The only minus had been the chauffeur's uniform he'd had to wear.

Nick hadn't liked that. Hadn't liked the way some people treated him when he was wearing it. As if he wasn't their equal. But he'd never told Ray that.

Ray, of course, had always treated him like an equal. There again, Ray was a man in a million. Nick thought the world of him.

'I'd like to name you as executor of my will,' Ray went on. 'If you don't mind, that is.'

'Of course I don't mind,' Nick replied. 'I'd be glad to do it.'

'Good. I'd also like to make you Sarah's legal guardian till she reaches the age of twenty-five.'

Nick stiffened in his chair for a split second. Until he reminded himself that this was just a hypothetical role. Sarah was some years away from turning twenty-five.

Also, the odds of Ray dying before he turned seventy were extremely remote.

Yet it was possible, he supposed. If by some incredibly unfortunate occurrence Ray did die in the foreseeable future, things could get very awkward indeed.

Nick had been avoiding his friend's one and only daughter ever since she'd shown up at Christmas lunch that year, looking very different from the thin, gawky, teenager of the year before.

Talk about the ugly duckling turning into a swan!

Where had those luscious curves come from? And that long, blonde-streaked hair? And that incredibly sexy walk?

Her eyes had been different, too.

Up till then Nick hadn't thought of Sarah's eyes as particularly beautiful. Cat-shaped and a murky green colour, they had seemed deeply set under thick straight brows, with dark shadows around them which had often given her a tired look.

Suddenly, under finely plucked brows and with the right makeup, they'd taken on an exotic beauty which was very striking.

Nick had looked into those eyes and been struck with a case of instant lust which had made even *him* feel shockingly guilty. Things had gone from bad to worse later that day, when she'd collared him under some mistletoe and given him a kiss which was as sweet and innocent as she basically still was, despite her physical transformation.

His reaction to her kiss had been far from innocent, however. It had taken all of his will-power not to pry her lips open and send his tongue deep into her oh-so-sweet mouth.

If she'd known what other forbidden thoughts had filled his head she would not have looked up at him with such hero-worship.

Knowing his own character better than anyone, Nick had steered well clear of Sarah after that, cleverly keeping his visits to Ray's home to those times when she was away at boarding school.

Except for Christmas Day, which inevitably drew him back to the one home where he felt accepted and respected.

But he'd always brought a girlfriend with him after that episode under the mistletoe. Which was just as well as with every passing year Sarah was becoming even more desirable to him.

As Nick gazed down the terrace steps at the pool below, an image filled his mind. That of another incident, last Christmas, when Sarah had sashayed down the terrace steps towards the pool below, wearing an extremely brief emerald-green bikini that had raised his testosterone level considerably.

He'd been in the pool himself at the time, trying to keep cool on what had to have been the hottest Christmas Day on record. Unfortunately Jasmine hadn't been in the water with him. She hadn't wanted to get her hair wet.

No such reservations for Sarah. She'd stepped up to the side and dived straight in, surfacing too close to him for comfort, her lovely green eyes sparkling with pleasure as she'd slicked back her long blonde hair and smiled at him.

'Want to have a race?' she'd said, reminding him of the many times when they'd done just that, during the years when he'd been her father's chauffeur and she'd been just a kid.

The trouble was she wasn't a kid any more. And he wasn't a chauffeur. He could have any woman he wanted these days. Except Sarah. Who looked like a woman, but wasn't.

But, hell on earth... He'd wanted her at that moment. Way, way too much.

He'd seen the hurt in her eyes when he'd made some lame excuse and climbed out of the pool. Had felt her eyes burning into his back as he'd reached for a towel and hurried off.

By the time she'd emerged from the pool, he'd collected Jasmine and left.

He hadn't seen Sarah since.

But he would see a lot of her if Ray died and he became her guardian.

'You don't seem too pleased about the prospect,' Ray said. 'Look, I know it's a lot to ask, but—'

'Not at all,' Nick broke in hurriedly. 'You know I'd do anything for you, Ray. I just wonder if I'm the best man for such a job.'

'Why? Because of your lack of fathering experience?'

'That, and other things.' *Like, I'm having enough trouble keeping my hands off your daughter as it is.* But how could he say that?

Nick could not have borne to have Ray look at him

with dislike and disgust. His mentor's trust and faith in him meant a lot to him.

'Don't you think Flora and Jim would be better suited?' he suggested.

Ray's housekeeper and her handyman husband had been with Ray for years. Although childless, they were decent people, and would make better parental substitutes than an ex-bad boy.

'I don't agree,' Ray said. 'They're not family.'

'Neither am I.'

'You're like a son to me, Nick. Look, I know exactly what's bothering you.'

Nick's head jerked back. 'You do?'

'Yeah. A man would have to be deaf, dumb and blind not to notice that Sarah has a schoolgirl crush on you. Has had for years. But she'll get over that once she leaves that all-girl boarding school and gets out into the big bad world. With her looks, she'll have the boys fighting over her. Not just boys, either. There'll be older men with their eye on my daughter, too. Men with more on their mind than just satisfying their carnal urges. Which is where your real-life experience will come in.'

'I'm not sure I know what you're getting at,' Nick said, struggling to overcome an unexpected stab of jealousy. But he'd honestly never thought about what it might be like to see Sarah with a boyfriend. Or, heaven forbid, some older guy...

The image did not sit well on him.

'You know the dark side of life, Nick,' Ray explained. 'You've seen it first-hand.'

And *lived* it first-hand, Nick could have added.

'You know what some men will do to get their hands on the kind of money which will one day be Sarah's.'

Nick nodded.

'The road to personal happiness is very hard for an heiress,' Ray continued. 'I hate to think what might happen to her if I die and she suddenly finds herself too rich at a tender age.'

'Ray, I think you're worrying for nothing. You'll probably live till you're a hundred.'

Ray shrugged. 'It's possible, I suppose. But to be on the safe side I intend structuring my will so that Sarah doesn't inherit my estate till she turns twenty-five. All she will get up till then is her educational expenses, which will also cease once she becomes employed.'

Nick frowned. 'That seems a little harsh.'

'I don't believe in children being given great sums of money. Sarah has to learn that money doesn't grow on trees.'

'What about this house?'

'I will instruct that you can live here, rent-free, till it becomes Sarah's. Naturally I will expect you to let Sarah live here, too, if she wishes.'

'You do realise Sarah could contest such a will?'

'She won't. Not unless she falls into the hands of some scoundrel. Your job will be to protect my little girl from the scoundrels of this world, Nick. The fortune-hunters, the con-men. And the corrupt.'

'That could be a tall order.'

'I have every faith in you. You are caring, and you have the intelligence and the necessary degree of cynicism to keep Sarah safe.'

Nick winced. 'I never thought of my cynicism as a virtue.'

'It's not usually. But my daughter is way too trusting. She needs a guardian who won't take her admirers at face value. And who won't turn a hair at having them investigated if needs be.'

Nick had to laugh. 'Set a thief to catch a thief? Is that it?'

Ray's expression carried surprise. 'Don't tell me you still think of yourself as a scoundrel.'

Nick shrugged. 'You can take the boy off the street. But you can never take the street out of the boy.'

'You're not a boy any more. You're a man—a fine man. I can't tell you how proud of you I am.'

Nick's heart contracted. 'I wish you'd stop talking like you're about to die any second, Ray. You have a good twenty years left in you at least.'

'I hope you're right. But if you're not and I am… Promise me that you'll look after my little girl till she turns twenty-five, Nick. Give me your word.'

Nick did the only thing he could do under the circumstances. He looked Ray straight in the eye and gave him his word.

But at the back of his mind he began hoping and praying that he would never have his word put to the test…

Nick had only been back on Happy Island for three weeks when the telephone call came from Ray's housekeeper. Between sobs, Flora choked out that Ray had passed away the night before.

'Can you fly home, Nick?' came her plaintive request. 'I know Ray made you executor of his will. He told me. He made you Sarah's guardian as well, didn't he?'

Nick closed his eyes against the wild mixture of emotions which consumed him. Shock. Grief. Frustration.

Life was both cruel and perverse, he decided.

But then, he already knew that.

'Sarah needs you, Nick,' Flora added. 'She doesn't have anyone else.'

This was true. Ray and Jess had had their only child rather late in life, after almost giving up on ever having a baby. Sarah had no siblings, and her grandparents on both sides were now deceased. Ray had been an only child, and Jess had only had one brother—a black-sheep bachelor who only ever came round when he wanted money. The bastard hadn't even bothered to come to his sister's funeral.

'The poor love is just devastated,' Flora sobbed.

Nick suddenly saw that his lust for Sarah simply had to be contained—and ignored. For he could not let Ray down. Or Sarah, for that matter. The last thing she needed was some sleazebag guardian taking advantage of her. Nick was pretty sure Ray hadn't had seduction on his list of things he wanted Nick to do for his daughter.

'I'll charter a plane straight away,' he told Flora briskly. 'Is Sarah still at school?'

'Yes.'

'Best she stays there till I get home. And, Flora, don't worry about the funeral arrangements. I'll attend to that.'

'God bless you, Nick.'

Nick wasn't sure he would ever have God's blessing. But neither did he aim to start batting for the other side.

The devil could take temptation when it came to Sarah. From this moment on she was off-limits, sexually speaking.

Ray had said to protect her from the scoundrels of this world.

Well, that obviously included him!

CHAPTER ONE

Seven years later...

A FROWN formed on Sarah's forehead as she watched Derek turn from the crowded bar and slowly make his way back to their table, a full champagne glass in each hand.

In the time it had taken him to be served, she'd begun to worry about having accepted his invitation for a Christmas drink.

Sarah comforted herself with the thought that in the six months Derek had been her personal trainer, he'd never made a pass, or crossed the line in any way, shape or form.

But there was a definite twinkle in his eye as he handed her a glass, then sat down with his.

'This is very nice of you,' she said carefully.

Sarah's heart sank when he beamed back at her.

'I *am* nice,' he said. 'And no, I'm not coming on to you.'

'I didn't think you were,' she lied before taking a relieved sip of the bubbly.

'Yes, you did.'

'Well...'

Derek laughed. 'This is just a little celebratory drink. One you deserve after all your hard work. But do be careful over the Christmas break. I don't want you coming back to me at the end of January in the same shape you were in six months ago.'

Sarah pulled a face at the memory. 'Trust me. I won't ever let that happen again.'

'Never say never.'

Sarah shook her head as she put down her glass. 'I've done a lot of thinking while you've been working my blubbery butt off these past few months, and I've finally come to terms with the reason behind my comfort-eating.'

'So what's his name?' Derek asked.

'Who?'

'The reason behind your comfort-eating.'

Sarah smiled. 'You're a very intuitive man.'

Derek shrugged. 'Only to be expected. Gay men are very *simpatico* to matters of the heart.'

Sarah almost spilled her wine.

'You didn't suspect at all, did you?'

Sarah stared across the table at him. 'Heavens, no!'

'I dislike guys who advertise their sexual preference by being obvious, or overly camp. Other gays sometimes guess, and the odd girl or two.'

'Really?' Even now that she knew the truth, Sarah couldn't detect anything obviously gay in Derek. Neither could any of the women who worked out at the gym, if the talk in the female locker room was anything to go by. Most of the girls thought him a hunk.

Whilst Sarah conceded Derek was attractive—he had nice blue eyes, a great body and a marvellous tan—she'd never been attracted to fair-haired men.

'So now that you know I'm not making a beeline for you,' Derek went on, 'how about answering my earlier question? Or do you want to keep your love life a secret?'

Sarah had to laugh. 'I don't have a love life.'

'What, none at all?'

'Not this last year.' She'd had boyfriends in the past. Both at university and beyond. But things always ended badly, once she took them home to meet Nick.

Next to Nick, her current boyfriend always came across as lacklustre by comparison. Time after time, Sarah would become brutally aware that she wanted Nick more than she ever did other men. Nick also had the knack of making comments that forced her to question whether her boyfriend was interested in her or her future inheritance.

Yet Sarah didn't imagine for one moment that Nick undermined her relationships for any personal reasons. That would mean he cared who she went out with. Which he obviously didn't. Nick had made it brutally obvious since becoming her guardian that he found the job a tiresome one, only to be tolerated because of his affection for and gratitude to her father.

Oh, he went through the motions of looking after her welfare, but right from the beginning he'd used every opportunity to shuffle her off onto other people.

The first Christmas after she'd left school, he'd sent her on an extended overseas holiday with a girlfriend and her family. Then he'd organised for her to live on campus during her years at university, where she'd specialised in early-childhood teaching. When she'd graduated and gained a position at a primary school out in the western suburbs of Sydney, he'd encouraged her to rent a small unit near the school, saying it would take her far too long to drive to Parramatta from Point Piper every day.

Admittedly this was true, and so she had done as he suggested. But Sarah had always believed Nick's motive had been to get her out of the house as much as possible, so that he was free to do whatever he liked whenever he liked. Having her in a bedroom two doors down the hallway from his was no doubt rather restricting.

A well-known man-about-town, Nick ate women for breakfast and spat them out with a speed which was breathtaking. Every time Sarah went home he had a different girlfriend installed on his arm, and in his bed, each one more beautiful and slimmer than the next.

Sarah hated seeing him with them.

Last year Sarah had restricted her home visits to Easter and Christmas, plus the winter school break, during which Nick had been away, skiing. This year she hadn't been home since Easter, and Nick hadn't complained, readily accepting her many and varied excuses. When she finally went home on Christmas Eve tomorrow, it would be nearly nine months since she'd seen Nick in the flesh.

And since he'd seen her.

The thought made her heart flutter wildly in her chest.

What a fool you are, Sarah, she castigated herself. Nothing will change. Nothing will ever change. Don't you know that by now?

Time to face the bitter truth. Time to stop hoping for a miracle.

'His name his Nick Coleman,' she said matter-of-factly. 'He's been my legal guardian since I was sixteen, and I've had a mad crush on him since I was eight.' She refused to call it love. How could she be in love with a man like Nick? He might have made a financial success of his life in the years since they'd first met, but he'd also become cold-blooded and a callous womaniser.

Sometimes Sarah wondered if she'd imagined the kindnesses he'd shown her when she was a child.

'Did you say eight?' Derek asked.

'Yes. He came to work for my father as his chauffeur on my eighth birthday.'

'His chauffeur!'

'It's a long story. But it wasn't Nick who started my eating binge,' she confessed. 'It was his girlfriend.' The one who was there draped all over him last Christmas, a drop-dead gorgeous, super-slender supermodel who'd make any female feel inadequate.

A depressed Sarah had eaten seconds at Christmas lunch, then had gone back for thirds. Food, she'd swiftly found, made her feel temporarily better.

By Easter—her next visit home—she'd gained ten kilos. Nick had simply stared at her. Probably in shock. But his new girlfriend—a stunning-looking but equally skinny actress this time—hadn't remained silent, making a sarcastic crack about the growing obesity problem in Australia, which had resulted in Sarah gaining another five kilos by the end of May.

When she'd seen the class photo of herself, she'd taken stock and sought out Derek's help.

Now here she was, with her hour-glass shape possessing not one skerrick of flab and her self-esteem firmly back in place.

'Amend that to two girlfriends,' Sarah added, then went on to fill in some more details of her relationship with her guardian, plus the circumstances which had led up to her coming to the gym.

'Amazing,' Derek said when she stopped at last.

'What's amazing? That I got so fat?'

'You were never fat, Sarah. Just a few kilos overweight. And lacking in tone. No, I meant about your being an heiress. You don't act like a rich bitch at all.'

'That's because I'm not. Not till I turn twenty-five, anyway. My father made sure in his will that I won't get a dime till I reach what he called a mature age. For years I had my educational and basic living expenses paid for, but once I could earn my own living I had to support myself, or starve. I was a bit put out at first, but I finally saw the sense of his stand. Handouts don't do anyone any good.'

'That depends. So this Nick fellow lives in your family home, rent-free?'

'Well, yes… My father's will said he could.'

'Till you turn twenty-five.'

'Yes.'

'When, exactly, does that happen?'

'What? Oh, next February. The second.'

'At which point you're going to turf that blood-sucking leech out of your home and tell him you don't want to see his sorry behind ever again!'

Sarah blinked, then laughed. 'You've got it all wrong, Derek. Nick doesn't need free rent. He has plenty of money of his own. He could easily buy his own mansion, if he wanted to.' In actual fact, he'd offered to buy hers. But she'd refused.

Sarah knew the house was way too big for a single girl, but it was the only connection she still had to her parents, and she simply could not bear to part with it.

'How come this Nick guy is so flush?' Derek asked. 'You said he was your father's chauffeur.'

'*Was* being the operative word. My dad took him under his wing and showed him how to make money, both on the stock market and in the business world. Nick was very lucky to have a man like my father as his mentor.' Sarah considered telling Derek about Nick's good fortune with *Outback Bride* but decided not to. Perhaps because it made Nick look as though he hadn't become success-ful in his own right. Which he had. 'Have you ever been to Happy Island on a holiday?' she said instead.

'No. But I know about it.'

'Nick borrowed money and bought Happy Island when it was going for a song. He personally supervised the remodelling of its largely derelict resort, built an airport on it, then sold the whole shebang to an international equity company for a fortune.'

'Lucky man.'

'Dad always said luck begins and ends with hard work. He also advised Nick that he'd never become rich working for someone else.' Which was why Nick had set up his own movie production company a couple of years back. He'd already had some success but nothing yet to rival *Outback Bride*.

'Your dad's right there,' Derek said. 'I hated it when I had a boss. That's why I started up my own gym.'

'You own The New You?'

Derek gave her a startled look. 'Don't tell me you didn't know that either.'

'No.'

He smiled, showing flashing white teeth. 'Talk about tunnel vision.'

'Sorry,' Sarah apologised. 'I can be like that. I'm a bit of a loner, if you haven't noticed,' she added with a wry smile. 'I don't make friends easily. Guess it comes from being an only child.'

'I'm an only child too,' he confessed. 'Which makes my being gay especially hard on my parents. No grand-kids to look forward to. I only told them a couple of years ago when Mum's pressuring me to get married got a bit much. Dad hasn't talked to me since,' Derek added, the muscles in his neck stiffening.

'That's sad,' Sarah said. 'What about your mum?'

'She rings me. But won't let me come home, not even for Christmas.'

'Oh, dear. Maybe they'll come round in time.'

'Maybe. But I'm not holding my breath. Dad is a very proud and stubborn man. Once he says something, he won't back down on it. But back to you, sweetie. You're simply crazy about this Nick fellow, aren't you?'

Sarah's heart lurched. 'Crazy describes my feelings for Nick very well. When I'm around him, I just can't stop wanting him. But he doesn't want me back. And he never will. It's time I accepted that.'

'But surely not till you've had one last crack at him.'

'What?'

'You haven't been working your butt off because some anorexic model said you were fat, sweetie. It's Nick you're out to impress, and attract.'

Sarah didn't want to openly admit it. But of course Derek was right. She'd do anything to have Nick look at her with desire. Just once.

No, not once. *Again.* Because she was pretty sure she'd spotted desire in his eyes one Christmas, when she'd been sixteen and she'd come down to the pool wearing an itsy-bitsy bikini that she'd bought with Nick in mind.

But maybe she'd imagined it. Maybe she was just

desperate to believe he'd fancied her a little that day, despite his actions to the contrary. Teenage girls were prone to flights of fantasy, as were twenty-four-year-olds, she thought ruefully. Which was why she'd spent all week buying the kind of summer wardrobe that would stir an octogenarian's hormones.

The trouble was Nick wasn't an octogenarian. He was only thirty-six, and he kept his male hormones well and truly catered to. Sarah already knew that the actress girlfriend had gone by the board, replaced by an advertising executive with a penchant for power-dressing.

Sarah might not have been home personally for several months, but she rang home every week to talk to Flora, who always gave her a full update on Nick's comings and goings before passing the call over to Nick. If he was home, that was. Often he was out, being a social animal with a wide range of friends. Or contacts, as he preferred to call them.

'I presume you spend the Christmas holidays back at home?' Derek asked, cutting into her thoughts.

'Yes,' she said with a sigh. 'I usually go home as soon as school breaks up. But I haven't this year. Still, I'll have to make an appearance tomorrow. I always decorate the Christmas tree. If I don't do it, it doesn't get done. Then I help Flora prepare things for the following day. The lunch is partially catered for, but Flora likes to cook some hot food as well. Flora is the housekeeper,' she added when she saw Derek frown at the name. 'She's been with the family for forever.'

'I have to confess I couldn't see your Nick with a girl-friend named Flora.'

'You'd be right there. Nick's girlfriends always have names like Jasmine, or Sapphire, or Chloe.' That was what the latest one was called: Chloe.

'Not only that,' Sarah went on waspishly, 'they never help. They always just swan downstairs at the last minute, with their fingernails perfect and their mi-nuscule appetites on hold. It gets my goat when they sit there, sipping mineral water whilst they eat abso-lutely nothing.'

'Mmm,' Derek said.

Sarah pulled a face at him. 'I suppose you think I'm going to get all upset and make a pig of myself again.'

'It's highly possible, by the sounds of things. But what I was actually thinking was that you need someone by your side at this Christmas lunch. A boyfriend of your own.'

'Huh! I've brought boyfriends to Christmas lunch before,' Sarah informed Derek drily. 'In no time, Nick makes them look like fools, or fortune-hunters.'

'And maybe they were. But possibly they were too young, and totally overawed by the occasion. What you need is someone older, someone with looks and style, someone successful and sophisticated who won't be fazed by anything your playboy guardian says and does. Someone, in short, who's going to make the object of your desire sit up and take notice. Of you.'

'I like the idea, Derek. In theory. But even with my improved looks, I don't think I'm going to be able to snaffle up the type of boyfriend you've just described at this late stage. Christmas is two days away.'

'In that case let me help you out. Because I know just such an individual who doesn't have anywhere to go on Christmas Day and would be happy to come to your aid.'

'You *do*? Who?'

'You're looking at him.'

Sarah blinked, then laughed. 'You have to be kidding. How can *you* be my boyfriend, Derek? You're gay!'

'You didn't know that till I told you,' he reminded her. 'Your Nick won't know it, either, especially if I'm introduced as your boyfriend. People believe what they're told, on the whole.'

Sarah stared at Derek. He was right. Why would Nick—or anyone else at lunch—suspect that Derek was gay? He didn't look it. Or act it.

'So what do you think?' Derek said with a wicked gleam in his eyes. 'Trust me when I say that nothing stimulates a man's interest in a woman as well as another man's undivided attention in her.'

Sarah still hesitated.

'What are you afraid of?' Derek demanded to know. 'Success?'

'Absolutely not!'

'Then what have you got to lose?'

Nothing at all, Sarah realised with a sudden rush of adrenalin. At the very least she would not feel alone, as she often did at Christmas, especially during that dreaded lunch.

This year she would not only be looking her best, but she would also have a very good-looking man by her side.

'All right,' Sarah said, a quiver of unexpected excitement rippling down her spine. 'You're on.'

CHAPTER TWO

SARAH's positive attitude towards Christmas lasted till she pulled her white car into the driveway the following morning and saw Nick's bright red sporty number parked outside the garages.

'Darn it,' she muttered as she pressed the remote to open the electronic gates.

She'd presumed Nick would be out playing golf, as he always did every Saturday, come rain, hail or shine. Come Christmas Eve as well!

If she'd imagined for one moment that Nick would be home, she'd have put on one of her sexy new sundresses this morning—probably the black and white halter-necked one that showed off her slender shoulders and nicely toned arms. Instead, she was sporting a pair of faded jeans and a striped yellow tank-top. Suitable clothes in which to decorate a Christmas tree. But not to impress a man, especially one who had a penchant for women who always looked as if they'd just stepped out of a beauty salon.

Still, with a bit of luck, she might be able to sneak up to her bedroom and make some changes before running into Nick. The house was, after all, huge.

Built in the 1920s by a wealthy mining family, Goldmine had been renovated and revamped many times since then. Its original stone walls were now cement-rendered white, with arched windows and lots of balconies, which gave it a distinctly Mediterranean look.

Because of the sloping site, the house looked double-storeyed from the road, but there was another, lower level at the back where the architecture incorporated a lot of glass to take advantage of the home's harbourside position.

Actually, there weren't many rooms in the house that didn't look out over Sydney Harbour, the view extending across the water to the bridge and the opera house in the distance. On the upper floor, all the bedrooms had individual balconies with water views, the master bedroom opening out onto a walled balcony that was big enough to accommodate an outdoor table-setting.

The enormous back terrace had the best vantage point, however, which was why it was always the place for Christmas lunch. Long trestle-style tables would be brought in, shade provided by huge canvas blinds put up for the day. Only once in Sarah's memory, when the temperature soared to forty degrees, had the lunch been held inside, in the family room, the only room large enough to accommodate the number of guests who swamped Goldmine every Christmas Day from midday onwards.

The tradition had been started by Sarah's father and

mother soon after they'd bought the house nearly thirty years ago, a tradition her father continued after her mother's death, and which Nick seemed happy to honour in the years he'd been living there.

Of course, the cynic in Sarah appreciated that Christmas lunch at Goldmine was more of a business lunch these days than a gathering of family and long-term friends. Most of the guests at the table would be the people Nick did business with, valuable contacts whose priorities were where the next few million were coming from.

Sarah was under no illusion that Nick was any different from the types he mixed with. He liked money as much—possibly more—than they did.

This last thought reminded Sarah of what Derek had implied over drinks last night: that Nick was taking advantage of his position as her guardian to live, rent-free, in her harbourside home. Although she'd defended Nick in this regard, Sarah had to concede that living in Goldmine was a huge social advantage. Not so much because of its size—some of the neighbours' homes were obscenely large—but because of its position. There was no doubt that having such an address had benefited Nick no end in the business stakes. Which was why he wanted to buy the place.

The gates finally open, Sarah drove through and parked next to Nick's car. She frowned over at it, still perplexed that he hadn't gone to golf today.

Thinking about golf, however, reminded her of the

Christmas present she'd bought him. It was a set of minia-ture golf clubs, with the club heads made in silver, the shafts in ebony and the bag crafted in the most beautiful red leather. She'd bought it on eBay and it had cost several hundred dollars, more than she usually spent on him.

The moment she'd seen it, she'd known Nick would like it.

But would he think it odd that she'd bought him something so expensive?

She hoped not.

Sarah grimaced when she realised he might think it even odder that she hadn't bought her new 'boyfriend' anything at all. Which she hadn't. She and Derek had discussed when he was to arrive tomorrow and what to wear, but they hadn't thought of presents.

Sarah sighed, her confidence about this subterfuge beginning to drop.

Not that it mattered all that much. She couldn't seri-ously expect to achieve the miracle of having Nick suddenly look at her and be carried away on a wave of uncontrollable desire. Why should that happen now, after all these years? It wasn't as though she hadn't dolled herself up for him before. She had. With abso-lutely no results at all.

The truth was she obviously wasn't his type. Even with her normally lush curves pared down to the bone, she'd never look or act like the kind of girlfriend Nick inevitably chose and obviously preferred: not only super-slim, but also super-chic and super-sophisticated.

A kindergarten teacher just didn't cut it with Nick, even with a future fortune attached. If anything, that she was her father's heiress was probably a turn-off for him. Nick would not like any reminders that he wasn't entirely a self-made man. Or the fact that she'd known him when he was a nobody.

With every new girlfriend, Nick came with a clean slate.

Sarah had no doubt he hadn't told this latest girl, Chloe, that he'd ever been in jail. Or that his ward's father had been a very generous benefactor. She felt sure Nick always represented her father these days as a long-term friend, thereby explaining his guardianship of her.

Sarah accepted these brutally honest thoughts with a mixture of emotions. There was disappointment, yes. But also a measure of relief. Because it made her realise that to harbour hopes of attracting Nick this Christmas was a case of desperation and delusion. It wasn't going to happen.

Whilst this realisation brought a pang of emotional pain—no one liked to have their longest and fondest dream dashed—the acceptance of reality also began to unravel the tight knots in her stomach. What she was wearing today no longer mattered. She could relax now and act naturally with Nick, which she would not have done with her previous pathetic agenda.

Sarah might have called Derek right then and there and cancelled his coming tomorrow, if she hadn't already told Flora when she rang last night that there'd be an added guest for Christmas lunch; her new boy-friend, Derek. Although Nick had been out at the time, Sarah had no doubt that Flora would have told Nick this news at breakfast this morning. Flora was a dear lady, but inclined to gossip.

No, there was nothing for it but to go through with this charade now.

'You'll probably be glad, come tomorrow,' Sarah told herself as she climbed out of the car and walked round to open the hatchback. Nick's new girlfriend sounded like a right bitch, if Flora's character assessment was to be believed. When Sarah asked what she was like, Flora had said she was up herself, big time.

'Just as good-looking as the last one,' Flora had added, 'but more intelligent. And doesn't she know it! Still, she won't last any longer than the others. Six months is tops for our Nick. After that, it's out with the old and in with the new. If that boy ever settles down, I'll eat my hat.'

Sarah pulled a face as she lifted her two bags out of the boot.

She would, too.

Nick was definitely not a marrying man; never had been and never would be. He wasn't into romance, either. Catering to his sexual needs was the name of his game where women were concerned.

Once Nick got bored with his latest game-partner, she was out.

He'd once admitted to Sarah when she'd been about

twelve—they'd just watched a very sweet romance on
TV together—that he could never fall in love the way
the characters had in that movie. He'd confessed rather
grimly that he didn't have any idea what that kind of
love felt like.

Sarah presumed his inability to emotionally connect
with women had something to do with his loveless upbringing, a subject she'd overheard being discussed by
her parents not long before her mother died. Apparently,
Nick had suffered terribly at the hands of a drunken and
abusive father, running away to live on the streets of
Sydney when he'd been only thirteen. After that, he'd
been reduced to doing some pretty dreadful things just
to survive.

Sarah never did find out exactly how dreadful, but
she could guess.

Just after turning eighteen, Nick had finally been
arrested—for stealing cars—and had been sentenced to
two years in jail.

It was during this term that he'd finally been shown
some kindness, and given some practical help. By a
man who'd spotted his natural intelligence, a man who,
for years, had generously given up many hours of his
time to help those less fortunate.

Nick was put into a special education programme for
inmates that this man had funded, and became one of
their most successful graduates, achieving his higher-
school certificate in record time.

That man had been her father.

'Sarah!'

Sarah almost jumped out of her skin at her name being called.

But when she saw who it was, she smiled.

'Hi there, Jim. You're looking well.' Flora's husband had to be over sixty by now. But he was one of those wirily built men who aged well and always moved with a spritely step.

'Got a lot of luggage there, missie,' he said, joining her behind her car and staring down at her two very large bags. 'Home for good, are you?'

'Not yet, Jim. Did you get me a good tree?'

'Yep. A beauty. Set it up in the usual spot in the family room. I put the boxes of decorations next to it. And I've hung up the lights out the back.'

'Great. Thanks, Jim.'

Jim nodded. He wasn't one for chit-chat, unlike his wife.

Jim was happiest when he was working with his hands. He loved keeping the extensive grounds at Goldmine spick and span, not such a difficult job after her father had come home from a visit to Tokyo a decade ago and had all the more traditional flower beds and lawns ripped out and replaced with Japanese-style gardens. Now there were lots of rocks and gravel pathways, combined with ponds and water features, all shown to advantage by interesting trees and plants.

Jim hadn't been too thrilled at first with the lack of

grass and flowers, but he'd grown to appreciate the garden's unique beauty and serenity.

Jim picked up Sarah's bags without her asking and started heading along the curved path towards the front porch, putting paid to her earlier plan to sneak in unnoticed through the garages.

To be honest, Sarah still wished she looked better for Nick's first sight of her. It would have been rewarding to see the surprised look on his face.

Sighing, she grabbed her carry-all from the passenger seat, locked the car and hurried after Jim, who by then had dropped her bags by the front door and rung the doorbell.

'I do have keys,' she said, and was fishing through her bag in search of them when the door was wrenched open.

Not by Flora—but by Nick.

If ever Sarah was glad she was wearing sunglasses it was at that moment.

Not because of Nick's reaction to her, but because of her reaction to him.

She'd been so caught up with worrying about her own appearance that she'd forgotten just how devastatingly attractive she found him, especially when he was wearing as little as he was wearing today: just board shorts and a sleeveless white surf top, the colour highlighting his beautifully bronzed skin.

Sarah's thankfully hidden gaze travelled hungrily down his body then up again before fixing on his mouth.

If Nick's black eyes hadn't been so hard, and his other

features strongly masculine, his mouth might have made him into a pretty boy. Both his lips were full and sensual, curving around a mouthful of flashing white teeth, their perfection courtesy of the top-flight dentist her father had taken him to as soon as he'd been let out of prison.

If Sarah had any criticism, it was of his hair, which she believed he kept far too short. Still, the buzz-cut style did give him an intimidating look that probably worked well for him in the business world.

'Well, hello, stranger,' he said, his dark eyes sweeping down to her sneakered feet, then up again.

Not a hint of admiration in *his* expression, however, or even surprise. No reaction at all. Zilch.

His lack of reaction—she'd been expecting some sort of compliment—exasperated Sarah. What did she have to do to make the man notice her, damn it?

'Thanks, Jim,' he said, bending to pick up her bags. 'I'll take these now.'

'Yes, thanks, Jim,' Sarah managed to echo through clenched teeth.

Jim nodded, then moved off, by which time Nick had picked up her luggage and turned to carry it inside.

Sarah wanted to hit him. Instead, she gritted her teeth even harder.

Suddenly, she couldn't wait to turn twenty-five. The sooner she got Nick out of her life, the better. He was like a thorn in her side, niggling away at her. How could she have what she wanted most in life—which was children of her own—if he was always there, spoiling things for her? How could she feel completely happy when she kept comparing every man she dated to him?

Out of sight would be out of mind. Hopefully.

Sarah closed the front door after her, smothering a sigh when she saw Nick heading for the stairs with her cases.

'I can take those up,' she said, desperately needing a few minutes away from the man to regain her composure.

As much as Sarah had subconsciously always known that nothing would ever come of her secret feelings for Nick, finally facing the futility of her fantasies was a soul-shattering experience.

He hadn't even noticed that she'd lost weight!

All that work. For *nothing*!

'It's no trouble,' he threw over his shoulder as he continued on up the stairs with the bags.

Sarah gritted her teeth, and hurried up the stairs after him. 'Why aren't you at golf?'

'I wanted the opportunity to talk to you,' he tossed back at her. 'Privately.'

'About what?'

He didn't answer her, instead charging on ahead with her bags.

'About what, Nick?' she repeated when she caught up, frustrated by his lack of reply.

He ground to a halt on the top landing, dropped her bags then turned to face her.

'Flora, for one thing.'

'What about her? She's not ill, is she?'

'No, but she can't do what she used to do. She gets

very tired. This last year, I've had to hire a home-cleaning service to come in twice a week to do all the heavy cleaning for her.'

'I didn't realise.'

'If you came home occasionally,' Nick pointed out drily, 'you might have noticed.'

It was a fair comment, evoking a large dose of guilt. Sarah recognised she'd been very self-obsessed this past year. But she'd been on a mission. A futile mission, as it turned out.

'I…I've been very busy,' she said by way of an excuse.

'With the new boyfriend, I take it?' came his next comment, this one quite sarcastic.

Sarah bristled. 'I have a right to a social life,' she retorted, taking off her sunglasses so that she could glare at him. '*You* have one.'

'Indeed. But it doesn't take over my whole existence.'

His critical tone was so typical of Nick when it came to her having a boyfriend, his condemning attitude often sparking a reckless rebellion in her that had her running off at the mouth.

Today was no exception.

'Derek and I are very much in love. Something *you* could never identify with. When people are truly in love they want to spend every minute of every day with them.'

'I'm surprised you came home today at all, then,' he countered quite sharply. 'Or will your lover be dropping by later?'

Sarah flushed. 'Derek's working today.'

'Doing what?'

'He owns a gym.'

'Aah. That explains it.'

'Explains what?'

'Your new shape.'

So he *had* noticed! 'You say that like there's something wrong with it.'

'You looked fine the way you were.'

Sarah's mouth dropped open. 'You have to be joking! I was getting fat!'

'Don't be ridiculous.'

Sarah rolled her eyes. Either the man was blind, or he cared about her so little that he'd never really looked at her before.

'Maybe you just didn't notice.'

Nick gave an offhand shrug. 'Maybe I didn't. Still, I suppose it's not up to me to tell you what to do.'

'I'm glad you've finally realised that!'

'Meaning?'

'I couldn't count the number of times you've interfered in my life, and my relationships. Every time I brought a boyfriend home in the past, you went out of your way to make him feel stupid. And me to boot.'

'I was only doing what your father asked me to do, Sarah. Which was to protect you from the money-grubbing creeps in this world.'

'They weren't money-grubbing creeps!'

'Indeed they were.'

'I'll be the judge of that from now on, thank you very much.'

'Not till your twenty-fifth birthday, madam. I have no intention of letting you fall into the hands of some gold-digging gigolo at this late stage. I wouldn't be able to sleep at night if I did that.'

'Huh. I can't see you ever losing any sleep over me.'

'Then you'd be dead wrong, sweetheart,' he grated out.

Their eyes met, with Sarah sucking in sharply at the momentary fury she glimpsed in Nick's face. It came home to her then just how much he'd hated being her guardian all these years. No doubt he would be very relieved when she turned twenty-five next year and his obligation to her father was over.

'I haven't given you that much trouble, have I?' she said, her softer voice reflecting her drop in spirits.

As much as she accepted Nick would never be attracted to her, she'd always thought that, underneath everything, he liked her. Not just because she was her father's daughter, but because of the person she was. When she was younger, he'd often told her what a great kid she was. He'd said she had character, and a good heart. He'd also said she was fun to be with, proving it by spending a lot of his spare time with her.

Of course, that had been a long time ago, before Nick had become a success in his own right. When that started to happen, he'd begun to ignore her. Then, after her father died, the rot had set in completely. It was patently obvious that she was now reduced to nothing more than a responsibility, a responsibility that he obviously found both tedious and exasperating.

'Does he know how rich you're shortly going to be?' he demanded to know.

Sarah's mouth thinned. Here we go again, she thought angrily.

Yet there was no point in lying. Better she answer Nick's questions now than to have him put Derek through the third degree on Christmas Day.

'He knows I'm going to be rich,' she bit out. 'But he doesn't know the full extent of my inheritance.'

'He'll know once he shows up tomorrow. People who live in this street have to be multimillionaires at least. It won't take him long to put two and two together.'

'Derek's not a fortune-hunter, Nick. He's a very decent man.'

'How do you know?'

'I just know.'

'My God, you know nothing!' he flung at her. 'Your father thought he was protecting you with his will. Instead, he set you up for disaster. He should have given most of his money away, donated it to some charity, not left it in the hands of a girl such as you.'

'What do you mean, a girl such as me?'

He opened his mouth to say something but then obviously thought better of it. Instead, he picked up her bags and carried them along the hallway to her room, the stiff set of his shoulders very telling. After dumping her cases just inside the door, he retreated back out into the hallway.

'We'll continue this discussion later,' he said in that deceptively quiet manner he always adopted on the odd occasion when he was in danger of losing his cool.

Over the years Sarah had learned to recognise this tactic of his. Nick hated losing his temper. Hated losing control. He preferred to act like the consummate ice-man, both professionally and personally. She'd rarely heard him yell. He didn't even swear any more, as he once had.

But his body language could speak volumes. So could his eyes.

Though not always. He did have the ability to make them totally unreadable. But not straight away. If you were watching him closely, you could sometimes glimpse what was going on in his head before he drew the blinds down.

'We'll have morning tea in the kitchen,' he pronounced, 'then we'll adjourn to my study and talk.'

'Not about Derek,' Sarah retorted. 'I have no intention of listening to you criticising someone you haven't even met.'

'Fair enough. But I have lots of other things to talk to you about, Sarah. Important issues connected with your inheritance. I want to have everything settled before Christmas.'

'But I don't turn twenty-five till February,' she protested. 'We have the rest of my summer break to settle things!'

'No, we don't. I won't be here.'

'Where will you be?'

'I'm spending most of January on Happy Island.'

Sarah's heart sank. She knew Nick had a holiday house there. But he rarely used it at this time of year.

'Flora never said anything about that when I called.'

'The subject probably didn't come up.'

'There's still the week between Christmas and New Year,' she argued, feeling very put out with Nick's choosing to go away for so long.

'Yes. But I'm having a guest stay during that week. And you have your new boyfriend, who you freely admit you wish to spend every minute of every day with. Better we settle everything whilst we have the chance.'

'But I have to decorate the tree today.'

'I just want a couple of hours, Sarah. Not all day.'

'What about tonight? Can't this wait till tonight?'

'I'm going present-shopping tonight.'

Sarah sighed. Wasn't that just like a man to go present-shopping at the last minute?

'Come on,' he said abruptly. 'Let's go downstairs.'

'I need to go to the bathroom first,' she said quite truthfully.

'Fine,' he replied with another offhand shrug. 'I'll go ahead and tell Flora to put on the kettle.'

Sarah shook her head as she watched Nick go. Derek didn't know what he was talking about. Dolling herself up tomorrow and sucking up to a pretend boyfriend wasn't going to make a blind bit of difference. She was nothing to Nick but an obligation that he obviously wanted over and done with. It was clear to Sarah that he couldn't wait for her twenty-fifth birthday to arrive.

Suddenly, she felt the same way. She was sick and tired of letting her feelings for Nick distress her. Sick and tired of secretly pining for what would never be.

Time to move on, girl. Time to get yourself a life. One that doesn't include Nick!

CHAPTER THREE

FLORA was in the kitchen, cutting up the caramel slice she'd made that morning, when Nick walked in with a face like thunder.

'Wasn't that Sarah at the door?' she asked.

'Yep. She won't be long. You can put on the kettle.'

Flora turned to pop the caramel slice back in the fridge before switching on the electric kettle. 'It's good to have her home,' she said. 'Isn't it?'

Nick scowled as he slid onto one of the four stools fronting the black marble breakfast bar. 'Speak for yourself, Flora.'

'Come, now, Nick. You've missed her. You know you have.'

'I know no such thing. Ray was out of his mind to make me that girl's guardian. I'll breathe a huge sigh of relief when February comes round, I can tell you.'

'I suppose it has been a big responsibility,' Flora agreed. 'Especially considering how much money she's going to inherit. What do you make of this new boyfriend of hers? Do you think he's on the up and up?'

'Who knows?'

'It's strange that she hadn't mentioned him before last night, don't you think? It makes me wonder what's wrong with him.'

'I've just been thinking the same thing. I guess we'll just have to wait and see.'

'I guess so,' Flora said. 'So how does she look?'

'What do you mean?'

'She told me last night that she'd been exercising and had lost weight. Don't tell me you didn't notice.'

'Yeah, I noticed.'

'And?' Flora asked, exasperated with Nick's reluctance to elaborate. He was just as bad as Jim sometimes. Why was it that men didn't like to talk? It would be nice to have Sarah home, just so she had someone to chat with occasionally.

'I thought she looked fine the way she was.'

'Isn't that just like a man? They never want the women in their life to change. Aah, there she is, the girl herself. Come over here, love, and give old Flora a hug.'

Sarah's heart squeezed tight when Flora enveloped her into a tight embrace. It had been a long time since anyone had hugged her like that.

There'd been no hug from Nick this morning. Not even a peck on the cheek. He never touched her, except accidentally.

Her gaze slid over Flora's shoulder to land on the man

himself. But he wasn't looking her way. He was staring down at the black bench top, looking highly disgruntled.

Probably wishing he were at golf.

'Oh, my,' Flora said when she finally held Sarah out at arm's length. 'You *have* lost quite a few pounds, haven't you? Still, now you can have a big piece of your favourite caramel slice without feeling guilty,' she added before turning away to open the fridge. 'I made it for you first thing this morning.'

'You shouldn't have, Flora,' Sarah chided, but gently.

'Nonsense. What else do I have to do? Did you know that the whole of the Christmas lunch is being catered this year? Nick says it's too much for me. All I'm allowed to do is make a couple of miserable puddings. I ask you!'

She rolled her eyes at Sarah, who was thinking to herself that Flora had aged quite a bit this past year. Her face was very lined and her hair had turned totally grey.

'Not that I'm complaining, Nick,' Flora went on. 'I do know I'm getting older. But I'm not totally useless yet. I could easily have baked a leg of pork and a turkey. And some nice hot veggies for those who don't like salad and seafood. Still, enough of that. What's done is done. Now, sit up there next to Nick, Sarah, and tell us all about your new boyfriend whilst I pour the tea.'

Sarah smothered a groan, but did as she was told, though she didn't sit right next to Nick, leaving one stool between them.

'What would you like to know?' she asked with brilliant nonchalance.

'How old is he, for starters?'

Sarah realised she had no idea.

'Thirty-five,' she guessed. One year younger than Nick.

Nick's head swung her way. 'Handsome?'

'Very. Looks like a movie star.'

Was she crazy, or did Nick's eyes glitter when she said that?

'How long have you been seeing each other?' Flora asked.

Sarah decided to use the truth as much as possible. 'We met shortly after last Easter. I hired him as my personal trainer.'

Nick made a small scoffing sound.

Sarah ignored him.

'Why haven't you mentioned him before?' Flora asked.

Sarah winced. She should have realised she'd get the third degree about Derek, from both Nick and Flora. Again, she decided to stick to the truth as closely as she could.

'We haven't been boyfriend and girlfriend all that time,' she replied. 'That's a more recent development. He asked me out for a drink one night after my workout, one thing led to another and…well, what can I say? I'm very happy.'

Sarah smiled, despite the lurch within her chest.

'And very healthy, too,' Flora said with a return smile. 'Don't you think so, Nick?'

'I think she looks like she could do with some of your caramel slice.'

Sarah found a laugh from somewhere. 'That's funny coming from you. All your girlfriends have figures like rakes.'

'Not *all* of them. You haven't met Chloe, have you?'

'I haven't had the pleasure yet.'

'You will. Tomorrow.'

'How nice.'

'You'll like her.'

'Oh, I doubt it. I never like any of your girlfriends, Nick. The same way you never like any of my boy-friends. I've already warned Derek.'

'Should I warn Chloe?'

Sarah shrugged. 'Why bother? It won't change anything.'

'Will you two stop bickering?' Flora intervened. 'It's Christmas, the season of peace and love.'

Sarah almost pointed out that Nick didn't believe in love, but she held her tongue. Sniping at Nick was not in keeping with her resolution to move on. But he'd really got under her skin with his remarks about her being skinny.

When Flora presented a plate full of caramel slice right in front of her, she couldn't really refuse. But she did take the smallest piece and proceeded to eat it very slowly between long sips of tea. Nick chose the biggest portion, devoured it within seconds, then had the gall to take a second salivating slice. The lucky devil had one of those metabolisms that allowed him to eat whatever he liked without getting fat. Of course, he did work out with weights every other day, and swam a lot.

Although thirty-six now, he didn't carry an extra ounce of fat on his long, lean body. Really, other than some muscling up around his chest and arms, Nick hadn't changed much since the day they'd met.

Physically, that was. He'd changed a good deal in other ways, matching his personality to suit whatever company he was in, sometimes warm and charming, at other times adopting a confident air of cool sophistication and *savoir-faire*, both personas a long way from the introverted and rather angry young man he'd been when he'd first come to live at Goldmine.

Though he was never angry with me, Sarah recalled. Never. He had always been sweet, kind and generous with his time. He'd made a lonely little girl's life much less lonely.

Oh, how she'd loved him for that!

Sarah much preferred the Nick of old to the one sitting beside her today.

In the beginning, when he'd launched himself into the business world, she'd admired his ambition. But success had made Nick greedy for the good life, feeding on hedonistic pleasures that were as fleeting as they were shallow. Other than the holiday house on Happy Island, he owned a penthouse on the Gold Coast and a chalet in the southern snowfields. When he wasn't working at making more money, he flitted from one to the other, always accompanied by his latest lady-love.

Whoops, no. Amend that to latest playmate. Love was never part of Nick's lifestyle.

Her father had always said how proud of Nick he was. He'd lauded Nick's work ethics, his intellect and his entrepreneurial vision.

Sarah could see that, professionally, there was much to be proud of. But surely her father would have been disappointed, if he'd been alive today, at the way Nick conducted his personal life. There was something reprehensible about a man whose girlfriends never lasted longer than six months, and who boasted that he would never marry.

No, that was unfair. Nick had never boasted about his inability to fall in love. He'd merely stated it as a fact.

Sarah had to concede that at least Nick was honest in his relationships. She felt positive he never spun any of his girlfriends a line of bull. They'd always known that their role in his life was strictly sexual and definitely temporary.

'Glad to see you're still capable of enjoying your food.'

Nick's droll remark jolted Sarah out of her reverie, her stomach contracting in horror once she realised she'd consumed a second piece of caramel slice without being aware of it.

She kept her cool, however, determined not to let Nick needle her further.

'Who could resist Flora's caramel slice?' she tossed at him airily. 'Next Christmas we'll get back to having a smaller Christmas lunch, Flora, and you can cook whatever you like.'

'You won't keep your father's tradition going?' Nick asked in a challenging voice.

'Is that what you think you've been doing, Nick?' she countered. 'When Dad was alive, Christmas lunch was a gathering of true friends, not a collection of business acquaintances.'

'Is that so? I think perhaps you're mistaken about that. Most of your father's so-called friends were business contacts.'

Nick was right, of course. But people had still liked her father for himself, not just for what they could get out of him. At least, she liked to think so.

But maybe she was wrong. Maybe she'd seen him through rose-coloured glasses. Maybe, underneath his *bonhomie*, he'd been as hard and cynical as Nick.

No, that wasn't true. He'd been a kind and generous man.

Not a brilliant dad, though. During her years at boarding-school he'd often made excuses for not being able to come to school functions, all of those excuses related to work. Then, when she came home for school holidays, she'd largely been left to her own devices.

If she was strictly honest, things hadn't been much better when her mother was still alive. A dedicated career woman, Jess Steinway had been totally unprepared for the sacrifices motherhood entailed upon the arrival of an unexpected baby at forty. Sarah had been raised by a succession of impersonal nannies till she went to kindergarten, after which Flora had taken over as carer before and after school. But Flora, warm and chatty though she was, had mostly been too busy with the house to do much more than feed Sarah and make sure she did her homework.

No one had spent quality time with her, or played with her, till Nick had come along.

She turned her head to look at him, a wave of sadness washing through her. Oh, how she wished he was still their chauffeur, and she the little girl who could love him without reservation.

Tears pricked at her eyes, right at that moment when Nick's head turned her way. She quickly blinked them away, but not before she glimpsed regret in his.

'Sorry,' he muttered. 'I didn't mean any disrespect for your father. He was a good man and a very generous one. Christmas was his favourite time of year. Did you know that every Christmas he gave huge donations to the various charities round Sydney for the homeless? Because of him, they always had a proper Christmas dinner. And no one, especially the children, went without a present.'

Sarah frowned. 'I didn't know that.' She knew about his good work with young prisoners. And he'd given lots of money to cancer research and cancer support groups. There were a few hospital wings named after him, too. But he'd never mentioned his Christmas donations. 'I hope his estate is continuing with that tradition, Nick. Do you know if it is?'

'It wasn't written into his will, so I do it in his name every year.'

'You?'

'Don't sound so surprised. I am capable of generous gestures, you know. I'm not totally selfish.'

'I…I never said you were.'

'But you think it. And, generally speaking, you'd be right.'

'Don't be so modest, Nick,' Flora piped up. 'You should see the huge plasma television Nick bought Jim and me a few weeks ago, for no reason at all except that he thought we'd like it. It has surround sound and its own built-in DVD. You can tape any number of shows and watch them later, when you have time. Jim's in seventh heaven, watching cricket and tennis at all hours of the day and night.'

'Why do you think I bought it?' Nick quipped. 'Had to do something to stop my right-hand man from spending every summer's day glued to that TV, when he should be outside working. My motivation was purely selfish, I assure you. And don't be expecting anything too expensive for Christmas, because I'm flat broke now.'

'Oh, go on with you,' Flora said laughingly.

'Don't laugh. I've made two dud movies already this year. And I'm damned worried about the one coming out in the New Year. We've had a couple of test audiences view it and they said the ending was way too sad. The director reluctantly agreed to reshoot it with a happy ending, but I've decided to go with his original vision. If this one flops, I might have to come to Sarah here for a loan.'

Sarah was shocked by this news. She knew better

than anyone that Nick's ego would not survive becoming poor again. 'I can give you as much as you need, come February. And it won't be a loan, either.'

'Lord, what am I going to do with this girl, Flora? I hope you haven't made any similar offers to this boyfriend of yours. Don't ever give a man money, Sarah,' he told her sternly. 'It brings out the worst in them.'

Sarah shook her head at him. 'How many times do I have to tell you? Derek doesn't want my money.'

'He will, when he sees how much you've got.'

'Not every man is a fortune-hunter, Nick. Now, if you don't mind, I do not wish to discuss Derek any further. I know there's no convincing you that no man could possibly love me for myself and not my money, so I'd prefer not to try.'

'Hear hear,' Flora agreed. 'I agree with Sarah. Another piece of caramel slice, love?'

The ringing of Nick's cellphone was a welcome interruption, not only to his incessant questioning about Derek, but also to her escalating exasperation. Tomorrow was not going to be a pride-saving exercise. It was going to be hell!

'Hi there,' she heard Nick say in that voice he reserved for girlfriends. 'Yeah, that'd be great, Chloe. OK. I'll pick you up tonight at seven. Bye.'

He clicked off his phone and slipped off the stool. 'Sorry, folks. Change of plan. Chloe's had a last-minute invitation to a Christmas Eve party at some bigwig's place, so I'll have to dash out and do my present-shopping now. We'll have to put off that talk till I get back, Sarah.'

'Fine,' she said, pretending not to care. But she did. She cared a lot. Not about the talk so much but about his going out this afternoon, then going out with Chloe tonight. Pathetic, really. The way she would accept the crumbs of his company.

'Don't forget I want a new car,' Sarah called after him as he walked away. 'A yellow one.'

Nick stopped walking, then glanced over his shoulder at her. 'Yellow,' he repeated drily. 'Any particular make?'

She named a top-of-the-range model. 'Of course. What else?'

When he smiled his amusement at her, Sarah's heart lightened a little. It was still there, that special bond between them. Because they *knew* each other.

Chloe didn't know Nick. Not the real him. She only knew the man who had graced the cover of Australia's leading financial newspaper last year.

'I'll see what I can do,' he said. 'Bye, girls.'

'Bye,' Sarah trilled back, smiling on the outside whilst inside she was already sinking back into the pit, that moment of pleasurable intimacy wiped away in the face of where Nick would be going tonight.

Do not succumb to jealousy, she lectured herself, or depression. Do not let him do this to you!

'You don't still have a thing for Nick, do you, love?'

Flora's softly delivered question was almost Sarah's undoing.

Gulping down the sudden lump in her throat, she

straightened her spine and adopted what she hoped was a believable expression. 'No, of course not.'

'That's good. Because it would be a mistake. There's no future for any woman with a man like Nick.'

Sarah laughed a dry little laugh. 'Don't you think I know that, Flora?'

'This Derek chap, is it serious between you two?'

Sarah hesitated to answer for a second too long.

'I didn't think so,' Flora said. 'You would have told me about him sooner, if that were the case.'

'Don't tell Nick,' she blurted out.

Flora's eyes narrowed. 'Is this Derek a real boyfriend or not?'

Sarah bit her bottom lip. She knew it would be wiser to lie, but she couldn't, not to Flora's face.

'He…he's just a friend.'

Flora gave her a long, searching look. 'What game are you playing at, girlie?'

Sarah sighed. 'Nothing bad, Flora. I just wanted to bring someone to the Christmas lunch and Derek volunteered. I'm sick and tired of Nick's girlfriends looking down their noses at me.'

'So it's a matter of female pride, is it?'

'Yes; yes, that's exactly what it is.'

'You do realise Nick is going to give this poor Derek the third degree?'

'Yes, he's prepared for that.'

Flora pulled a face. 'I hope so. Because Nick takes his job as your guardian very seriously, love.'

'Derek can hold his own.'

'None of your other boyfriends could.'

'Derek's not a real boyfriend.'

'But he's pretending to be one.'

'Yes.'

Flora sighed. 'Good luck to him, then. That's all I can say.'

CHAPTER FOUR

SARAH decorated the Christmas tree on automatic pilot, her mind still on Flora's last words.

Flora was right, of course. Derek was going to be in for a rough time tomorrow.

But I did warn him, she reminded herself. And he still wanted to do it. In fact, he seemed to find the prospect of pretending to be my boyfriend an exciting challenge.

Sarah was beginning to find the thought terrifying. Nightmarish possibilities kept popping into her mind. What if Nick somehow discovered that Derek was gay? Or that their so-called relationship was just a sham? How could she explain such a crazy deception? Surely saving her pride wasn't worth the risk of feeling more of a fool in front of him.

And in front of Chloe.

Chloe…

Already she didn't like the woman and she hadn't even met her.

Nick had implied earlier that Chloe wasn't as skinny as his usual girlfriend. Was she blonde as well?

She would have to ask Flora later for a more detailed description.

Finally, all of the ornaments and lights were hung, except for the star that went on top of the tree. A glance at her watch showed that it was ten past six, way past time for a toasted sandwich and some coffee. She'd bypassed lunch after having eaten two pieces of that dreaded caramel slice, believing that they would easily sustain her for the whole afternoon.

Serious hunger pangs told her she'd been wrong. But the Christmas star came first.

Sarah climbed up the stepladder once more, this time having to go up on tiptoe to reach the right spot.

'That's a great-looking tree.'

Sarah jumped at the unexpected sound of Nick's voice, the star dropping from her hands as the back feet of the ladder lifted off the floor and she began to over-balance forwards. How Nick managed to save her she'd never know, but one second she was about to crash head-first into the tree, the next the ladder was abruptly righted and she fell backwards into Nick's arms.

'Oh, lord!' she gasped, her arms flailing wide whilst his wound tightly around her back, pulling her hard against his chest.

'You're all right,' he told her.

Her arms finally found a home around his neck, her heart thudding loudly behind her ribs.

'You…you frightened the life out of me,' she blurted out.

'Sorry. Didn't mean to.'

Sarah opened her mouth to say something more, *anything* to defuse the excitement that had instantly been sparked by finding herself in Nick's embrace. Such physical closeness, however, was not conducive to sensible brain activity, her mind going totally blank when his dark eyes dropped down to her softly parted lips.

For several, highly charged seconds Nick just stared at them.

Time seemed to slow around her, the air stilling whilst her pounding heart suspended its beat, her eyes closing as her head tipped invitingly sideways.

He was going to kiss her. She was sure of it!

To suddenly find herself being lowered onto her feet came as a shock.

'Oh,' she cried out, her eyes flying open to discover Nick frowning down at her with nothing but concern in his face.

'Steady now,' he said.

Sarah could have cried. Clearly, she was so *desperate* in her infatuation with this man that she'd conjured up passion where there was none. Not on his part, anyway.

'I'm fine, thank you,' she said curtly, pride demanding she cool her overheated blood and still that foolish, treacherous heart of hers.

'For a second there, I thought you were going to faint.'

'Faint? Why on earth would I faint?'

'Some girls do, after a shock.'

'I'm fine,' she reiterated.

'In that case, how about thanking me for saving you from a nasty fall?'

'Which you caused in the first place,' she pointed out stroppily. 'What are you doing home, anyway? I thought you were going to a party at seven. It's not far off that now.'

'Chloe forgot to tell me that it was black-tie. So I came home to change.'

Sarah had seen Nick in a dinner suit. Of course, he looked devastatingly handsome. Jealousy jabbed at her as she thought of Chloe on his arm tonight, then possibly in his bed…

Sarah's stomach somersaulted at the thought.

'I'm surprised you're not going out tonight yourself,' Nick said.

'What? Oh, yes, well…Derek wanted to take me somewhere, but I…I told him I'd be too busy with the tree and present-wrapping.' She was babbling and stammering! Why, oh, why did she have to think about Nick with Chloe?

'You should do what I do,' Nick said. 'Only buy presents at shops that do free gift-wrapping.'

And in shops where some smitten female sales assistant did all the choosing for him as well, Sarah thought ruefully.

'I'd better get going,' Nick went on. 'See you at present-opening in the morning. And before you ask, no, Chloe will not be in attendance. So you won't have to sulk.'

'I never sulk,' Sarah snapped.

'Oh, yes, you do, madam. But I agree with you on one score: some of my girlfriends have not been all that nice to you. Still, that's because most of them are jealous.'

'Of *me*?' Sarah could not have been more surprised.

Nick's smile was wry. 'How would you like to discover that your Derek was living with an attractive young female ward? Now I really must go,' he pronounced abruptly, and spun away.

'We still haven't had that private talk,' she called after him.

He stopped and glanced over his shoulder at her, his body language impatient. 'I realise that. It'll just have to wait till after Christmas Day.'

'But won't Chloe be here then?'

Nick had said this morning that he had a guest between Christmas and New Year. Who other than his current girlfriend?

'Chloe and I don't need to spend every minute of every day together,' he said rather pointedly. 'See you in the morning, Sarah.'

Sarah watched him stride across the family room, then leap up the two steps that led to the foyer. She heard him run up the stairs, depression descending at the sound of his hurrying to take out his girlfriend.

'I'm glad Derek is coming tomorrow,' she muttered under her breath.

'Talking to yourself is never a good idea, love.'

Sarah turned, then smiled at Flora. 'I have some of my best conversations with myself.'

'Better than that tea towel you used to talk to when you were a child, I suppose.'

Sarah stared at Flora. 'You knew about that?'

'Nothing much gets by me, love. So was the tea towel your other self? Or a special friend?'

'A special friend,' she confessed.

'Boy or girl?'

'Um…boy. Sort of.'

'He wasn't called Nick, was he?'

Sarah flushed.

'Like I said, love,' Flora continued as she went over and turned the switch that lit up the tree, 'nothing much gets by me. My, now, that is one lovely tree.'

'Jim chose a really good one this year.'

'He did indeed. Was that Nick I heard a minute ago?'

'Yes. He came home to change. The party's black-tie.'

'I'm not surprised. Chloe's a social climber, if ever there was one.'

Sarah shook her head. 'She sounds awful. What on earth does Nick see in her?'

'What does Nick see in any of his girlfriends? I suppose he doesn't much care about their characters as long as they're beautiful and do whatever he wants them to do in bed. He doesn't keep any of them, after all.'

'Flora! I've never heard you talk like this about Nick before.'

Flora shrugged. 'I'm getting old, I guess. When you get old you say things you wouldn't dare say before. Don't get me wrong. I'm very fond of Nick. But where women are concerned, he's bad news. He's never made a pass at you, has he, Sarah?'

'What? Me? No, never!'

'Just as well, with you having that crush on him.'

'I'm over that now.'

'You might think you are, but he'd still be able to turn your head, if he tried.'

Flora had never said a truer word. 'Why would he bother, when he has the likes of Chloe in his bed?'

Flora wrinkled her nose. 'I suspect Madame Chloe is fast reaching her use-by date. I'd watch myself, if I were you, when you swan downstairs tomorrow wearing one of those sexy new dresses of yours.'

Sarah's mouth dropped open. 'How do you know about them?'

'Couldn't sit around doing nothing all afternoon, so I unpacked for you. Which one are you wearing tomorrow? The red and white one, I'll bet.'

'Flora, you're an old sticky-beak!'

Flora remained quite nonplussed at this accusation. 'How do you think I get to know everything? I also put all those lovely Christmas cards you got from your pupils on your dressing table. Didn't leave room for much else, I'm afraid, so I set out all your new make-up and perfume and skin-care stuff on the vanity unit in your bathroom.'

Sarah didn't know whether to be appreciative, or annoyed. 'So, did everything get your seal of approval?'

'Let's just say I think you'll give Chloe a run for her money in the beauty stakes.'

'I sure hope so.'

'And who knows? Maybe your Derek will take one look at you and decide to take your friendship to a different level.

'Somehow I don't think that's likely to happen.'

'You never know, love. You just never know.'

CHAPTER FIVE

SARAH woke to a less than gentle shake of her shoulder and an unshaven Nick leaning over her. Surprise and shock sent her eyes instantly wide and her heart racing.

'What is it?' she exclaimed. 'What's wrong?'

When he straightened she saw he was already dressed, in jeans and a T-shirt. 'Nothing's *wrong*,' he said.

Then what on earth was he doing in her bedroom at some ungodly hour in the morning?

'Flora sent me to wake you,' he went on, his voice carrying a measure of exasperation.

'What for?' Confusion in her own voice.

'For breakfast and present-giving.'

Sarah blinked. '*This* early?'

'The men with the tables and blinds are due to arrive at nine and it's already eight.'

'Eight!' Sarah sat bolt upright, pushing her hair back from her face as she glanced first at her sun-drenched balcony, then at her bedside clock, which confirmed that it was indeed, just after eight. Yet she had set her alarm for six, wanting to be looking her very best for present-opening with her hair done, make-up perfect and dressed to impress in her sexy new jeans and a very pretty green top.

'I must have slept through the alarm,' she said with a groan.

Or perhaps she'd fallen asleep without actually setting it. She'd stayed up quite late, doing everything she could the night before in preparation for Christmas Day.

'Just get up and come downstairs,' Nick said impatiently before whirling and striding from the room.

'I…I'll be down shortly,' she called after him.

'You'd better be,' he called back.

It wasn't till Nick left that Sarah realised she hadn't wished him a happy Christmas. Still, he hadn't thought to wish her the season's greetings, either. He'd sounded tired and grumpy. Probably hadn't had enough sleep. She hadn't heard him come in last night, so it had to have been very late. Probably went to Chloe's place after the party and…

'Don't think about last night,' she lectured herself aloud. 'Just get up and get on with things.'

Scooping in a deep breath, Sarah threw back the bed-clothes and dashed into the bathroom, where she washed and cleaned her teeth in two minutes flat.

Then she stared at herself in the mirror.

D-Day, she thought with a wild fluttering in the stomach.

In a way it was a good thing that she didn't have time to dress. It would make her transformation later on all the more eye-catching and dramatic.

At the same time, she didn't want to look a total dag.

No time to do much with her hair except brush it, then twist it up into a loose knot on top of her head. Definitely no time for make-up.

Thankfully, her nightie was new and pretty, a lavender satin petticoat that had a matching robe. She slipped the robe on, looped the sash belt and hurried back into her bedroom, only then realising she had nothing suitable for her feet.

She never wore slippers. Sandals didn't seem right and neither did her flip-flops.

Oh, well, it wouldn't be the first time she went downstairs for Christmas breakfast barefooted and in her night things, though usually the latter were a bit longer. This nightie only reached mid-thigh, the robe to her knees. She would have to watch herself when she sat down. At least her legs were nice and smooth, all the way up. Sarah had taken herself off to a beautician late last week and had a full wax. Painful, but worth every penny not to have to worry about shaving for ages.

It felt a bit odd when she wasn't wearing panties, however. Like now, for instance.

Sarah might have slipped some panties on, but there really wasn't time for any more delay. It was already seven minutes past eight. And it wasn't as though anyone would know.

Sarah sucked in one last, long, calming breath, exhaled slowly, then set forth for the staircase.

Breakfast on Christmas morning was always very light; croissants and coffee served in front of the tree during present-opening. The family room in Goldmine was huge, with three distinct sitting areas. The Christmas tree was always placed down the far end, where there were two brown leather sofas facing each other, and a sturdy wooden coffee-table between them.

Everything was set out in readiness by the time Sarah made it downstairs, delicious aromas hitting her nostrils as she padded down the steps into the family room.

Her entry was quiet, due to her bare feet, giving her a second or two to survey the situation and work out in advance where she would sit.

Flora and Jim occupied opposite ends of the sofa facing the terrace, with Nick sitting in the middle of the sofa opposite, sipping coffee. She didn't want to sit next to him, not after what had happened yesterday. She certainly didn't want to sit next to him without her panties on. Physical proximity to Nick made her body—and her mind—go absolutely haywire.

Whilst Sarah was still resolved to go through with her plan to doll herself up for Christmas lunch—and to pretend Derek was her new boyfriend—she no longer held any hope whatsoever that Nick's eyes would be opened to her attractions as a female. She'd come to the dampening conclusion that after her father died Nick had mentally placed her in a box marked 'legal responsibility', thereby killing off any possibility of a personal relationship between them.

Suddenly his head turned her way, his dark eyes travelling swiftly from her tousled hair down to her scarlet toenails before moving back up again.

Was she mistaken, or did his eyes stop to linger on her breasts?

Whatever, her body responded instantly, a tingling feeling spreading over her skin whilst her heartbeat quickened and her nipples peaked alarmingly against the satin.

Sarah swallowed. Surely she was imagining it, as she'd imagined yesterday that he'd been going to kiss her. Yes, of course she was. The man was just looking, the way any man would when a pretty young female presented herself in front of him in her night things. He'd always *looked* at her, just not the way she wanted him to.

'Merry Christmas, everyone!' she trilled, determined not to let the deluding nature of her feelings for Nick spoil present-opening.

Flora and Jim glanced round at once, their kind faces breaking into warm smiles.

'And merry Christmas to you too, love,' Flora returned happily. 'Come on, come over here and sit next to me,' she said, patting the spot next to her.

'Sorry to keep you waiting.' Sarah angled herself past Flora's plump knees to take her place in the middle of the sofa directly opposite Nick. 'I must have slept through my alarm,' she added, once she was safely leaning back with her knees modestly pressed together and her robe arranged to cover as much of her bare thighs as possible.

'That's perfectly all right, love,' Flora said. 'You're here now. Coffee?' she offered, already leaning forward to pick up the coffee-pot.

'Yes, please.' Ignoring Nick—whose eyes had remained on her as she sat down—Sarah picked up a bread plate and helped herself to a croissant. 'Have you all eaten yet?'

'Jim and I have,' Flora said. 'Nick hasn't. He said he wasn't hungry. But I think he's got a hangover.'

'I do *not* have a hangover,' Nick protested. 'I feel fine. I'm just saving my appetite for lunch. But I will have a top-up of coffee, Flora,' he said, putting his mug on the coffee-table and pushing it towards her. 'With cream and sugar. That should keep me going for the next couple of hours.'

'Did you enjoy yourself at the party last night?' Sarah asked before she could snatch the words back. Truly, she was stupid sometimes.

Nick picked up his refilled coffee mug and took an appreciative sip before answering. 'It was a typical party of that type. To be honest, I think I'm partied out at the moment. That's one of the reasons I'm going to Happy Island. So that I can relax and do absolutely nothing for a while.'

'You could do absolutely nothing here,' Sarah pointed out, still hating the thought of his going away.

His dark eyes connected with hers over the rim of the mug. 'I can't, actually.'

'Why not?'

'People will bother me here,' he stated matter-of-factly. *And get in the way of your spending private time with your girlfriend.*

Sarah could picture them skinny-dipping in his swimming pool on Happy Island, making leisurely love in the water and everywhere else in the no doubt luxurious holiday house.

It was a depressing train of thought.

'I think we should get on with present-giving,' Flora suggested. 'Jim, why don't you play Santa this year? Is that OK with you, Sarah?'

'Sure.' She was more than happy to sit there and devour her croissant, telling herself all the while that she would stop at just one. Because if she didn't, she'd be on her way back to Blubbersville.

But she needed the comfort the croissant gave her, needed to combat the dismay which was crushing her at that moment.

It was all so hopeless, Sarah thought wretchedly as she finished the first croissant in no time flat, then picked up another. Nick was never going to be hers. Not in bed, or anywhere else.

But then, you knew that, didn't you? You were a fool to listen to Derek, even for a moment.

Flora's gentle hand on her arm stopped her from stuffing the second croissant into her mouth.

'Perhaps that can wait till after we've opened the presents,' she suggested. 'Pick one of Nick's presents first, Jim, so that Sarah can drink her coffee.'

'Thank you, Flora,' Sarah whispered under her breath as she put down the croissant and picked up her coffee instead.

Jim rose and began moving the pile of presents around, Sarah's stomach contracting when he selected a smallish rectangular gift, wrapped in sparkling gold paper that had Christmas trees all over it.

'That's from me,' she said with false brightness when Jim handed it over to Nick.

Instead of Sarah feeling joyful anticipation at Nick's opening her present, her main emotion now was anxiety over his reaction. Sarah knew he would like it. She just hoped he wouldn't read anything into it. She would hate him to guess how she secretly felt about him. Hate the humiliation that would go with any such discovery.

Nick put down his coffee and ripped off the wrapping paper, frowning when confronted with the plain white cardboard box.

'Not cologne this year?' he said as he struggled to open the tight top, his short nails not helping with the task.

'No,' she replied. 'Do you want me to open it for you?'

'No. I'll get it. Eventually. There. Done.' Nick frowned some more as he upended the box and slid the bubble-wrapped gift into the palm of his hand. 'I have no idea what this could be,' he said with genuine puzzlement in his voice as he unwrapped it.

Sarah found herself holding her breath, rewarded when she saw pure, unadulterated delight fill his face.

'I…I hope you like it,' Sarah said, her cheeks colouring when his eyes lifted to stare over at her. Oh, goodness, she hoped he wasn't jumping to any embarrassing conclusions.

'What is it?' Flora piped up before Nick could answer her. 'Show me.'

Nick placed the miniature golf bag on the coffee-table for everyone to see before shaking his head at her.

'Words fail me, Sarah,' he said. But with amazement, not speculation.

'Look at this, Jim,' Flora said. 'It's a tiny little golf bag, full of the most beautiful little golf clubs.'

Jim leant over to take a closer look. 'It looks expensive.'

'Yes,' Nick agreed. 'It does. You shouldn't have spent so much money on me, Sarah.'

'Oh, it wasn't too dear for a soon-to-be heiress,' she replied airily. 'I thought you deserved something special for having put up with me all these years. The clubs are made from real silver, you know. English silver. They have hallmarks on them.'

'Where on earth did you get it?' Nick asked.

'I bought it on eBay. They have things you just don't see in the shops.'

'It's an exquisite and thoughtful present,' he said as he picked it up again. 'I'll treasure it always.'

Sarah's heart swelled with pleasure. If nothing else, she'd pleased him with her gift today, his genuinely warm reaction lifting her spirits and making her realise that he did care about her. She'd seen the affection in his eyes just now.

If she could not spark his sexual interest, then she would settle for his affection. It was better than nothing. For a while there, over the last few years, she'd begun thinking he didn't even like her any more.

But it was clear that he did. Maybe, once she grew up and got over this mad sexual obsession that had been tormenting her for far too long, they could even become friends again.

'Now it's your turn,' Nick said. 'Jim, give me that box with the red bow on it, please. Yes, that's the one.'

Nick smiled as he handed Sarah the store-wrapped package. 'Sorry it's not quite what you asked for.'

'What are you talking out? Oh, you mean the car. Well, I was only joking, you know. I can't imagine what you've bought me,' she said a bit breathlessly as she removed the bow then lifted the lid off the box.

Inside was a yellow car. A model of the one she'd mentioned to Nick. Not a miniature, but quite a large one. And not cheap, either.

Sarah laughed as she drew it out. 'Look what the wicked devil bought.'

Flora clucked her tongue at Nick. Jim liked it, though, calling it a beauty.

'If you open the driver's door,' Nick said, 'you might find something of more use to a soon-to-be heiress.'

Sarah did as she was told, and discovered a small, rectangular-shaped box made in dark red velvet. She knew, before she opened it, that it contained jewellery, but what?

Nerves claimed her stomach when she started to lift the lid. Nick never bought her jewellery. So why had he this time?

The sight of what was inside took her breath away.

'Oh, my God!' she gasped before gazing with wide eyes up at Nick. 'Tell me they're not real diamonds. Tell me they're zircons, or cut glass.'

'Of course they're real diamonds,' Flora said, leaning over to gaze at Sarah's present.

'They do look expensive,' Jim said, not for the first time that morning.

'Don't you like them?' Nick said drily. 'If you want to return them, I'm sure I still have the receipt somewhere.'

'Over my dead body!' Sarah retorted, snapping the box shut and hugging it to her chest.

Nick smiled. 'I do realise that you have all your mother's jewellery, but what suits one woman doesn't necessarily suit another. I thought these were more you.'

Sarah opened the box again, then picked one of the earrings out of the box for closer viewing. It had a large diamond at the lobe, and two dangling drops of smaller diamonds that shimmered and sparkled with the slightest movement.

'You think I'm a girl who favours flashy jewellery?'

'Diamonds aren't flashy, they're classy. And they never go out of fashion. You can wear them with any outfit.'

'Then I'll wear them today,' she decided immediately. 'To the Christmas lunch.' And I'll make sure Chloe knows who gave them to me, she vowed with uncharacteristic bitchiness.

'Yes, do that,' he agreed, an odd glitter in his eyes.

Sarah wished she knew what was going on in his head. But he was a closed book when he wanted to be.

'I'd like my present from Nick now,' Flora piped up.

'Oooh, did I get diamonds, too?' she added when Jim handed her a beautifully wrapped gift that was almost as small as Sarah's.

'Sorry,' Nick returned. 'I thought you'd prefer sapphires, to go with your pretty blue eyes.'

'Oh, go on with you,' Flora said laughingly.

But he *had* bought her sapphires, in the form of an utterly stunning, sapphire-encrusted watch. Jim got a watch, too, a very expensive gold one. Both were thrilled to pieces.

Sarah had never known Nick spend so much money on Christmas presents. He couldn't possibly be having serious financial worries, she thought with some relief, if he was throwing money around like this.

Flora and Jim seemed to like the gifts Sarah had chosen for them, Flora gushing over her favourite perfume and a cookbook, a new one that featured healthy meals. Jim was notoriously difficult to buy presents for, but a bottle of really rare port, plus a special glass engraved with his name, found favour.

In return, Flora and Jim gave Sarah a truly beautiful photo frame and a lovely feminine diary for the following year. It had pictures of flowers on every page, along with a special thought for the day. Nick became the proud owner of a new leather wallet, along with a very stylish gold silk tie.

'For the rare occasions when you're forced to wear one,' Flora informed him.

Which was, indeed, rare. Nick looked drop-dead gorgeous in a tux, or any suit for that matter. But he hated wearing them. He much preferred casual clothes. When circumstance demanded, he did wear a business suit, but he mostly teamed it with an open-necked shirt, or a crew-necked designer top. Only when protocol insisted on a tie did he wear one.

Around the house, he lived in shorts and jeans. Like now. Of course, he would change for Christmas lunch into a smart pair of trousers and an open-necked shirt, its length of sleeve depending on the weather. Today the forecast was for twenty-eight degrees, a very pleasant temperature for this time of year.

Sarah was glad it wasn't going to be cool, or rainy, as she would have frozen in her outfit.

'OK, folks,' Nick said, and abruptly stood up. 'Time to clean up the mess we've made here and shake a leg. Jim, I'll need your help getting everything ready outside. But Flora, you're not to rush around working yourself into a lather like you usually do. The caterers are due here at ten. All they require is a clean kitchen. They're providing everything, right down to the crockery, cutlery and glasses. Though not the wine. I bought that last week and stored it in the cellar. Jim, we'll need to bring that up as well. I'll put my presents away first, then meet you on the back terrace in five minutes. The guests are due to arrive from midday on, so, Sarah, leave plenty of time to dress and be back downstairs by five to twelve, ready to help me greet people at the door as they arrive.'

'How many are coming this year?' she asked.

'Twenty, if they all show up. Twenty-four, including us. OK?'

'Fine.'

They all rose to do as they were told, Sarah's heart beating faster when she thought of what lay ahead. Ok, so maybe it had been foolhardy of her to go along with Derek's plan without thinking it fully through, but now that the moment was at hand, it was still better than facing Christmas lunch alone. If nothing else, Derek wouldn't let her eat everything in sight.

But would he be able to withstand Nick's scrutiny?

Flora had told her yesterday that Nick took his job as her guardian very seriously indeed. Which in the past had obviously included vetting her boyfriends and making sure they weren't fortune-hunters.

Bringing Derek home so close to her inheriting her father's estate—not to mention telling Nick that they were very much in love—would only make him extra-protective. And paranoid.

She'd feel more confident if Derek weren't gay. And if she'd met this Chloe before. The unknown made her nervous. And she didn't want to be nervous. She wanted to swan downstairs just before midday, the epitome of cool composure and worldly sophistication. She wanted Nick to take one look at her and think to himself that she was the most beautiful and desirable woman that he had ever seen!

CHAPTER SIX

By ELEVEN, Nick had done everything that needed to be done downstairs. The tables and shady blinds had been set up, and the wine brought up from the cellar and delivered to the family-room bar. The caterers had arrived right on ten, the staff consisting of three females and two males, a highly efficient group of people whose job it was to take the stress out of Christmas Day dinners.

Nick smiled ruefully to himself as he went upstairs. He had no doubt that they did a very good job with the food, the serving and the clearing up afterwards. But nothing—and no one—was going to take the stress out of *this* Christmas dinner. Not for him, anyway.

He'd thought he'd finally got a handle on the unwanted desires Sarah had been evoking in him since she turned sixteen. But no, he'd just been deluding himself. Her staying away from home for most of this year had lulled him into a false sense of security. That, and meeting Chloe, whose sexy body and entertaining company had banished his secret lust for Sarah into the dungeon of his mind; that dark, dank place in which Nick imprisoned memories and emotions that were best forgotten. Or, at least, ignored.

He'd honestly thought he was prepared for Sarah's presence at Christmas. Thought he'd taken every precaution to keep the door to that mental dungeon firmly locked.

It had been Flora's news over breakfast yesterday that Sarah was bringing a boyfriend to the Christmas Day lunch which had shattered his illusion of iron self-control, stirring up a hornet's nest of jealousy within him. Next thing Nick knew, he was staying home from golf, just so that he could be here when she arrived. He'd made the excuse that he needed to talk to her about her inheritance, when in fact what he'd wanted most was to question her about the new man in her life.

Finding out that she was madly in love with this Derek didn't do his jealousy any good. OK, so on the surface he'd managed to control himself around Sarah. He gave himself full marks for not kissing her when he'd had the chance yesterday afternoon.

But he'd given in to temptation over those diamond earrings, hadn't he? Spent a small fortune on them, with the full intention of letting dear Derek know who'd bought them for her.

The truth was Nick had behaved badly every time Sarah brought home a boyfriend. He'd always pretended to himself that he was only doing what Ray had asked him to do, justifying his actions with the excuse that he was protecting her from fortune-hunters.

But that was actually far from the truth. None of those poor boys in the past had been gold-diggers. How could they be, when Sarah had never told anyone she was an heiress? They'd just been young men who'd had the good fortune—or was it misfortune?—to be where Nick had always wanted to be.

With Sarah.

The savage satisfaction he'd experienced every time he broke up one of her relationships showed just what kind of man he was: rotten to the core and wickedly selfish.

What would he do this time? he wondered grimly as he mounted the top landing and gazed down the hallway towards Sarah's bedroom.

Nothing, he hoped. The same way he'd done nothing yesterday when she'd been in his arms. He'd wanted to kiss her. Hell, he'd *ached* to kiss her.

But what would that have achieved, except make her look at him not with adoration as she'd once done, but with disgust? Sarah had finally fallen in love; possibly she was on the verge of having what she'd always wanted: marriage and children.

If this Derek was a decent fellow, then it would be cruel and callous to try to put doubts in Sarah's head about him.

Yet he wanted to…

Still, wanting to do something and actually doing it were two entirely different things. He'd wanted to seduce Sarah for years, but he hadn't, had he?

Nick shook his head agitatedly as he forged on across the carpeted landing into the master bedroom. It wasn't till he shut the door behind him that his mind shifted from his immediate problem with Sarah to another problem he would have to face in the near future.

Come February, he had to leave this house.

It would be a terrible wrench, Nick knew. He'd grown very attached to the place, and the people in it. He could not imagine coming home to any other house, or any other bedroom.

Strange, really. Eight years ago, after Ray died and Nick moved into the house, he hadn't much liked this bedroom.

Ray had gone Japanese-mad after his trip to Tokyo; the gardens hadn't been the only thing around Goldmine to be changed: the master-bedroom suite had been totally gutted, its walls painted white, the plush gold carpet ripped out and polished floorboards laid. The heavy mahogany bedroom suite had been given to charity, to be replaced by black lacquered Japanese-style furniture. The king-sized bed was now large and low, the duvet and pillows covered in scarlet silk with sprays of flowers at their corners.

Other than two matching black lacquered bedside tables, there'd been no furniture in the room, the walk-in wardrobe being spacious enough to accommodate all Ray's clothes.

The bathroom had been changed with an all-white suite during this refurbishment, enlarged as well to accommodate a huge spa bath that you could practically swim in.

Nick liked the bathroom, but had found the bedroom

rather stark, and not evocative of the atmosphere he wanted his bachelor boudoir to evoke. So he'd bought three fluffy white rugs to surround the bed, and some white cane chairs for the corners. A huge plasma television now hung on the wall opposite the bed with access to every satellite television channel available. Black silk sheets were his final purchases, along with some new shades for the chrome-based bedside lamps: red, of course.

The effect at night was erotic and sensual.

When in his bedroom, Nick didn't pretend to be anything but what he was: a very sensual man.

Which made his actions last night after the party almost incomprehensible.

Why, when he'd taken Chloe home, hadn't he gone inside and made mad, passionate love to her? She'd been all over him like a rash at the door. Normally, he loved it when she was sexually aggressive, loved it that he didn't have to be gentle with her. At any other time, he would have pushed her inside and had her up against the wall.

Instead her rapacious mouth had repelled him for some reason, and he found himself telling her he had a headache. A *headache*, for pity's sake!

Chloe had been surprised, but reasonably understanding, sending him off with a kiss on the cheek and the advice to have a good night's sleep.

'You won't get off so easily tomorrow night,' she'd added as he walked back to his car.

Nick hadn't gone straight home. He'd driven round and

round, trying to work out why he wasn't in Chloe's bed right at that moment, sating his desires to a degree where he wouldn't be capable of feeling any lust for anyone!

Then, when he'd finally come home, he'd fallen into a fitful sleep, his dreams filled with disturbingly erotic images involving the bane of his life. In one dream, Sarah had come down to the Christmas lunch wearing that minute bikini that had tormented him all those years ago. In another, she had been decorating that damned Christmas tree in the nude. In yet another, she'd been in his arms and he was kissing her the way he'd wanted to kiss her yesterday.

He'd woken from that dream incredibly aroused.

When Flora had sent him into Sarah's bedroom to wake her this morning, he'd stared down at her sleeping form for longer than was decent, the dungeon door in his mind well and truly open. Then, when she'd waltzed down to present-giving in that sexy little nightie, he'd been consumed with a desire so strong it had taken every ounce of his will-power to keep himself in check.

Her giving him that exquisite and very expensive miniature golf set had tormented him further, giving rise to the provocative possibility that, despite her new boyfriend, she still secretly fancied *him*. But her rather offhand words that her present was a parting gift of gratitude had propelled Nick back to cold, hard reality.

Sarah was well and truly over her schoolgirl crush on him. He'd lost his chance with her, if he'd ever had one.

It was this last thought that was bothering him the most.

'You should be glad she's over you,' he muttered as he marched towards the bathroom, stripping off his T-shirt as he went. 'Now all you have to do is concentrate on getting through today without behaving badly.'

Nick wrenched off his jeans, before walking over to snap on the water in the shower.

'No sarcastic remarks,' he lectured himself as he stepped under the ice-cold spray. 'No telling Derek you bought his girlfriend thirty-thousand-dollar earrings. And definitely no looking, no matter *what* she wears!'

CHAPTER SEVEN

'LET's go, Sarah.'

Nick's loud command—called through her bedroom door—was accompanied by an impatient knocking.

Sarah's bedside clock showed it was three minutes to twelve, two minutes after Nick had asked her to be downstairs.

'Coming,' Sarah called back after one last nervous glance in her dressing-table mirror.

She did look good: the red and white sundress clung to her shapely but slender body, and her choice of hairstyle— she'd put it up—showed off her new diamond earrings.

It wasn't Sarah's sexy appearance that had the butterflies gathering in her stomach. It was this silly charade with Derek. Nick was going to spot something strange about their relationship, she felt sure of it!

But it was too late now. Derek was on his way, having texted her a while back to say the taxi he'd ordered had just arrived and he should be at her place by twelve.

Sarah pulled her scarlet-glossed mouth back into

what she hoped passed for a happy smile and hurried across the room, movement setting her earrings swinging. When she wrenched open the door, Nick glanced up from where he was leaning with his back against the gallery railing. He still looked tired, she thought, but very handsome in fawn chinos and a brown and cream striped short-sleeved shirt.

'I'm ready,' she said breezily.

Nick's dark eyes swept over her from head to toe, his top lip curling slightly, as it did sometimes. 'Yes, but ready for what?'

His sarcasm rankled, as always.

Sarah planted her hands on her hips, just above where her skirt flared out saucily. 'It wouldn't hurt you to say something nice to me for a change.'

His eyebrows lifted, as though she'd surprised him with her stance. 'That's a matter of opinion. But if you insist…' His eyes travelled over her again, this time much more slowly.

A huge lump formed in her throat when his gaze lingered on her breasts before lifting to her mouth, then up to her eyes. If she'd been hoping to see desire in his detailed survey, however, she was doomed to disappointment.

'You look utterly gorgeous today, Sarah,' he said at last, but in a rather dry fashion. 'Derek is a very lucky man.'

Sarah was tempted to stamp her foot in frustration when the doorbell rang, saving her from her uncharacteristic temper tantrum.

'That'll probably be Derek now,' she tossed off instead, and bolted for the stairs, eager to answer the door without Nick being too close a witness to their greeting.

It wasn't Derek at the door, but an attractive, thirty-something brunette wearing a wrap-around electric-blue dress and a smile that would have cut glass.

Sarah knew immediately who it was.

'Sarah, I presume,' the woman said archly after a swift once-over that made her ice-blue eyes even icier. 'I'm Chloe, Nick's girlfriend.'

Of course you are, Sarah thought tartly. Nick's girl-friends might look different from one another—this one had a very short, chic hairdo, plus a much curvier body than the others. But underneath their varied physical features always lay a hard-nosed piece with no genuine warmth or niceness.

Sarah despised Chloe on sight.

'Hi there,' she managed politely before spinning round to see where Nick was. No way was she going to be caught having to make small talk with the bitch *du jour*.

Nick was still coming down the stairs, his expression none too happy.

'Chloe's here,' she called out to him.

For a split-second, Sarah could have sworn he had no idea who she was talking about. But then the penny dropped and he hurried to the door, his disgruntled face breaking into a smile.

'Happy Christmas, darling,' Chloe gushed as she threw herself into Nick's arms.

Sarah turned away so that she didn't have to watch them kiss, her stomach contracting when she heard Chloe whisper something about giving him his main Christmas present later that night.

It was extremely fortunate that Derek chose that moment to arrive, Sarah's nervous anticipation over their charade was obliterated in the face of her need to have someone by her side *on* her side.

'Derek, darling!' she gushed in much the same way Chloe had. 'Merry Christmas. Oh, it's so good to see you.' She let out a mental sigh of relief when she took in the way he was dressed. She'd been a bit worried he might wear a pink Paisley shirt, or something equally suspect. But no, he looked very attractive and sportily masculine in knee-length cargo shorts and a chest-hugging sky-blue top that complimented his fair colouring and showed off his great body.

'And you too, babe,' Derek returned, startling Sarah with his choice of endearment, not to mention his leaning over the rather large present he was holding to kiss her full on the mouth, taking his time.

'You look incredible,' he said on straightening. 'Doesn't she look incredible, everyone?'

Neither Nick nor Chloe said a word.

Sarah flushed with embarrassment, but Derek was undeterred.

'I hope this fits, babe,' he said, then pressed the present into her hands. 'I saw it in a shop window and I thought straight away that it was you to a T.'

Sarah didn't know whether to be pleased, or afraid of the contents. Derek had a wicked streak in him that was proving to be as entertaining as it was worrying.

'I...I'll open it a bit later,' she hedged. 'I have to help Nick greet our guests. Which reminds me. Nick, this is Derek,' she said by way of a formal introduction. 'Derek, this is Nick, my guardian.'

'No kidding,' Derek said as he shook Nick's hand, 'I got the impression you'd be older.'

Sarah tried not to laugh. But it was rather funny, seeing the expression on Nick's face.

'And I'm Chloe,' Chloe said with a sickeningly sweet smile. 'Nick's girlfriend.'

It never ceased to amaze Sarah how females like Chloe possessed split personalities—a super-sweet one for dealing with the male sex, a super-sour one, for their own.

'Why don't you go open your Christmas pressie in private?' Chloe suggested to Sarah with pretend saccharin-sweetness. 'I can help Nick answer the door, can't I, darling? I mean, all of the guests—other than Derek, of course—are Nick's friends.'

'What a good idea!' Sarah said, jumping at the chance to remove herself from Chloe's irritating presence. Of all Nick's girlfriends, she disliked this one the most, the conniving, two-faced cow!

'No, not down there,' Derek whispered when she grabbed his elbow and began steering him across the foyer towards the sunken family room. 'Take me upstairs. To your bedroom.'

'My *bedroom*!' she squawked, grinding to a halt.

'Ssh. Yes, your bedroom,' he went on softly. 'Don't ask why, just do it. And don't look back at either of those two. Just giggle, and then skip up those stairs with me.'

'I *never* giggle.' She hated females who giggled.

'You're going to today. That is, if you don't want to wonder for the rest of your life what it would be like to spend a night in Mr Dreamy's bed.'

Sarah finally saw what he was up to. 'This won't work, Derek, trust me.'

'No, you trust me. I know what I'm doing here, Sarah. I'm a master at the art of sexual jealousy. All gays are.'

'Ssh. Don't say that out loud.'

'Then do as you're told.'

Sarah refused to giggle. But she did laugh, then let Derek usher her with somewhat indecent speed up the stairs.

'Which room is yours?' he asked once they reached the landing.

'The third one on the right.'

'Nice room,' he said on closing the door behind them.

'Nick thinks it's too girlie. He also thinks I'm too thin now. He still doesn't fancy me, Derek. You're wasting your time trying to make him jealous.'

Derek smiled. 'That's not the impression I got when I kissed you.'

'What do you mean?'

'I kept my eyes open a fraction and watched your guardian's reaction over your shoulder.'

'And?'

'He hated it. And he hated me. I could feel his hatred hitting me in waves. Then, when he shook my hand he tried to crush my fingers.'

Sarah shook her head as she walked over and placed Derek's present on her pink quilt. 'I don't believe you,' she said as she sat down next to it.

'Why not?'

'Because I...Because he...Just because!' she snapped.

'You know what, Sarah? I think you're afraid.'

'Afraid of what?'

'Of success. You've lived with this fantasy for far too long. It's time to either let it go, or try to make it real. Which is it to be?'

Sarah thought of lying alone in this bed tonight whilst Nick cavorted with Chloe in his bed. She squeezed her eyes tightly shut for several seconds whilst she made up her mind. Then she opened them and looked into Derek's patiently waiting face.

'So what's the plan of action?'

Derek grinned. 'Stay right where we are, for starters. What time is lunch served?'

'Actually it's not served as such. It's a buffet. Nick usually tries to get everyone heading for the food at one o'clock.'

Derek glanced at his watch. 'In that case we'll make a reappearance downstairs at around five to one.'

Sarah frowned. 'We're going to stay up here till then?'

'Yep.'

'You do realise what Nick is going to think we're doing.'

'Yep.'

'He'll think I'm a slut!'

'If I'm right about him, he'll have trouble thinking at all. Now open your present. And make sure, when you come downstairs, you tell him what I gave you.'

CHAPTER EIGHT

NICK tried to hide his growing agitation, but where the hell was Sarah and what in God's name was she doing? It didn't take *that* long to open one miserable present. Damn it all, it was getting on for one o'clock.

The obvious answer just killed him: she was up in her bedroom, doing unspeakable things with that lounge lizard she was madly in love with and who had obviously pulled the wool over her eyes.

If ever Nick had seen a fortune-hunter it was darling Derek, with his fake smile, his fake blonde hair and his equally fake suntan!

Unfortunately his muscles didn't look fake, a fact that irritated the death out of Nick. He'd never thought Sarah was the sort of girl whose head could be turned by such superficial attractions. But clearly she was. She even seemed to like being called babe.

Didn't she know darling Derek probably called every one of his girlfriends babe? Saved him having to remember their names, since it was obvious he didn't have enough brains to make his head ache.

'Nick, Jeremy's talking to you,' Chloe said somewhat waspishly.

'What? Oh, sorry.' Nick dragged his mind away from his mental vitriol to focus back on the man talking to him.

Jeremy was his production company's location manager. Quite brilliant at his job, and gayer than gay.

'What were you saying, Jerry?'

Jeremy gave him a sunny smile over the rim of his martini. 'Just that I'm super-grateful to you for inviting *moi* for lunch today. Christmas is the one time of year when gays are severely reminded that lots of people are still homophobic. We try telling ourselves that Sydney is a very sophisticated city these days, but it's not as sophisticated as it pretends to be.'

'Really?' Nick said, his eyes returning to the foyer through which Sarah would have to come. If she ever came back downstairs, that was.

'You'd think the world had more important things to worry about than what people do in their private lives, wouldn't you?' Jeremy rattled on. 'I mean…what business is it of others who or what you have sex with, as long as you're not hurting anyone?'

But what if you were? came Nick's savage thought. What if having sex with someone—right at this moment—was tearing someone else's insides out?

'Well said, Jeremy,' his partner complimented.

Nick's eyes swung to Kelvin, who was a tall, skinny fellow of indeterminate age.

Nick was about to open his mouth and make some possibly rude remark—he suspected he was on the verge of behaving very badly indeed—when the movement he'd been waiting for caught the corner of his eye.

Nick's guts crunched down hard as he watched the object of his agitation waltz across the foyer with a smug-looking Derek hot on her heels.

That Sarah's hair was down—and tousled—did not escape Nick. Neither did her flushed cheeks.

'If you'll excuse me,' he said abruptly, 'there's someone I must speak to. Chloe, could you show our guests out to the terrace? The lunch is a buffet, but there are place cards on the table.'

Nick ignored the flash of annoyance that zoomed across Chloe's face, just before he spun away and marched across the family room to confront Sarah. What he thought he was going to say he had no idea. But he needed to say something; anything to give vent to the storm of emotion building to a head within him.

'Sarah,' he bit out when he was close enough to the lovebirds.

Her eyes jerked round towards him.

'I need to talk to you. *Now*. In private.'

'But we were just going out to the terrace for lunch,' she returned, oh, so sweetly.

He gritted his teeth as his furious gaze fastened on her mouth, where her red lipstick was an even glossier red than it had been before. Courtesy, no doubt, of having had to be retouched.

But the *coup de grâce* to his already teetering control was noticing that she'd removed his diamond earrings.

'I'm sure you won't mind not eating for a further five minutes,' he snapped, his stomach turning over at the thought of why she wasn't still wearing his Christmas gift.

Her shrug seemed carefree, but he detected a smidgeon of worry in her eyes.

'I won't be long, darling,' she said to her lover with a softly apologetic stroke on his arm. 'The buffet's all set up on the terrace out there. You go ahead and I'll join you shortly.'

'Sure thing, babe. I'll choose for you. And get you some of that white wine you like.'

'Would you? That would be wonderful.'

The schmaltzy exchange almost made Nick sick to his stomach. The moment Derek departed he grabbed Sarah by the elbow and steered her back out to the foyer, then along the front hallway towards his study.

When she tried to wrench her arm free, his hand tightened its hold.

'Is this caveman stuff really necessary?' she protested.

Nick said nothing, just pushed her into his study, then banged the door shut behind them. When he glowered over her, she did look a little shamefaced.

'OK, you're mad at me for not coming downstairs earlier and helping you with your guests,' she said. 'That's it, isn't it?'

'Not only was your behaviour rude, Sarah, it was embarrassing.'

'Embarrassing! I don't see how. I mean, it's not as though I know any of the guests this year. Flora told me beforehand that all of them are from your production company.'

'That's no excuse for ignoring them,' he lashed out. 'They have heard me speak of you. They *expected* to meet you, but you were nowhere to be seen. On Christmas Day, of all days! It would have been polite of you to be in the family room, offering drinks and making conversation. Instead, you were upstairs in your bedroom, having sex with that obsequious boyfriend of yours. I would have thought you had more pride, and a better sense of decorum.'

Her cheeks went bright red. 'Derek is not obsequious. And I was *not* having sex with him.'

Nick's laugh was both cold and contemptuous. 'Your appearance rather contradicts that.'

Her mouth fell open, then snapped shut. 'What Derek and I do in the privacy of my room is none of your business. Just as it's none of my business what you'll be doing with Chloe tonight in your bedroom. We're both adults now, Nick. I've been an adult for quite some time, in case you haven't noticed. In six weeks' time, I'll be twenty-five and you'll no longer have any say in my life whatsoever. I will be able to do whatever I like in this house because you won't be in it!'

'And no one will be more pleased than me,' he threw

back at her, his frustration making him reckless. 'Do you think I've enjoyed being your bloody guardian? Do you think it's been fun, trying to keep you safe from all the sleazebags? Do you have any idea how hard it's been for me, keeping my own hands off you?'

There! He'd said it. It was out in the open now. His dark secret, his guilty obsession.

Nick hated the shock in her face. But it was a relief, in a way.

'You never guessed?' he said, his soul suddenly weary.

She shook her head. 'You…you never said anything.'

Nick's smile was wry. 'I owed it to Ray to do what he asked me to do.'

'He asked you to keep away from me?'

'He asked me to protect you from the scoundrels of this world.'

If anything, this statement shocked her more than his admitting his desire.

'But you're not a scoundrel!'

'Trust me, Sarah. I'm a scoundrel of the first order. Always was. Always will be. Believe me, if you were any other man's daughter I would have seduced you when I had the chance. Because I did have a chance with you, didn't I? When you were sixteen.'

'You mean when I kissed you that time? You actually wanted me back then?'

'That's putting it mildly. Don't imagine for a single moment that I was worried about your age. Such things have never mattered to me. I just couldn't bear the thought that the one man in the world whom I liked and respected might look at me with disgust. Ray's words of praise and acceptance meant more to me than my intense but inconvenient desire for you.'

'I...I see...'

Nick doubted it. How could someone as basically sweet and naïve as Sarah understand the dark and damaged undercurrents of his character?

'Go on. Go back to your Derek,' he commanded.

'He...he's not my Derek.'

'What? What do you mean by that?'

'Derek's not my lover. He's just a friend. He's also gay.'

'Gay!' Nick repeated, his mind whirling as he tried to make sense of Sarah's confession.

'You've just been brutally honest with me, so I'm going to be brutally honest with you. I brought Derek to today's lunch so that I wouldn't be alone. And hopefully, to make you jealous.'

Nick stared at her.

Sarah looked as if she was about to cry. 'I've had a crush on you for as long as I can remember,' she blurted out.

Nick grimaced. He hated that word, crush. It sound so schoolgirlish. Of course, Sarah was still very young, compared to him. He'd been old from the time he was thirteen.

'You still have a chance with me, Nick,' she went on, her green eyes glistening. 'If you want it...'

If he wanted it. Dear God, if she only knew.

But what he wanted bore no resemblance to what she wanted.

'I'm no good for you, Sarah,' he bit out, surprising himself that he could find the will-power to resist what she was foolishly offering him.

'Why not?' she demanded to know.

'You know why not. I hid nothing from you when you were a youngster. I told you more than once: I can't fall in love.'

'I'm not asking you to.'

He glowered at her. 'Don't you dare lower yourself in that fashion. Don't you dare! I know you, Sarah. You want love and marriage and children. You do not want some decadent affair with a man of little conscience and even less moral fibre.'

'So you're knocking me back again. Is that the bottom line?'

'I already have a girlfriend,' he said coldly. 'I don't need you.'

The hurt in her eyes showed Nick that he'd done the right thing. Sarah's crush would have deepened into love if he slept with her. It had happened to him before, which was why he always stuck to partners like Chloe these days.

But that didn't mean he felt good about rejecting Sarah. His body was already regretting it.

'You'll find Mr Right one day,' he said stiffly.

'Oh, don't be so bloody pompous,' she snapped at him. 'If I wanted Mr Right, do you think I'd have just propositioned *you*? But that's all right, there are plenty of other good-looking studs around. Once I inherit all Daddy's lovely money, I don't think I'll be wanting for lovers, do you? Now I'm going to go eat my Christmas lunch. You can please yourself with what you do!'

CHAPTER NINE

'DOES that face mean good news or bad news?' Derek asked after Sarah had dragged the chair out next to him, and plonked herself down.

'Don't talk to me just yet. I'm so mad I could spit.'

'Oooh. I wish I'd been a fly on the wall. Here, have some wine. It's a very good Chardonnay from the Hunter Valley.'

'I don't give a damn what it is as long as it's alcohol.'

Sarah lifted the glass to her lips and swallowed deep and hard.

'I hope you like seafood,' Derek said, indicating the plateful he'd collected for her.

'At this point in time, I like anything which is edible. And drinkable!'

Sarah could still hardly believe what had just happened. Her fantasy man had confessed that he fancied her. Had claimed he'd fancied her way back when she'd been fifteen!

She'd been within a hair's breadth of having her most

longed-for dream come true and what had he done? Rejected her, in favour of the brown-haired witch sitting two chairs down from her.

'Sarah!' the witch suddenly snapped. 'Where on earth is Nick? I got his meal for him and now he's not here to eat it.'

Sarah gained some pleasure from seeing that Chloe was not pleased with her lover's absence. Not pleased at all!

'I have absolutely no idea where he is,' came her seemingly nonchalant reply, which was followed up by another large gulp of wine.

'But weren't you just talking to him?'

'Yes,' she replied airily.

The witch's eyes narrowed. 'So what were you two talking about? Or weren't you talking at all?'

Sarah blinked, her wine glass stilling in mid-air. 'What?'

'You don't fool me,' Chloe spat. 'I know what's going on here with you and Nick. I knew it the moment I clapped eyes on you.'

'Knew what, Chloe?'

Both Sarah and Chloe jumped at Nick's reappearance, Sarah quite stunned by the ice in his voice. And his eyes.

Chloe's own eyes stayed hard. 'Don't take me for a fool, Nick. I know jealousy when I see it. And I know you. No way could you have lived all these years with a girl of Sarah's—shall we say?—attractions—without sampling them for yourself. '

Sarah's mouth gaped open whilst Nick's hands tightened over the back of his chair, his knuckles going white. 'Are you accusing me of sleeping with my ward?'

'For want of a better word—yes.'

Sarah suddenly became aware that a silence had fallen over the long, trestle-style table. In the distance she could hear the sound of a speedboat on the harbour. Up close, all she could hear was her own heart beating loudly in her chest.

'If that's what you think,' Nick said, 'then I suggest you leave.'

Chloe looked rattled for a moment, but only for a moment. Her face became a sour mask as she scraped her chair back and stood up. 'I couldn't agree more. I'm not a girl who tolerates being cheated on.'

'I never cheated on you,' Nick stated curtly.

'If that's so, then it's only because Sarah decided she temporarily preferred Derek to you. I am well aware she hasn't been home lately. But be warned, Derek,' she flung in Derek's direction, 'she belonged to Nick first. Isn't that right, Sarah?'

Sarah could have lied. But she wanted this creature gone from Nick's life.

'Yes, that's right,' she said, and there was a immediate buzz around the table. Chloe's face showed a savage satisfaction, whilst Nick's expression carried alarm.

'But not the way you're implying,' Sarah went on, determined not to let this witch-woman ruin Nick's reputation in the eyes of his business colleagues. 'Nick has always had my love, and he always will. He has not, however, ever acted in any way with me but as my protector, and my friend. So yes, I agree with Nick. If you believe he's behaved in such a dishonourable fashion, then you should leave. There is no place in my home for anyone who doesn't hold Nick in the same high regard in which my father did, and in which I do. So please,' she said, and stood up also, 'let me show you to the door.'

'No,' Nick said, and pressed a gentle but firm hand on her shoulder. 'Let me.'

Sarah threw him a grateful glance before sinking back down into her chair, only then realising her knees were very wobbly indeed.

'Good luck,' Chloe grated out with one last vicious look at Sarah. 'You're going to need it.'

As Nick shepherded Chloe from the terrace, Derek began a slow clap, joined by several of the guests.

'Very impressive, sweetie,' Derek said softly. 'But also rather telling.'

Sarah's head jerked around towards him. 'In what way?'

'Blind Freddie can see you're in love with the man.'

Sarah sighed. 'Was I that obvious?'

'Afraid so.'

'Oh, dear.'

'No matter. Now, tell me what happened a little while back that made you so mad. Was Nick as jealous as Chloe said he was?'

'Yes.'

'I *knew* it! He fancies you, doesn't he?'

Sarah shook her head. 'I couldn't believe it when he told me he did. And not just lately. Since I was sixteen.'

'Wow. Did you tell him you fancied him right back?'

'Yes.'

Derek looked confused. 'Then I don't get it. What's the problem? Not me, I hope. You did tell him I wasn't your real boyfriend, didn't you?'

'Oh, yes. I was totally honest with him. I even told him you were gay.'

'*And?*'

'He still rejected me. Said he was no good for me.'

'*What?*'

'He told me my father asked him to protect me from the scoundrels of this world, of which he rates himself the gold-medal winner.'

'For crying out loud, can't the man see that his not sleeping with you all these years makes him one of the good guys?'

'Obviously not.'

'This calls for even sneakier action. Now, tonight I suggest you—'

'Stop, Derek,' she broke in. 'Just stop.'

'You're giving up,' he said, disappointment in his voice.

'No, I'm moving on. And so is Nick. He's already told me he can't wait to leave here.'

'That's because he can't trust himself around you. You've got him on the ropes, sweetie, and he's running for cover.'

'Then let him run. It's over, Derek.'

'How can it be over when it hasn't even begun?'

'Could we just leave this conversation and eat?'

Derek shrugged, then fell to devouring some prawns.

Sarah was doing her best to force some food down her throat when Nick returned to the table. Her hand tightened around her fork whilst he removed Chloe's chair, along with her plate, before pulling out his own chair and reseating himself.

'Sorry about that, Sarah,' he muttered as he shook out his serviette. 'Thank you for standing up for me.'

'That's all right. Chloe shouldn't have said what she did.'

'No, she shouldn't have. But I can understand why she did. Jealousy can make you do…stupid things.'

'Yes, I know. I'm truly sorry for this whole charade today, Nick.'

'I wasn't talking about you, Sarah. I was talking about myself.'

Her head turned and their eyes connected.

'You *were* jealous, weren't you?' she whispered.

'We're not going to go there again, Sarah,' he warned her abruptly. 'Do I make myself clear?'

If his harsh voice wasn't sufficiently convincing, his cold eyes were.

'Crystal clear,' she said.

'Good. Now let's forget about everything that has happened today so far and enjoy our Christmas lunch.'

Sarah sat there in stunned silence when Nick tucked into his food with apparent relish. She was even more amazed when he started up a very lively conversation with the man on his immediate right.

Was he just pretending, or hadn't he been genuinely upset by the events of the day? Chloe had been his girl-friend for the last six months and she'd just been dismissed in an instant.

Hadn't he cared about her at all?

Obviously not.

Maybe Nick was right. Maybe he was a scoundrel.

Sarah slid her eyes to her right, where she surreptitiously watched him eat half a dozen oysters; watched him lift each oyster shell to his lips, tip his head back, then slide the tasty morsel down his throat, after which .he would lick his lips with relish.

Sarah finally found herself echoing this action with her own tongue, moving it over her suddenly parched lips, her heartbeat quickening when his head turned her way.

He stared at her wet lips for a long moment, before his mouth pulled back into a twisted smile. 'You just can't stop, can you?'

'Stop what?' she choked out.

'The tempting. No, don't bother to deny it. Or defend yourself. Everything you've done today has been leading to this moment. Very well. You've won. Though I doubt you'll see it as a win by tomorrow morning.'

'What do you mean?'

Again, that cold, cryptic smile. 'I did warn you. If you insist on playing with the devil, then you have to be prepared to take the consequences.'

CHAPTER TEN

THE rest of the afternoon was endless, an eternity of wondering and worrying exactly what Nick meant by his provocative yet threatening words.

Several times Sarah tried to draw him into further clarification but he would have none of it, always turning the conversation away from the subject, or turning away from her altogether. After the lunch was over he deserted her to play the role of host, mingling with all his guests and making sure they had a good time. Coffee was served around the pool, with a few of the guests changing afterwards for a swim. Unfortunately Nick joined them, the sight of him in his brief black costume not doing Sarah's agitated state of mind any good.

It was around this time that Derek received a call on his cellphone from his mother, saying that his father had had a change of heart and wanted him to come home for Christmas after all. A delighted Derek called a taxi straight away and rushed off, leaving Sarah pleased for him, but even more lonely and agitated herself. In desperation, she left the party and escaped to the privacy of her bedroom.

But there was no peace for her there. She could still hear the gaiety downstairs through the French doors, the sounds tormenting her. What kind of man was Nick to say what he'd said to her and then ignore her? Finally, she could not bear her solitude any longer and made her way out onto the balcony, where she had a perfect view of the pool below…and Nick.

He saw her watching him, she knew. But he still ignored her, choosing instead to put his head down and swim, up and down, up and down. He must have swum for a good fifteen minutes straight before he stopped abruptly at one end and hauled himself out of the pool. Grabbing a towel, he draped it around his dripping shoulders before throwing her a savage glance, then striding up the terrace steps and disappearing under the roof created by the canvas blinds.

Every female nerve-ending in Sarah's body went on high alert. He was coming upstairs. To change? Or for something else?

She gripped the wrought-iron railing of the balcony, hot blood rushing around her veins at the possibility that it was *her* he was coming for; that he was about to put his teasing words into action. It didn't seem possible that he would do such a thing with the house still full of guests. But he'd said he was a scoundrel, hadn't he?

Sarah did not hear him enter her bedroom. But she

felt his presence in every pore of her body. She whirled to find him standing in the doorway that led out onto the balcony. The towel was no longer draped around his shoulders. His legs were set solidly apart, his hands balled into fists by his sides.

Sarah had seen him dressed in nothing but his swimming costume many times, but never in her bedroom, and never with that look on his face.

She shivered under the impact of the dark passion emanating from his coal-black eyes.

'Come here,' he commanded, his voice low and harsh.

Shock—and a sudden wave of fear—held her motionless.

He stunned her further by stripping down to total nudity, leaving her to confront the physical evidence of his desire.

Now, *that* she'd never seen before, and a dark excitement sent her head spinning and her pulse racing.

'Come here,' he repeated in gravelly tones.

She moved across the balcony like some robot, her mouth dry, her heart thudding loudly behind her ribs. When she was close enough he reached up to cup her heated face, his eyes holding hers captive whilst his mouth lowered to her still parched lips.

But he didn't kiss her. He just slowly licked her lips with his tongue. She found it incredibly erotic, her eyes shutting as her lips fell further apart on a soft moan.

Another moan punched from Sarah's throat when his tongue suddenly slid into her mouth. Surprise swiftly gave way to a wild craving to draw him in deeper and yet deeper. The need to pleasure him was great; the need to possess him even greater.

Her eyes flung wide when he wrenched his tongue away, her cry the cry of dismay. But then his hands fell to her shoulders and he was pushing her down onto her knees in front of him.

Any shock was momentary. If this was what he wanted, then she wanted it too.

He tasted clean and salty from the swimming pool. But it wasn't the taste of him that mattered to Sarah. All the years of wanting him to want her made her both reckless and wild. Her secret passion was finally unleashed.

Afterwards, she had no detailed recollection of how long it was before he came. A minute perhaps. Maybe two.

All she could recall was her satisfaction in his release, thrilling to the raw groans that filled the room, exulting in his uncontrolled surrender.

She glanced up at him, still unbearably aroused by what she'd just done. Her body was on fire, her conscience in danger of being totally routed. She did not care if he was a scoundrel. Did not care if he was only using her. She'd never been so excited in all her life.

'You do realise there's no going back now,' he grated out as he lifted her to her feet.

She just stared at him, unable to formulate any reply at that moment.

He stared back with hard, glittering eyes. 'I should have known you'd do this to me today.'

'Do what?' she choked out.

'Make me cross the line. You think you know what you're doing but you don't.'

'I'm not a child, Nick.'

He laughed. 'You are, compared to me. But that's all right. That's your attraction. I like it that you're relatively innocent. It excites me. It'll almost be worth it to open your eyes, to make you see what kind of men there are in this world. And how easily it is for them to seduce girls like you. Hopefully, by the time I've finished with you, you'll have enough experience to protect yourself in future.'

'I'm not that innocent,' she threw back at him.

'No? Why do you say that? Because you think you know how to go down on a man?'

Sarah's face flamed.

'I'm not saying that I didn't enjoy it,' Nick went on, reaching out to stroke a perversely loving hand down her cheek. 'But I'll enjoy teaching you how to do it properly a lot more.'

His hand drifted across to her mouth, where he inserted a finger between her lips.

'Most men prefer not to be gobbled up like fast food,' he advised, sliding that knowing finger back and forth along the middle of her tongue. 'Once you master the art, you can love a man more times than you would think possible. Have you ever been made love to all night long, Sarah?'

A shudder rippled down Sarah's spine at the images he was evoking.

'I think not,' he purred, his dark gaze narrowing on her wide eyes.

His finger retreated, leaving her feeling weirdly bereft and empty.

'But tonight you will, my love,' he promised. 'Tonight, I will take you to places you've never been before. If that's what you want, of course. Do you want it, Sarah? This is your last chance to tell me to go to hell.'

She stared into his heavily lidded eyes, afraid now of the power he had over her.

But her fear was not as strong as her desire.

'So be it,' he snapped when she said nothing. 'Just remember that you must live with the consequences of your decision.'

'What consequences?'

'That one day, I will have had my fill of you and you will go the way of all the others,' he said so coldly it was scary.

'Are you trying to frighten me off?'

His laugh was hard, and lacking in humour. 'Good God, no. I want nothing more than to have that gorgeous body of yours at my daily disposal till at least the end of the summer holidays. But I have a policy of brutal honesty with all my girlfriends. Chloe knew the score. Now you do too.'

'Can I tell Flora that I'm your new girlfriend?'

His face darkened at this suggestion. 'Absolutely not!'

'I thought that might be the case. You want to keep me your dirty little secret, don't you?'

'I do have my pride. Don't you?' he threw at her challengingly.

Her chin lifted. 'Yes.'

'Then it will be *our* dirty little secret. If you're not happy with that, then we can still call it quits. Right now. After all, one swallow doesn't make a summer.'

Sarah sucked in sharply at this most outrageous *double entendre*. 'You really are a wicked devil, aren't you?'

'I did warn you about my character. So what's your final decision? I can leave you and this house asap. Or…' He walked over to the bed, where Derek's present was lying spread out on the pink quilt. It was a black satin and lace teddy, which left little to the imagination, bought with the idea of making Nick jealous.

He picked it up, his eyebrows arching as he turned it this way and that. 'Or you can agree to come to my bedroom tonight, wearing nothing but this and my diamond earrings.'

Sarah tried to feel disgusted with him, and herself. But it was no use. There was no room in her quivering body at that moment for anything but a wild rush of dizzying excitement. She could not wait to do what he asked, could not wait to present herself to him the way he asked.

What did that make her?

A masochist, or just a girl in love, a girl who'd lived for far too long with her romantic fantasies.

Yet he wasn't offering her romance, just a few weeks of the kind of lovemaking she hadn't experienced before. He was right about that. All her lovers so far had been youngish men of little *savoir-faire*.

But the way Nick was talking made her wonder if there were ways nice girls didn't know about.

The thought only excited her further.

'What time tonight?' she asked, and looked him straight in the eye.

No way was she going to let him think he'd seduced her into this. She would come to him willingly, with courage, not fear.

His smile was wry. 'I've always known you had spirit, Sarah. That's another of your many attractions. Shall we say nine? Flora and Jim will have retired to their quarters by then.'

'Nine,' she repeated in pained tones. That was over four hours away!

'Yes, I know. But it will be all the better for the waiting. Now I must go and dress,' he said, bending to snatch up his swimming costume and towel from where they lay on the cream carpet. 'Meanwhile I suggest you go downstairs. People might begin to wonder where we are, and jump to the conclusion that there's some truth in Chloe's accusations. Just don't forget to replenish your lipstick before you go.'

Sarah stared after him as he left. Then she whirled and hurried into the bathroom.

CHAPTER ELEVEN

'I KNEW Chloe had just about reached her use-by date,' Flora remarked as she packed the dishwasher for the last time that evening. 'But I still can't believe Nick broke up with her on Christmas Day.'

Sarah glanced up from where she was sitting, having a cup of coffee. The clock on the wall showed twenty-two minutes past eight.

'He's a right devil with women,' Flora rattled on, 'but I've never thought of him as cruel.'

Strangely enough, Sarah agreed with Flora.

'He really had no option after Chloe accused him of carrying on with me in front of everyone,' she defended.

Flora pulled a face. 'I suppose not. I just wish I'd been there. Trust something exciting to happen the first year Jim and I decide to eat Christmas dinner back in our rooms. So tell me, what led up to it?'

Sarah shrugged. 'I have no idea. One minute everything seemed fine, the next she just came out with it. We were both shocked, I can tell you.'

'I'll bet it was because of the way you look today. She was probably blind with jealousy.'

'That's what Nick said.'

'He'd have been furious with her for saying something like that in front of his work colleagues. But I heard you set her to rights.'

'Really? Who told you that?' She'd done her best not to provide Flora with too many details, in case she slipped up with her story.

'One of the waiters. He said it was the most interesting Christmas lunch they'd ever catered for.'

'It was darned embarrassing. I'm glad it's over. Next year, things are going to be very different.'

Sarah wished she hadn't said that. Because she didn't want to think about next year. She didn't want to think about anything but tonight.

But once the thought was put in her head, it was impossible to banish it. If Nick had been telling the truth earlier, then by next Christmas she would be long gone from his life, and from his bed.

'You won't change your mind?' Flora asked.

'About what?'

'About letting me cook a hot meal next year. Call me old-fashioned, but Christmas just doesn't feel like Christmas without a turkey and a plum pudding. I know Nick won't mind. He really likes turkey.'

'Nick probably won't be here,' Sarah said a bit stiffly.

'What? Why not?'

'He's moving out in February.'

'So what? You'll invite him here for Christmas, surely. You and he are like family.'

'He might not want to come.'

'Rubbish! He loves having Christmas here. Even when he was building that resort on Happy Island, he always came back for Christmas. And it's not as though he'll go off and get married and make a home of his own.'

'True,' Sarah agreed ruefully, her eyes dropping to her coffee. 'That's never going to happen.'

So don't start secretly hoping that it will. He's not going to fall in love with you, no matter how much you love him. You're just another sexual partner, a temporary object of desire, a source of physical pleasure.

And when that pleasure begins to wane, when boredom sets in, you'll be replaced. That's the way it's always been with Nick and that's the way it will continue.

It might have been a seriously depressing train of thought if she'd been in a sensible, looking-after-her-future-happiness mood. But Sarah was anything but sensible at that moment. Excitement was fizzing through her veins, her insides wound so tight she was having trouble swallowing her coffee. How she managed to appear so composed in front of Flora, she had no idea. Obviously, she had the makings of an Oscar-winning actress!

'Where is Nick, by the way?' Flora asked.

'He went upstairs a little while ago,' Sarah replied as cool as you please. 'He said he was tired.'

'You finished with that?' Flora reached out for her coffee-mug.

Sarah handed it to her. 'I think I'll go up to bed, too,' she said, this time with a slight catch in her voice. 'It's been a long day.'

'There's a good movie on at eight-thirty,' Flora said. 'Got that film-star fellow in it that I like. Sexy devil. Now, he can put his slippers under my bed any time he likes.'

'Mmm,' Sarah murmured as she slid from the stool. Not as sexy as the devil she was about to spend the night with. 'Goodnight, Flora. Don't worry about breakfast. I'm going to sleep in. You should too. You look tired.'

'I am a bit. What about Nick?'

'I'll tell him to get himself something in the morning. I doubt he's asleep yet.'

'Before you go, Sarah, I just want to say how lovely you looked today. I wouldn't mind betting that by next Christmas you'll have a real boyfriend sitting at the Christmas table. Or even a fiancé. Which reminds me, did anything further develop with Derek today?'

'Er—no. He's not interested in me in that way.'

'What a pity. Still, there are plenty of other fish in the sea. Off you go, then.'

'Goodnight, Flora. Enjoy the movie.'

'Oh, I will.'

Sarah's pretend composure began to disintegrate the moment she left the kitchen.

'What on earth do you think you're doing?' she muttered to herself as she walked up the stairs on suddenly shaky legs. 'He's going to break your heart. You know that, don't you?'

Sarah stopped in front of his bedroom door. She even lifted her hand to knock. What she was going to say to him, she had no idea, though *go to hell* came to mind.

But then she heard the sound of Nick's shower running.

He was getting ready for her.

She could picture him standing naked under the jets of warm water, washing himself clean with long, soapy strokes of a sponge. In her mind's eye, he was already wanting her.

It was the thought of his wanting her that was the most corrupting. She'd wanted him to want her like this for years.

Impossible to turn her back on his desire.

Impossible to ignore her own.

Sarah's hand fell back to her side and she stumbled on to her bedroom.

Nick stood under the lukewarm spray, his hands braced against the shower-stall tiles, his eyes down.

Half an hour to go and already he was in agony.

Gritting his teeth, he turned the water to cold. Ten minutes later, he had his flesh under control again. But not his mind.

You should not be doing this, Nick, came the reproachful thought. She's in love with you. Or she thinks she is.

'You're a total bastard,' he growled to himself.

His mouth twisted into a sneer as he emerged from

the shower stall and snatched up a towel. 'So what's new, Nick?'

Still, he *had* given her every chance to escape. She'd been right when she'd accused him of trying to frighten her off. He'd honestly thought when he pushed her to her knees the way he had that she would jump up and run a mile. But she hadn't...

Of course, his desire for Sarah had been building in his head for years. It was no wonder he'd found it difficult to control himself this afternoon.

Still, it was a worry, his lack of control. From the moment she'd taken him into her mouth, he'd just lost it. Totally.

As he stared at his reflection in the bathroom mirror, Nick vowed that tonight would be different. Tonight he would be the coolly confident lover he usually was, patiently taking her on an erotic journey that initially might feel romantic to a girl as young and naïve as she was.

By morning, however, she would see him for what he really was: a cold-blooded and ruthless bastard who used women for nothing but his own pleasure and satisfaction. She would see that any finer feelings would be wasted on him, at the same time becoming a lot wiser to the wicked ways of the world, and of men.

It was a perverse way to protect her, but then, he'd always been perverse when it came to Sarah. Hadn't he lusted after her when she'd been little more than a girl? A lust which had been as obsessive as it was unwanted.

This moment had been inevitable, Nick conceded as

he finished drying himself. The only surprise was that he'd held back as long as he had.

Nine o'clock saw Sarah once again at Nick's door, her hands curling into white-knuckled balls as she struggled to find the courage to knock.

The black teddy fitted her perfectly, the skin-tight mid-section outlining her newly defined waist, the built-in lace bra cut low. More transparent lace inserts covered her hips, making the already high-cut sides seem even higher. But it was the back of the teddy that shocked her, mostly because there wasn't much of it. A couple of inches of material above her waist and next to nothing below, where it narrowed into a satin thong.

The door suddenly being wrenched open brought a gasp to her lips. Nick stood there, a dark red towel slung low around his hips, the expression on his face not a particularly happy one.

But his eyes changed as they swept over her, that white-hot desire she'd always wanted to see making her stomach flip right over.

'I knew you'd look beautiful in that. I didn't realise just how beautiful. And how damned sexy.'

He looked pretty damned sexy himself, she thought breathlessly.

His sudden frown worried her, as did his ragged sigh. 'You've made my life really difficult, Sarah.'

'No more than you've made mine,' she countered. Quite bravely, considering she was quaking inside.

He shook his head as he took her right hand in his and pulled her into the bedroom, kicking the door shut behind them.

'I presume you haven't changed your mind,' he said drily as he drew her across the room towards the bed.

'If I had, I wouldn't be wearing this, would I?' she threw at him with more feigned boldness whilst her gaze flicked nervously around.

She noted the bed, its red quilt thrown back, the black satin sheets glowing under the soft light of the red lampshades.

His suddenly scooping her up into his arms shattered her brave façade.

'You're trembling,' he said.

'Am I?'

'Very definitely.' He sighed for the second time, his eyes shutting for a moment. 'What am I going to do with you?'

'Make love to me, I hope. All night long, you promised.'

His eyes flicked open to glower down at her.

'No, Sarah. That's not what's going to happen here.'

Her heart plummeted to the floor.

'What I'm going to do is have sex with you. Don't mistake it for lovemaking. I never make love. I have sex with women. Of course,' he added with a sardonic smile as he lowered her gently into the middle of the bed, 'it will be great sex.'

Relief—and a rush of excitement—flooded through Sarah as her head and shoulders came to rest against the pile of satin-covered pillows. At this moment, he could call it whatever he liked. Nothing he could say would deter her from seeing this through.

But for Sarah, it would be lovemaking. For her, this was going to be the night of her life!

The satin sheets felt cool against her heated skin. Nick's eyes were cool as well, that white-hot desire she'd spotted earlier now not in evidence.

'Relax,' he advised as he straightened.

'I...I guess I am a bit nervous,' she admitted when he joined her on the bed.

'Yes, I can see that.'

Propping himself up on his side, he ran a teasing fingertip around the edge of the low-cut neckline, making her skin break out into goose-pimples. When he traced the neckline a second time, almost touching one of her nipples, she sucked in, then held her breath.

'Do you have extra-sensitive breasts?'

His question rattled her. Actually his talking rattled her. None of her previous lovers had talked. They'd simply got on with it.

Sarah finally let go of her long-held breath. 'I...I don't know,' she said, her head spinning.

'Let's see, shall we?'

Sarah held her breath again as he levered the satin straps off her shoulders and peeled them slowly downwards till the lace cups gave up their prizes.

'Mmm. Delicious,' he said, and bent to lick her right nipple.

Sarah clenched her teeth hard in her jaw, lest she cry out. But oh, the dizzying pleasure of it.

When he drew her nipple into his mouth, she could not prevent a moan escaping.

When he nibbled at it with his teeth, she squirmed and whimpered.

His head lifted, his eyes glittering now.

'As much as this teddy looks fantastic on you, right at this moment I prefer you without it.'

Sarah gulped but said nothing as he peeled it down her body and off her feet before tossing it carelessly aside. His eyes were like laser beams, honing in on that private part of her body.

'I love looking at you,' he rasped, caressing her smooth pubic bone before sliding his fingers through the already damp folds of her sex.

'Oh,' Sarah choked out, stunned by the sensations that came crashing through her.

'You are so beautiful,' he crooned as he continued to explore her down there, touching her everywhere. Inside, outside, then inside again. More deeply this time, finding erotic zones she didn't know she had. She pressed herself urgently against his hand, her head twisting from side to side, her wide eyes pleading with his as her body raced towards a climax.

'It's OK,' he said, his voice rough, his eyelids heavy. 'I want to watch you come.'

Sexy words, sexy eyes. Pushing her over the edge in a free-fall of pleasure that was wonderfully wanton, till she came to earth with a thud and realised this was *not* what she'd waited a lifetime to experience: Nick watching her come.

But no sooner did these rather dismaying thoughts flash through her mind than he was kissing her, not wildly but gently, his mouth sipping softly at hers.

'Don't be upset,' he murmured between kisses. 'You needed that. You were wound too tight. Next time…I'll be inside you…and it'll be much better.'

She blinked up at him when his head rose.

The corner of his mouth lifted in a quirky smile. 'You don't believe me?'

'Oh, no,' she said truthfully, 'I believe you.'

'Then what is it?'

'I…I'm sorry, but I thought…before we go any further, what…what about protection? I mean…Oh, you know what I mean,' she said, annoyed with herself for stuttering and stammering. 'You've been around.'

His expression carried an element of reproach. 'Sarah, you don't honestly think I would risk making you pregnant, do you?'

'Well, actually, you can't,' she admitted. 'Make me pregnant, I mean. I'm on the Pill.'

'I see. But you still want me to use condoms?'

'I'm not a total fool, Nick.' Even if he thought she was for being here with him.

'You've no need to worry. I've got that taken care of. Relax. No way are you getting out of here, sweetheart. Not till your old Uncle Nick lets you.'

'Don't call yourself that!' she snapped as she struggled to suppress an involuntary moan. Dear heaven, but he was good at that. 'There's nothing wrong with our being together,' she threw at him in desperation.

'That depends on your definition of wrong,' he countered, his devastatingly knowing fingers not missing a beat as he touched her breasts again. 'But no matter. It's like I said this afternoon,' he went on, that knowing hand sliding slowly down over her stomach and back between her legs. 'I'd reached the point of no return.'

'I...I think I'm just about reaching it again, too,' she choked out.

'So soon?'

She squirmed against his hand, her still sensitised flesh unable to bear too much more.

'You have to stop that,' she cried.

He stopped, leaving her panting whilst he rolled away and yanked open the top drawer of his bedside table. He selected a condom and drew it on. When he returned to her body, he did not rush. Neither did he attempt any kind of weird or wonderful position, for which she was grateful. Sarah wanted to look into his face when he was inside her; wanted to hold him and love him as she'd always wanted to.

She tried not to cry out when he finally entered her. But she couldn't quite manage to contain herself, a raw sound escaping her throat. Do not fall apart, for pity's sake, she lectured herself. But there was a great lump in her throat and tears were threatening.

Nick's concern was instantaneous. 'Are you all right?' he asked, smoothing her hair back from her face and staring deep into her by then glistening eyes. 'I'm not hurting you, am I?'

What an ironic thing to say!

'No, no, I'm fine,' she insisted, though her voice sounded artificially high. 'Would you mind kissing me, please? I like to be kissed a lot.' Anything to stop him staring down at her in that thoughtful fashion.

'My pleasure,' he said, and lowered his mouth to hers.

It was a kiss that might have been the kiss of true love, if she hadn't known differently.

How hungry it was, how passionate…how heart-breaking.

When his body began to move in tandem with his tongue, her fragile emotions were forgotten as the physical experience took over. With each surge of his flesh she could feel the coil of desire tighten within her. It was exciting, yet frustrating at the same time. She wanted to come. But as the seconds turned into minutes there was no release for her, only an all-consuming heat that flooded her body and quickened her heartbeat to a point where her mouth was forced to burst away from his.

'Help me, Nick,' she sobbed as she dragged in some life-saving breaths.

'Look at me,' he commanded, cupping her face and stilling his flesh inside her.

She stared up at him, her eyes wide and wild, her mouth panting heavily.

'Wrap your legs higher around my back,' he advised. 'Then move *with* me. Lift your hips as I push forward, then lower them when I withdraw. There's no hurry, Sarah. Just look into my eyes and trust me.'

Just look into my eyes…

She never wanted to look anywhere else.

Trust me…

Oh, God. How she wanted to do that too.

This is all a big mistake, Nick thought as she blindly followed his instructions. How long had it been since he'd been so damned nice and considerate in bed?

Who was this Nick who was suddenly caring so much?

He didn't approve of him. Couldn't trust him. He might start thinking he'd changed.

Which was impossible. He was what he was and he'd never change. This was just a momentary aberration. He'd get over it.

The trouble was he didn't think he'd get over it in one night.

He began moving faster, and so did she, her eyes growing wider and more desperate-looking.

Her first spasm was so strong Nick almost came then and there, but he held on, watching with wonder as her face became suffused with a seductive mixture of surprise and sheer joy. He'd never seen a woman look like that before. Never felt a woman who felt the way she did, either.

Finally he surrendered his control, astonished at the

intensity of his own climax, and the strange lurch to his heart when she pulled him down on top of her.

'Oh, Nick,' she cried, and nuzzled into his neck. 'Oh, my darling…'

Nick didn't say a word. He couldn't.

He'd never felt so confused. All he was sure of was that he'd never felt what he'd felt just now when she'd called him her darling. The endearment had wrenched at his very soul, that soul which he'd always imagined was too dark for such sentiment.

As he lay there with her cuddled up to him, Nick gradually became sure of something else: he didn't want to frighten Sarah off any more.

Which rather changed his plans for the rest of the night.

Nick didn't delude himself that this more romantic side he'd unexpectedly discovered within himself would last. But, for now, he found it quite irresistible. He could not wait to make love to Sarah again, could not wait to see the delight in her eyes.

But first, there was something he had to do. Carefully he disentangled himself from her arms and headed for the bathroom, where he washed himself fresh and clean then returned to the bed. He was about to stir her with some kisses when the phone next to his bed began to ring.

CHAPTER TWELVE

SARAH woke to the sound of a phone ringing. For a split-second she had no idea where she was. But the feel of Nick's naked body pressed up against hers swiftly cleared the haze in her head, everything coming back in a rapid series of flashbacks.

Her, coming to his bedroom wearing that outrageous teddy.

Him, carrying her to the bed.

Her, lying back against these satin pillows.

Him, making love to her.

But then came another memory: she'd called him darling afterwards.

When the phone continued to ring, Nick sighed then rolled over to reach for it.

No, don't, was her instinctive reaction.

But his hand had already swept the receiver up to his ear.

'Yes?' he said rather abruptly.

Sarah clutched the sheet up over her breasts as she

sat up, pushing her hair back off her face at the same time. Who on earth could it be?

Not Chloe, she hoped, trying to worm her way back into Nick's life with a million apologies.

'For how long?' Nick asked in concerned tones. 'How bad are they?'

She had no idea whom he was talking to or what it was about. But it didn't sound like Chloe.

'No, I think you're right, Jim. Don't listen to her. She has to go to hospital. *Now.*'

Sarah sucked in sharply. Something was wrong with Flora!

'I don't think we should wait for an ambulance,' Nick told Jim quite firmly. 'Get her into the back of the Rolls and I'll drive you straight to St Vincent's. I'll just throw some clothes on.'

Slamming down the phone, he tossed back the sheet and jumped up.

'Flora's having chest pains,' he threw over his shoulder as he strode across the floor towards his walk-in wardrobe. 'I'm taking her to the hospital.'

'Can I come too?' Sarah asked, her heart racing with alarm.

'No, it'll take you too long to dress,' he said as he returned to the bedroom, jeans already on, a blue striped shirt in his hands.

'But I—'

'Let's not argue about this, Sarah.' He shoved his

arms into the shirt's sleeves and drew it up over his shoulders. 'I'll call you from the hospital.'

'You haven't got any shoes on,' she pointed out when he headed for the door, shirt flapping open. 'You can't go to a hospital without shoes!'

He grumblingly went back for some trainers, then flew out of the door. Sarah heard him running down the stairs. Then she heard nothing.

A shiver ran down her spine, nausea swirling in her stomach at the possibility that Flora could be having a heart attack. She might even die!

The thought brought back all those horrible feelings she'd had when her father had been struck down by a coronary. Aside from the emotional trauma of losing her last parent, she'd been besieged with regret that she hadn't even been able to say goodbye to him, or tell him that she loved him.

Flora might not be a parent but Sarah loved her dearly. It pained her that Nick hadn't let her go with him, even though he was probably right—she would have taken longer to dress than him. He'd taken all of thirty seconds!

But that doesn't stop you from dressing now and following him to the hospital in your own car, does it?

Sarah was out of the bed in a flash, dashing for her room.

She didn't dress as fast as Nick, but she managed to make herself respectable in under ten minutes. Getting out of the house, however, took her another few minutes, because she had to lock up. Then she had difficulty finding the hospital, not having been there since her mother fell ill all those years ago. At last she located the right street, along with a parking spot not far from the emergency section.

She'd just made it to the ER waiting room when her mobile rang.

It had to be Nick, she reasoned as she retrieved it from her handbag.

'Nick?' she answered straight away.

'Where in hell are you?' he grumbled down the line. 'I tried the home number and you didn't answer.'

'I couldn't just sit there, Nick. So I got dressed and drove myself to the hospital. I've just arrived at the emergency waiting room. How's Flora?'

'Not too bad. They whipped her in and gave her some medication to thin her blood straight away. Then they hooked her up to some kind of heart-monitoring machine that does ECGs and other things. The doctor thinks it might just be angina.'

'But that's still not good, is it? I mean, angina can lead to a heart attack.'

'It can. But at least we've got her where she can have some further tests, and proper treatment. You know Flora. She doesn't like going to doctors, or hospitals. I'm going to make sure she stays in for a couple of days till we get a full picture of her condition. I've rung a colleague whose uncle is a top cardiac specialist here. We're going to transfer her to a private room after the doctor in ER is finished with her, and he'll come in in the morning and take over.'

Sarah felt the tension begin to drain out of her. 'That's wonderful, Nick. How's Jim doing?'

'To be honest, I've never seen him so distressed,' Nick whispered. 'He's sitting by Flora's bed as white as a sheet himself. I'm going to try to persuade him to come with me for a cup of tea and a piece of cake. I think he's in shock. Look, just sit down where you are and I'll be with you shortly. Then we can all go together. There has to be a cafeteria somewhere in here.'

'Couldn't I see Flora myself before we do that? I need to see her, Nick.' To tell her old friend that she loved her. Also that she was coming home to live. Permanently. She would put in for a transfer to a nearer school. No, she'd resign and find work in one of the many local preschools. They were always crying out for experienced infant teachers.

'She's not going to die, Sarah,' Nick said gently.

'You don't know that. What if she took a bad turn while I was sitting near by, having a cup of tea? I'd never forgive myself.'

'Fine. Stay where you are and I'll come and get you. I'll just tell Jim where I'm going.'

Sarah sat down in an empty chair against the wall, only then absorbing her surroundings. The place was very busy, with people rushing to and fro, and lots of people just sitting and waiting to be treated, several of them dishevelled young men with cuts and bruises over their faces. There were half a dozen mothers with crying children, and wailing babies. They all looked poor and wretched. Some of them even smelt.

She dropped her eyes away, upset by this brutal confrontation with the cold, cruel world. Not that she hadn't come across neglected children before. Just not on Christmas Day.

'Sarah? You OK?'

Sarah jumped up from the plastic chair. 'Oh, Nick, I'm so glad you're here.' She grabbed his arm and steered him away to one side.

'Did any of those louts bother you?' he asked.

'No, no, nothing like that. I just…Oh, Nick, the world's a horrible place, isn't it?'

'It can be,' he agreed soberly.

'We are so lucky to be healthy. And rich.'

His smile was wry. 'You're right there, sweetheart. Healthy and wealthy are the daily double. Come on, I'll take you to Flora.'

The sight of Flora's dull eyes and pale face alarmed Sarah. But she tried not to show it. 'What a scare you gave us,' she said lightly as she bent and kissed Flora on the cheek.

'It's just indigestion,' Flora protested. 'But no one believes me.'

The attending nurse surreptitiously rolled her eyes at Sarah, indicating that it certainly wasn't indigestion.

Sarah pulled up a chair by Flora's bed and picked up her hand. It felt oddly cold, which was another worry.

'Best we make sure, now that you're here,' she said.

Flora pressed her lips together. 'That's what Nick and Jim say but, truly, I'd much rather go home to my own bed. All I need is a rest.'

'Now, Flora, love,' an ashen-faced Jim began before his voice trailed weakly away. He'd never worn the trousers in the family and it looked as if he wasn't about to now.

'You'll do as you're told, madam,' Nick intervened firmly. 'Now I'm taking Jim for a cuppa. Sarah's going to sit with you for a while.'

Sarah flashed him an admiring smile. Truly, Nick's command of this situation had been wonderful from the word go. He hadn't panicked, he'd acted decisively and quickly—and possibly saved Flora's life in the process.

'See you soon,' he said to her, then turned and shepherded Jim away.

Sarah's gaze followed him for a while before returning to Flora.

'Have you something to confess, missie?' Flora said softly, but in a very knowing fashion.

Sarah had no intention of letting herself be railroaded into any admissions about Nick. She would not hear the end of it if she told Flora that she and Nick were having an affair.

'I just wanted to say I love you dearly, Flora, and I've been a selfish cow, staying away from home as much I have. Things are going to change from now on, I assure you. I'm going to get a job near by so that I can be there, in person, to make sure you take it much easier, as well as look after your diet. I've become a very good cook of low-fat meals this past year, and you, madam, need to lose a few pounds. If you must work, then you can help Jim in the garden. And you're going to start walking. *Every* morning.'

'Goodness, you're sounding just like Nick.'

'Who has your best interests at heart as well. So I don't want to hear any more nonsense about your coming home just yet. Nick has organised a specialist to come in tomorrow to do some tests and you're going to have them.'

'Heavens to Betsy, is this my sweet little Sarah talking?'

'No, it's your grown-up Sarah.'

'I can see that. And so does Nick. He couldn't take his eyes off you today, Sarah. Or tonight, for that matter.'

Sarah eyed Flora sternly. 'Don't start matchmaking, Flora. You and I both know Nick is not a marrying man.'

'If anyone could make him change his mind about that, it's you, love.'

Sarah bit her tongue, lest she give the game away. But there was a part of her that agreed with Flora.

Nick hadn't just 'had sex' with her tonight. He'd made love to her, with tenderness and caring.

Who knew? Maybe there was a chance of a real relationship between them, no matter what Nick said.

'You're in love with him, aren't you?' Flora said.

Sarah could not bring herself to lie any longer. 'Yes,' she admitted.

'Then go after him, girl.'

'That's what I am doing.'

'And?'

Sarah felt a betraying smile tug at her lips. 'Let's just say it's a work in progress.'

'Ooooh, I like the sound of that.'

'Well, I don't,' the nurse interrupted firmly. 'Your blood pressure is on the rise again. Sorry,' she said to Sarah. 'I think it would be better if my patient rests quietly for a while. Perhaps you could join her other visitors in the coffee lounge for the next half-hour at least. It's thatta way.'

Sarah went reluctantly, with the solemn promise to return. She followed the direction of the nurse's finger, but still had to ask for more directions before she found the cafeteria.

Jim and Nick glanced up with questioning eyes at her arrival, Jim looking particularly anxious. She didn't have the heart to tell him that she'd raised his wife's blood pressure, saying instead that the nurse wanted Flora to rest quietly and they weren't to go back to her bedside for half an hour at least.

'If you want anything, you have to order at the counter,' Nick informed her.

Sarah shook her head. 'I don't want anything.'

'Don't be silly. I'll get you some coffee and cake. You have to be hungry. I know I was.'

Jim said nothing during the time it took Nick to return with the coffee and piece of carrot cake. He just kept staring blankly into space.

'You haven't eaten your cake, Jim,' Nick said as he sat back down.

Jim turned his head towards Nick, his eyes remaining vacant. 'What did you say?'

'Your cake,' Nick said, nodding towards the untouched plate.

He shook his head. 'I can't eat it.'

'She's not going to die, Jim.'

'But what if she does?' he said plaintively. 'I can't live without her. She's all I have.'

'I know, Jim.' Sarah reached over to press a gentle hand on his arm. 'But you won't have to live without her. Not yet, anyway. We've caught this in time. We'll look after her together and make her better.'

His eyes filled with tears, shocking Sarah. She'd only ever seen a man cry once before in her life—her father, at her mother's funeral. Jim's crying propelled her back there, to her mother's graveside and the awful sound of her father's broken sobs as they lowered her coffin into the ground.

'I'm just so worried,' Jim choked out.

'We all are, Jim,' Nick said gently.

'I never thought I'd get married, you know,' Jim went on, his voice cracking some more. 'At forty, I was a crusty old bachelor. Not ugly exactly, but not the kind of chap women went for. Flora used to shop in the same supermarket as I did. Not sure why she took a liking to me but she did. Before I knew it, we were hitched.'

A huge lump filled Sarah's throat as she watched the tears run down Jim's sun-weathered cheeks.

'Best thing I ever did,' he finished up, pulling a hankie from his pocket.

An emotion-charged silence descended on their table. They all fell to drinking and eating, no one saying a word. Sarah noted that the people at the other tables weren't saying much either.

Cafeterias in hospitals, she decided, were not places of joy, especially late at night.

When her eyes returned to their table, she found Nick staring at her.

What are you thinking? she longed to ask.

But she said nothing, her eyes dropping back to her coffee.

Nick could not believe the crazy thoughts going through his head at that moment. Jim's touching little story about his romance with Flora must have totally unhinged him. Because, suddenly, he was thinking that that was what *he* should do: get married…to Sarah.

An incredibly bad idea. Even worse than giving in to his lust and sleeping with her. An affair with a scoundrel could have the beneficial side-effect of educating and protecting her, in a perverse kind of way. But marriage to the same scoundrel had nothing going for Sarah at all. Because such a union would not give her the one thing she wanted most in life: children.

This last thought steeled Nick's strangely wobbly heart,

reaffirming his resolve to keep their affair strictly sexual. That way, when it was over, Sarah wouldn't be too hurt.

Meanwhile, it would be kinder of him if their affair didn't last too long. Best it be over by the time she turned twenty-five. Which gave him what time with her?

Six short weeks. Not long to burn out a lust that had been growing for years, and which he now had little control over. Despite all that had happened tonight, he could not wait to get her home, to bed. Which underlined just what type of man he was; not fit to marry a lovely girl like Sarah, that was for sure.

'I think we should go back to the ward now. See what they've discovered.'

Nick's abrupt suggestion jerked Sarah back to the moment at hand.

'The nurse didn't seem keen on Flora having too many visitors,' she told him. 'I think it would be best if I went home to bed. I'll come back and visit Flora tomorrow morning, bring her some things she might need.'

'That sounds like a good idea,' Nick agreed.

'I'm not going home,' Jim said somewhat stubbornly. 'I'm going to stay with my wife. They said I could.'

'Of course,' Nick soothed. 'I'll stay till I find out the doctor's verdict, then I'll go home too. I'll come back with Sarah in the morning.'

Nick stood up first, coming round to hold the back of Sarah's chair as she rose.

'*My* bed,' he whispered. 'Not yours.'

Shock held her rigid. How could he possibly be thinking about sex at this moment? It was the last thing on her mind.

But by the time she unlocked the front door and made her way upstairs, the thought of being with Nick again was slowly corrupting her. She kept telling herself that she was as wicked as he was; that she should be consumed with worry for Flora, not desire for him.

Nick's brief phone call from the hospital informing her that it had just been angina, and not a heart attack, did soothe her conscience somewhat, though her emotions were still very mixed as she showered and perfumed her body, then slipped, naked, back between those black satin sheets.

She'd heard about people having wildly tasteless sex at wakes, just to prove that they were still alive. Maybe this was something like that.

But she suspected not.

Sarah wanted to believe that it was love behind her behaviour. But she was beginning to wonder if it was more a matter of lust. She'd never experienced the kind of sexual pleasure that she'd had earlier that evening. And she wanted more.

By the time she heard the Rolls throttle down in the driveway, Sarah was beside herself with excitement. When Nick strode into the room already stripping off as he went, desire had rendered her totally mindless.

This time he did not speak and neither did she. Their coupling was fast and furious, a raw, animalistic mating that sent them both hurtling over the edge in seconds. Afterwards, they clung to each other, their skin pearled in sweat, their bodies stuck together.

'I didn't use a condom,' he muttered into her hair.

'I know,' she rasped.

'I'm sorry.'

'Don't be,' she shocked herself by saying. 'I liked it.'

Oh, what an understatement. She'd gloried in his hard, unprotected flesh surging into hers, wallowed in his flooding her womb.

His head lifted, dark eyes gleaming. 'But you're not safe. You've just opened the dungeon door, Sarah, big time.'

Her sex-glazed eyes searched his. 'What dungeon is that?'

'The one I've kept my X-rated fantasies about you imprisoned in all these years.'

Sarah's eyes widened at the rather menacing metaphor.

'Don't ever imagine I'm in love with you,' he snarled. 'Love doesn't live in a dungeon. Now, go to sleep. I've had enough for one night and I'm bloody exhausted.'

CHAPTER THIRTEEN

'SOMETHING to drink, Sarah?'

Sarah's head turned. She'd been staring through the plane window at the panoramic vista below. They'd not long taken off from Mascot Airport and hadn't yet reached any clouds.

'Yes, please,' she said to both Nick and the hovering stewardess. 'What can I have?'

'How about a glass of champagne?' Nick suggested.

'At seven-fifteen in the morning?'

'Why not?'

'Nick, you *are* terrible,' she chided, but jokingly. 'OK, champagne it is.'

'And you, sir?' the flight attendant asked.

'I'll have what she's having.'

Sarah's laugh enchanted him, as did she. There was no artifice in her, no pretend sophistication. She was a pleasant change from the kind of woman he usually dated.

Once she was handed her glass of champagne, Sarah

turned back to gaze intently through the window, her nose close to the rim.

Truly, she was like a child on her first flight.

Nick stared at her as he waited for his drink. She looked about sixteen this morning, wearing little make-up, no jewellery and a simple black and white sun-dress. Her hairstyle was young too, the sides scooped up into school-girlish combs, the rest falling loosely down her back.

The flight attendant was probably thinking he was a shameless cradle-snatcher. Nick detected a knowing glint in the woman's eyes as she handed him his glass of champagne.

Not that he cared what she thought, or anyone else for that matter. Nick had become so besotted by Sarah that he was already considering extending the length of their affair.

Of course, a month of non-stop sex with her at his holiday house on Happy Island might return him to a wiser course of action. He really hadn't had enough time to burn out his lust for Sarah since the first night they'd spent together.

Apart from anything, they'd been very busy, visiting Flora at the hospital and seeing to her health needs.

Fortunately, the specialist had located the source of the angina, a minor blockage in one artery that had been successfully cleared without the need for open-heart surgery. When the doctor had suggested a holiday for his quickly recovering patient, Nick had offered Jim and Flora his penthouse on the Gold Coast, which was fully serviced, with meals readily available, either in the restaurant downstairs or delivered to their apartment door. They'd jumped at the chance of an all-expenses-paid jaunt and Nick had seen them off at the airport three days ago, New Year's Eve.

Which had left him alone in the house with Sarah.

As Nick settled back to sip his champagne, his mind drifted back to the thirty-first of December...

He'd chilled some white wine, ordered in a five-star meal from a local restaurant, then set everything up on the balcony to the master bedroom, the perfect setting for a romantic, candlelit dinner. The perfect setting for New Year's Eve as well, with the uninterrupted view of Sydney Harbour—the water, the city and the bridge—which was always the showpiece of the fireworks.

Not that they got to see the fireworks, either at nine or at midnight, each occasion finding them otherwise occupied inside. After nearly a week of abstinence, he was insatiable, both for Sarah's beautiful body and her rapturous responses, Nick wallowing with wicked selfishness in the transparency of her feelings for him.

Nick could not get enough of her that night. Or the next day. Oddly enough, he didn't want to try out lots of different positions. He was content to just be in bed with her.

That evening, however, she suddenly called a halt, claiming she was exhausted. That night she slept alone, in her pink-quilted, little-girl bed.

Nick didn't argue. He could see she was determined. But he wasn't happy, resolving during that long, restless

night that the following morning he would persuade her
to go away with him to Happy Island, where she
wouldn't be able to escape him.

Fortunately, he hadn't cancelled the airline tickets
he'd booked for himself and Chloe.

Sarah's reaction to his invitation over breakfast seriously surprised Nick.

'Surely you can't expect me to go away with you
on the same holiday you planned with Chloe!' she
threw at him.

Nick quickly saw that his sensitivity meter was reg-
istering very low, Sarah making it clear what she
thought of his suggestion.

He had to work hard all day to make Sarah see he
wasn't treating her as a substitute for Chloe. Some
tender lovemaking seemed to soften her stubborn
attitude a little. But he finally struck the right note when
he said that he'd never taken Chloe—or any of his other
girlfriends—to Happy Island before. She would be the
first female to share his holiday house with him.

It was both the truth, and a lie. He had taken Chloe
there for one short weekend back in September. But, as
it had turned out, she'd fallen ill with food poisoning on
the flight there. She'd been unwell the whole time,
unable to do anything but stay in bed and read. Nick
decided in his male mind that that didn't count.

After agreeing to go with him, Sarah had surprised
him once again when she'd insisted on spending last
night alone in her bedroom. She'd said she needed a

good night's sleep, since they had to get up so very, very early.

Nick had been wide awake well before his alarm went off, his desire more intense than ever.

But it wouldn't be long now. Soon he would have her all to himself again in a place where she had nowhere to run to. Or to hide.

'Oh, I can't see anything any more,' Sarah said wistfully as she slumped back into her seat, her champagne glass still untouched. 'The clouds are in the way.'

Nick smiled. 'Anybody would think you hadn't flown before.'

'It's been years since I have,' she said, then finally took a sip of champagne.

'Really?'

'I haven't had much money left for holidays, what with paying for my rent and my car and general living expenses.'

Nick frowned. 'You could have asked me for some money for a holiday,' he said. 'I never did agree with Ray for leaving you that short of funds.'

'It was probably good for my character. At least I'm not spoiled.'

Nick's frown deepened. No, he thought. She certainly wasn't. But would spending time with him change her character? He wanted to educate her, not corrupt her. He would hate for her to turn out like Chloe, who thought of no one's pleasure but her own.

'Now, what's that frown all about?' she asked him.

'You're not worrying about Flora and Jim, are you? I spoke to them last night and they're as happy as can be up there on the Gold Coast. It was a brilliant idea of yours to lend them your penthouse. Very generous, too.'

Nick decided not to let her go back into hero-worship mode. Bad enough that she probably thought she was in love with him.

'Come, now, Sarah, you know very well it wasn't generosity that inspired my offer. It was a strictly selfish proposition. I wanted them right out of the way.'

'You're not the only one,' she said, then blushed.

It got to him, that blush, sparking a desire so intense that his flesh ached.

'I wish I could kiss you right now,' he said.

'Why can't you?' she returned, her cheeks still pink.

'Because I wouldn't want to stop there,' he ground out. 'Next thing you knew, we'd be joining the mile-high club.'

Her nose wrinkled with distaste. 'No way could you get me to do that. I've always thought sex on a plane to be the height of tackiness.'

'Hear! Hear!' Nick said, and raised his glass to her. No way, he realised with considerable relief, would she ever become like Chloe.

It would be damned difficult to go back to girls like Chloe after being with Sarah…

As Sarah sipped her champagne, she wondered if Nick really approved of her view. Maybe he thought her prudish, since he'd always claimed to be a roué.

But surprisingly, other than that first incident, when he'd pushed her down to her knees, her sexual encounters with him had not been the least bit decadent. Passionate, yes. But not dark.

On New Year's Eve he'd been very romantic, something he'd claimed he would never be.

Sarah held the opinion that people were as good, or as bad, as you let them be. Certainly, that applied to children. She'd discovered during her teaching years so far that if she had high expectations of her pupils they usually lived up to them.

Especially the so-called bad boys.

Nick was a bad boy. But he wasn't bad through and through, no matter what he thought of himself, and no matter what he'd done in the past. Her father had seen his worth. Her dad had also expected a lot of Nick. And Nick had lived up to those expectations.

Admittedly, he'd lost his way a bit since Ray's death. Sarah could not deny that he had earned his playboy reputation. Women had been relegated to sex toys in his life for so long that it probably was foolish of her to think he would ever embrace a better way of life. With her.

Very foolish.

But love was foolish, wasn't it?

Why else was she sitting here, in a seat that had been booked for Chloe? The bottom line was that if Chloe hadn't made that *faux pas* on Christmas Day, she'd be the one sitting here today.

This pessimistic train of thought irritated Sarah to death. Hadn't she decided last night to be positive, and not negative; to view Nick's invitation to share a whole month with him as a step towards a real relationship? Hadn't she vowed to use this time not just to explore the sexual chemistry between them, but also to revive that special bond which had sprung up all those years ago when they'd both been so very lonely?

She hoped that, besides the sex, they would have deep and meaningful conversations during which Nick would tell her everything about himself, and vice versa.

'You're not drinking your champagne,' Nick pointed out.

Sarah turned a rueful smile his way. 'It *is* a little early. I think coffee would have been a better choice.'

'It's a woman's privilege to change her mind,' he said amiably, and pressed the button for service.

Sarah watched with pride as he gave the stewardess back the champagne and asked for coffee instead. She loved his decisiveness, his 'can-do' attitude. Nick was a natural leader, something her father had once commented on.

Sarah believed he would make a great husband and father. But would Nick ever believe it?

'I have a confession to make,' he said after the coffee arrived.

Sarah's stomach contracted. 'Nothing that will upset me, I hope.'

'No reason why it should.'

'Out with it, then.'

'I read all your Christmas cards. The ones on your dressing table.'

Her stomach relaxed. 'Oh? When?'

'Yesterday. When you were having a shower.'

'And?'

'I don't think I've ever seen such glowing words. It's a privilege to be in the company of the "bestest" teacher in the whole wide world.'

Sarah laughed. 'A slight exaggeration. But I am pretty good.'

'And yet you've resigned?'

'Only from my current school. I'll find another position closer to home. Possibly at a preschool. I'm very fond of small children. They have such open minds.'

'I don't have any patience with small children.'

'Lots of men don't. But they change, once they have their own.'

His glance was sharp. 'I won't. Because I don't intend having any of my own.'

Sarah kept her expression calm. 'Why's that?'

'Fathering is a learned skill, passed on from generation to generation. The only example I ever had of fathering is not something I'd like to pass on.'

'Not every child of abusive parents becomes an abuser themselves, Nick,' she said carefully.

'Perhaps not. But why take the chance? The world has enough children. They won't miss mine.'

'You might change your mind if you were presented with one.'

He whipped his head round to glare at her. 'You have brought your pills with you, haven't you? You're not going to try that old pregnancy trap. Because it won't work, Sarah. Not with me.'

The coldness in his eyes sent a chill running down her spine.

But she refused to give up on him. For now, anyway.

'I have no intention of trying to trap you with a baby, Nick. And yes, I have brought my pills. You can feed me one every day, if you'd like.'

'I just might do that.'

'Have you always been this paranoid about pregnancy?'

'Let's just say you're the first female I've ever had sex with without a condom.'

'It's nice to know that I'm unique.'

He smiled wryly as he shook his head at her. 'You are that, all right. Now, drink your coffee before it goes cold and I have to call the stewardess again.'

She drank her coffee quickly, anxious to get back to their conversation. It would be a couple more hours before they landed on Happy Island, with Nick imprisoned by her side all that time. Sarah didn't think she'd ever have a better opportunity to find out all the things she'd ever wanted to know about him. She suspected that once they hit Happy Island, there might not be too much talking done.

'Tell me about your life, Nick,' she said when she finally put the coffee down. 'Before you came to work for Dad. I'm curious.'

'I never talk about that part of my life, Sarah.'

'But that's silly. It's not as though I don't already know quite a bit. I know you had a horrible father and that you ran away from home to live on the streets when you were only thirteen. And I know that you were put in jail for car-stealing when you were eighteen.'

'Then you know enough, don't you?'

'Those are just the bare facts. I want you to fill in the details.'

Nick sighed. 'You do pick your moments.'

'I think I have the right to know some more about the man I'm sleeping with, don't you? You used to give my boyfriends the third degree.'

'But I'm not your boyfriend. I'm your secret lover. Secret lovers are often men of mystery.'

'Sorry, but you're not my secret lover any longer. I told Flora last night that we were together.'

'You *what*?'

Sarah shrugged. 'I said I was sorry.'

'Like hell you are. You're a conniving, manipulative little minx.'

Sarah could see that he wasn't as angry as he was trying to sound. And she had no intention of backing off.

'So are you going to tell me your life story, or not?'

'Do you think you're up for it, little girl?'

'Don't insult my intelligence, Nick. I might not have

been around like you, but I watch the news at night, and I can read. I know about the big, bad world. Nothing you say will shock me.'

What a naïve statement, Sarah was to discover over the next quarter of an hour as she listened to Nick's dreadful life story.

His mother had run off when he'd been too young to remember her, his lone-parent father a violent and drunken good-for-nothing who taught his son to shoplift when he was only five and beat him every other day. Sarah was appalled as Nick described being not only punched and slapped, but also beaten with belts and burned with cigarettes.

Naturally, Nick's schooling had been limited—he was kept away a lot—but he was smart enough to learn to read and write. Love, of course, had been an unknown emotion. He'd counted himself lucky to be fed. Survival had been the name of the game.

When he'd gone into puberty at thirteen, he'd suddenly shot up in height and was able to look his father straight in the eye. For the first time when his father hit him, Nick had hit back.

He hadn't actually run away from home as she'd thought. He'd been literally thrown out into the street with only the clothes he was wearing.

He'd stayed in a refuge for a while, but was unfortunate enough to find one that was run by someone who wasn't interested in helping, just in pocketing his salary. Not the best introduction to the welfare system for an already emotionally scarred child. After running away from there, Nick had made his way to King's Cross in Sydney, where he squatted in derelict buildings and made money the only way he knew: by stealing. Not shoplifting. Mostly he broke into parked cars and stole the contents.

He'd resisted joining a gang, not wanting to rely on anyone but himself. He had made a few friends, but they were all low-life, pimps and prostitutes and drug-dealers. Inevitably, he'd been drawn into drug use himself. Anything to make his existence more bearable.

Addiction of any kind, however, took money. So he had started breaking and entering, plus stealing the cars themselves, rather than just the contents.

'One night,' he said, 'I made a mistake and got caught. I went to jail, met your father and the rest is history, as they say.'

Sarah was close to tears. 'Oh, Nick...'

'I did warn you.'

'You survived, though.'

'Let me tell you about that kind of survival,' he bit out. 'It makes you think of no one but yourself. You become hard, and cold, and capable of just about anything. When I first met your father when I was in jail, I didn't give a damn about him, only what he could do for me. I saw a means of escape and I grabbed it with both hands. When I finally got out of jail and came to work as Ray's chauffeur, I thought he was a sucker. I had no feelings for him whatsoever.'

'But you did, in the end,' she said. 'You *loved* him.'

'I respected him. That's not the same as love.'

'I see…'

'No, you don't. You don't see at all. You can't, till you've lived in my shoes. I've told you once, now I'll tell you again: men like me can't love anyone.'

'I don't believe that,' she muttered. She couldn't. For if she did, her future was unbearable. 'You weren't that bad when you came to live with us. You were kind to me for starters.'

'Was I? Or was I just trying to get in good with the boss?'

Sarah frowned. She'd never thought of his actions in that light before.

'Damn it all, don't look at me like that. OK, so I did like you. You were a nice kid.'

'You still like me,' she said with a smile of relief.

'Yeah. I still like you.'

As admissions went, it wasn't much, but it made Sarah feel better. Things suddenly looked a bit brighter. But she felt a change of subject was called for.

'Have you heard anything about your movie yet?'

She'd never seen Nick look so confused. *'What?'*

'Didn't you say that movie you'd put so much money into was coming out in the New Year? Well, it's the third of January. That's past the New Year.'

The penny dropped for Nick. His lurid background was too much for Sarah. Hopefully, she wouldn't bring it up again. Talking about movies he could cope with. His past was best kept locked in the dungeon.

'It came out yesterday to mixed reviews,' he told her. 'It'll take a few more days before the public's verdict has come in.'

'What's it called?'

'*Back to the Outback*. It's a sequel to *Outback Bride*. It has the same writer-director.'

'That should do well, surely. Everyone who saw and loved *Outback Bride* will come to see it.'

'That's what we're hoping.'

'Is it any good? Sequels often aren't as good as the original.'

'I think it is.'

'But the critics didn't.'

'A couple of them did. The others hated the tragic ending.'

'Who dies? Not Shane, I hope.'

'No, Brenda.'

'*Brenda!* That's even worse. You can't kill off the heroine in a romance. There has to be a happy ending, Nick.'

'Rubbish. Lots of romances have unhappy endings.'

'Only the ones written by men,' she said disgustedly. 'How does she die?'

'She's shot saving her child from the baddies,' he said defensively, as if that made it all right.

'No excuses. She simply cannot die. Why couldn't she have been shot, but still live? Truly, you should have talked to me about this earlier, Nick. I would have advised you.'

'She *needed* to die. She was no good for Shane. Their romance was flawed and their marriage was a disaster waiting to happen. She hated life in the country and was threatening to go back to the city and take the child when the baddies from her earlier life show up. The sequel isn't really a romance, Sarah, it's a drama.'

'You can call it what you like. It sounds awful.'

'Thank you for the vote of confidence.'

The captain announcing that they were expecting some turbulence and everyone was to belt up terminated what was becoming a heated exchange.

'Typical,' Nick muttered as he snapped his seat belt shut.

'What do you mean?' Sarah asked, grabbing at the armrests when the plane shuddered.

'January is cyclone season in this neck of the woods.'

'I wish you'd told me that earlier. We could have just as easily stayed home, especially once Flora and Jim went away.'

'I wanted to show you Happy Island.'

'The island itself, or your fancy holiday house?'

Nick smiled. 'A man's allowed to show off to his girlfriend, isn't he?'

Sarah's heart flipped over. 'You…you called me your girlfriend.'

Nick shrugged. 'I reserve the right to rescind the title if you get stroppy with me.'

'I only get stroppy during cyclones. I also get hysterical.'

Nick laughed. 'Now she tells me. Don't worry. My place is cyclone-proof. Actually, Happy Island hasn't been directly hit by a cyclone in decades. Mostly, it just gets lots of wind and rain. Unfortunately, we might have to stay indoors for days on end,' he added with a wicked twinkle in his eyes.

Sarah grinned. 'Just as well I brought all my old board games with me, then, isn't it?'

Nick groaned. 'Oh, no, not the Monopoly! You always whipped my butt at that.'

'Monopoly and Snakes and Ladders, and Chinese Checkers. I found them in the bottom of my wardrobe when I was packing.'

When Nick looked pained, she gave him a playful dig in the ribs.

'Come on. We used to have great fun playing those games.'

'I had some different kinds of games in mind now that you've grown up.'

Sarah shook her head at him. 'If you think this holiday is going to be just a sex-fest, Nick, then think again. I picked up a brochure about Happy Island from a local travel agent and there's heaps I want to do.'

'Really. Such as?'

'Aside from a tour around the island to all the scenic spots, I'd like to take a boat trip to the barrier reef and a helicopter ride over the Whitsundays. Then there's windsurfing and souvenir-shopping. Oh, and mini-golf. You can have your revenge on me with that. I also saw pictures of a lovely white beach with the most beautiful turquoise waters where I'd like to go for a swim.'

'Uh-uh,' he said with a shake of his head. 'You won't be doing that.'

'Why not?'

'Because of the irukanji.'

'The what?'

'They're a jellyfish. Toxic as all hell. They can put you in hospital for days. Two people have died from their sting since 2001. Summer is their peak season.'

'Oh, great. No swimming.'

'Actually, you *can* go in the sea, if you wear a full body suit. But they don't look too glamorous. Still, not to worry. There are more swimming pools on Happy Island than you can poke a stick at. Mine is fabulous, and solar-heated as well.'

'I didn't doubt it.'

His smile carried amusement. 'You have a tongue on you at times, don't you?'

'I never said I was perfect.'

'Just nearly,' he murmured, and leant over to kiss her on the cheek.

Her head turned fully to face him. 'I thought you said you weren't going to kiss me.'

'You call that a kiss? I'll show you a kiss when I get you to my place.'

A quiver ran through her body at the desire gleaming

bright in his eyes. This was what she'd always wanted, to have him look at her like this. But would it be enough, just being the recipient of Nick's passion? The truth was she wanted more now. She wanted that happily-ever-after ending. She wanted Nick's love, the very thing he claimed he could never give anyone.

'You can relax your hands now,' he said. 'We're through the turbulence.'

Not so, she thought with a tormented twist to her heart. The turbulence has only just begun.

CHAPTER FOURTEEN

THE beauty of Happy Island just blew Sarah away. The pilot circled it once before landing, giving all the window-seat passengers a splendid view.

Talk about a tropical paradise!

She'd heard people wax lyrical about the colour of the sand and the water in this region, but the beaches and bays were just magic to the eye, framed by lots of palm trees and environmentally friendly buildings that blended beautifully with the green vegetation.

Nick was right about the number of pools, though. They did stand out from the air, because there were so many, in all sorts of shapes and sizes.

Any worry she was still harbouring about the eventual outcome of their relationship was put aside as excitement took hold. It would be wonderful to have a romantic holiday here, with the man she loved. Wonderful to have him all to herself for a whole month.

If nothing else, she would have this marvellous memory.

'No point in rushing off the plane,' Nick said when everyone else jumped up from their seats. 'We'll only have to wait in the heat for our luggage. There's no carousel in the terminal here, just a collection area down near where all the resort shuttles are parked.'

'Will we be taking a shuttle?'

'No. I own a golf buggy, which I keep at the airport.'

'Oh, yes, I read about those in the brochure. It said there weren't many cars on the island, and everyone got around in golf buggies.'

'That's right.'

'Can I drive it?'

'Sure.'

'Oh, wow. That'll be fun.'

Sarah and Nick finally exited the plane next to last, with Sarah surprised to find it not quite as hot outside as she'd been expecting. 'Am I wrong, or is it not all that hot out here?'

'No, you're quite right. But the weather forecast says there'll be a change later in the week. It's going to gradually get hotter, with higher temperatures and humidity. They're predicting a storm on Saturday after-noon, with strong gusts of wind and tons of rain.'

'How do you know all that?'

'Looked on the internet last night for the forecast up this way.'

'You didn't bring your laptop with you, I hope.'

'No need. I have a full computer set-up here.'

'What *don't* you have here?' Sarah heard herself saying half an hour later.

She was standing in the main living room of Nick's holiday house, looking through a wall made totally of glass at the most magnificent pool she had ever seen. It was called a horizon pool, so named because the far side of the pool seemed to have no edge, the water meeting the sky the way the horizon did out at sea.

'It cost me a pretty penny,' Nick agreed.

'You mean the pool, or the rest of this place?'

Actually, the house wasn't all that huge. Only three bedrooms. But everything was beautifully and stylishly decorated in cool greens and blues that complemented its tropical setting. There was also every mod con available, including a kitchen to die for and a king-sized plasma television.

'The foundations cost the most,' he told her.

Sarah could understand why. The house was built on the side of a cliff, its half-hexagonal shape creating one-hundred-and-eighty-degree views. All the rooms had huge glass windows or walls that looked out to sea and the other islands beyond. The glass was specially toughened to withstand even the worst storms, Nick told her, and tinted to soften any glare.

'It took two years to build,' Nick said. 'It was only completed last June.'

'Really?' Sarah said. So that was why Nick hadn't brought any of his girlfriends here before. He hadn't had the opportunity. Still, it was nice to think she was the first girl to stand here with him. And the first to share this particular master bedroom. She could hardly make the same claim about the bedroom back home.

'It's spectacular, Nick,' she said, throwing a warm smile up at him. 'So's this view.'

Nick slid an arm around her waist and pulled her close. 'Wait till you see it at sunrise.'

When he turned her towards him, Sarah knew he was going to kiss her. And this time, there would be no stopping him. Not that she wanted to. Her heart was already pounding by the time his lips met hers.

'I don't think I'm going to let you unpack,' Nick said to her some considerable time later. 'I like you like this.'

They'd eventually made it to the master bedroom, though Sarah's clothes were still on the living-room floor. Nick's as well.

Sarah sighed with pleasure as Nick gently caressed her stomach.

'I like you like this as well,' she returned dreamily.

The lovemaking between them was getting better and better, and gradually more adventurous. Sarah had thought she preferred the missionary position with Nick, where their eyes could meet and she could hold him close in the traditional way. But she found this spoon position very much to her liking, thrilling to the hot feel of Nick's body cocooned around hers. She loved that it left his hands free to play with her breasts and the rest of her body whilst he was inside her. The sensations had sent her head spinning.

He hadn't withdrawn afterwards, and she could feel

him slowly coming back to life. He groaned when her bottom moved voluptuously against him.

His hands lifted to her breasts, where he pinched her nipples.

'Oh,' she gasped, startled by the odd mixture of pain and pleasure.

'You liked that,' he muttered thickly in her ear.

'Yes…no…I don't know.'

'*I* liked it,' he said, and did it again.

She moaned, then squirmed. Yes, she definitely did like it.

'Do it again,' she urged breathlessly.

He obliged and her head whirled with the dizziest pleasure. Now he was fully erect again, and began thrusting harder than the first time. Heat enveloped her, her forehead breaking into a sweat.

'Yes,' she bit out, everything inside her twisting into exquisitely expectant spirals. 'Yes. Yes,' she cried out as her body broke into little pieces, splintering apart with a violent release.

With a raw groan Nick rolled her over onto her stomach, cupping her breasts and lifting her up onto her hands and knees. Sarah thought she was done, but she was wrong. When he reached down and rubbed her clitoris, another orgasm ripped through her. This time he came too, hot and strong. At last she fell, face-down, onto the bed, his body collapsing on top of hers.

For a couple of minutes they just lay, glued together by sweat, their breathing ragged.

'See?' he said at last, his voice low and thick. 'A woman can come lots of times in a row. I could keep you coming all day, if you want me to.'

Sarah went weak with the thought of his doing such a thing.

'I...I think what I need right at this moment,' she said shakily, 'is a shower.'

'Mmm. What a good idea. I'll join you.'

CHAPTER FIFTEEN

NICK lay stretched out next to Sarah's sleeping form, his hands linked behind his head, his body temporarily sated but his mind not even remotely at peace.

It wasn't working, his plan to burn out his lust for Sarah. It seemed the more he had her, the more he wanted her.

Thirty-six hours had passed since their arrival, with their hardly leaving the master suite, except for food and the occasional dip in the pool.

Nick's flesh began to stir once more as he recalled their erotic encounter by the pool last night, not to mention the wildly passionate one in the kitchen this morning.

Sarah had confessed afterwards she'd never had sex whilst sitting on a granite bench-top before. Or sitting anywhere, for that matter.

It seemed her sex life so far had been limited and unimaginative, a fact that Nick found surprising, yet primally satisfying. He was beginning to understand why some men married virgins. There had to be something intensely pleasing about being a female's first lover.

At the same time, Sarah's lack of sexual experience troubled him. Young, naïve girls like her fell in love so very easily.

Though she'd never said she loved him, he'd seen adoration in her lovely but very readable eyes. Seen it, and wallowed in it.

Was that the reason behind his growing addiction for her? Not the sex so much but the way Sarah made him feel whilst he was making love to her?

How would it be to always have her in his bed? he began to wonder. To put his ring on her finger? To legally bind her to him?

Crazy thoughts, Nick. Crazy.

Shaking his head, he rolled over and propped himself up on one elbow to stare down at her, his eyes roving hotly over her lusciously naked body. Before he knew it he was touching her again, waking her, *wanting* her. He groaned when she opened her arms to him on a sigh of sweet surrender.

Say no, damn you, his mind screamed as he plunged into her.

But she didn't.

Sarah crept from the bed, lest she wake Nick. Night had fallen and he was sleeping soundly at long last.

Pulling on her lavender satin robe—her only item of clothing as yet unpacked—she made her way quietly out to the kitchen, where she began to search the large freezer for something substantial to eat. During the past two days they'd only eaten enough to survive—mostly toast and coffee—and Sarah was suddenly feeling ravenous.

Half an hour and two microwaveable meals later, Sarah carried a second mug of coffee into the living room and curled herself up in a corner of the blue sofa. She sighed as she sipped, only then allowing herself to think about what they'd been doing since they'd arrived on Happy Island.

So much for her saying this holiday was not going to be just a sex-fest!

Truly, she should put her foot down and demand that they leave the house occasionally. It wasn't right to just loll around, having sex all the time.

Sarah pulled a face. Maybe it wasn't right, but it felt good. *She* felt good. Better than she'd ever felt.

But enough was enough, she decided. Come tomorrow, she would insist on their getting dressed and going out somewhere.

Hopefully Nick would not make a fuss, or start seducing her again. Her head whirled at how good he was at doing that. And how successful. She just couldn't seem to say no to him.

But she would, come tomorrow morning.

Easier said than done, Sarah thought ruefully. He only had to roll over and start touching her, and she was a goner.

Maybe she should spend the rest of the night out here on this sofa; it was big enough to sleep on.

Whatever, she didn't need sleep for a while. After her eating binge, she was wide awake. Watching television was not an option, however. The noise might wake Nick. Maybe she would read for a while. There were a few paperbacks on the shelves that flanked the large built-in entertainment unit.

Sarah put down her coffee and made her way across the tiled floor. There was only one title that appealed, called *Dressed to Kill*, the back blurb promising a page-turning thriller with twists and turns and a spine-tingling climax.

Sarah's spine certainly tingled when she opened it and saw the handwritten name on top of the first page.

Chloe Cameron.

Her mouth went dry as she stared down at that hated name, her head filling with a hundred horrible thoughts, the main one being that Nick had lied to her. Chloe *had* been to Happy Island with him—how else would this book be here? Nick was not a reader.

Various repulsive images popped into Sarah's mind. Of Nick having sex with Chloe by the pool and on the kitchen counter. Of his doing all the things with Chloe that he'd done with her.

The hurt was overwhelming. So was the humiliation. What a fool she'd been to be so easily tricked! A besotted fool!

But no more.

Gripping the book tightly in both hands, Sarah marched back into the bedroom, snapping on the overhead light, then slamming the door with deliberate loudness.

* * *

Nick woke with a start, blinking madly as he sat up. Sarah's glowering at him from the side of the bed brought confusion, then a jolt of alarm.

'What is it? What's wrong?'

She threw something at him. A book. It struck his bare chest before he could catch it, tumbling down into his lap.

'You said you'd never brought her here,' Sarah bit out. 'You lied, you bastard.'

The penny dropped for Nick, as did his stomach.

'It's not what you're thinking,' he defended.

Her laugh had a hard, hollow sound to it. 'And why's that, Nick?'

'I didn't have sex with her.'

She laughed again. 'You expect me to believe that? Mr I-have-to-have-it-ten-times-a-day!'

'Chloe was sick, with food poisoning. She spent the whole weekend in bed in the guest room.'

Sarah crossed her arms, her expression scornful. 'If that's the truth, why didn't you tell me?

'I'll tell you why,' she went on before he could say a single word. 'Because that might not have got you what you wanted, which was stupid me, filling in for Chloe on this holiday. Better to let the silly little fool think she's unique and special. Make her believe your inviting her to come with you here is a one-off. Whatever way you look at it, Nick, you lied to me for your own selfish ends.'

Nick was not at his best when backed into a corner. He always came out fighting.

'And you haven't done the same?' he counterattacked. 'I seem to recall your telling me in my study on Christmas Day that all you wanted from me was sex. Obviously that wasn't the truth, was it? You want what you've always wanted: marriage. That's why you've been so damned accommodating all the time. And why you're so upset right now!'

Her face flushed with a shaming heat, her hurt eyes making him feel totally wretched.

'If that's what you really think, Nick,' she choked out, 'then I can't stay here with you. I just can't.'

In all his life, Nick had never felt so dreadful. Even when he'd been in jail. But it was for the best, wasn't it? He was no good for her. Better they call it quits now before she got even more hurt.

'If that's what you want,' he snapped.

'What I want...' She shook her head, her shoulders slumping as a soul-weary sigh escaped her lips. 'I'm never going to get what I want. Not with you. I can see that now.' She straightened, putting her shoulders back and lifting her chin up. 'I'm sorry for throwing that book at you, Nick. Generally speaking, you have been honest with me. Quite brutally at times. I just didn't want to hear what you were saying.'

Now Nick felt even worse, his heart like a great lump of iron in his chest. The temptation to jump up and take her in his arms was almost overwhelming. He wanted to tell her that *he* was the sorry one, that she *was* unique and special and that he *did* want to marry her.

But he resisted the temptation. Somehow.

'I…I'll move my things into one of the spare bedrooms for tonight,' she went on, her eyes glistening. 'Then first thing tomorrow I'll see if I can get on a flight back to Sydney.'

'Fine,' he said, and threw back the sheet. 'Now, if you'll excuse me, I need to go to the bathroom.'

CHAPTER SIXTEEN

SARAH couldn't sleep. Not only was she still very upset, but she was also hot. The weather forecast had been right: the temperature had risen sharply over the last few hours, so the air-conditioning was struggling in the higher humidity.

In the end, Sarah got up, put on the pink bikini she'd bought before Christmas, grabbed a towel and headed for the pool. Who cared if it was the middle of the night and pitch-black outside? The pool had underwater lighting.

The strength of the wind surprised her. She had to anchor her towel underneath a banana lounger to stop it from blowing away. The same banana lounger, she realised, that she and Nick had had sex on the day before. Wild, wanton sex, with herself a very willing partner.

Shuddering at the memory, Sarah dived into the water, and began stroking vigorously up and down, hoping to make herself so exhausted that when she returned to bed she would immediately fall asleep.

Fat chance, she thought wretchedly, but continued

to punish herself with lap after lap. Finally, the lactic acid in her joints forced her to stop. Slowly, she swam over towards the lounger that was down near the far edge of the pool.

Sarah shivered as she hauled herself out of the water. The wind was much stronger than before. That storm couldn't be far off now. Hopefully, it wouldn't last too long. She didn't want there to be any reason for the airport to be closed tomorrow. She needed to get off this island and away from Nick as soon as possible.

Sarah was bending to retrieve her towel when a wildly swirling gust of wind lifted a nearby table and umbrella off the tiled surrounds and hurled them against her back. She screamed as she was catapulted with tremendous force into the air and right over the horizon edge of the pool. She screamed again when she hit the water-catching ledge below with a bruising blow to her shoulder, another scream bursting from her mouth when momentum carried her right off the edge and into the void.

Nick was lying on top of the sheets, wide awake, when he heard Sarah's terrified screams. He was off the bed in a flash, fear quickening his heartbeat—and his legs— as he raced in the direction of her cries.

The pool area.

The security light was already on, indicating that Sarah must have come outside here recently. But he couldn't see her anywhere.

And then he saw them: the table and umbrella floating in the far end of the pool.

'Oh, my God!' he exclaimed, his first thought being that she was under them in the water, knocked unconscious and already drowning.

When Nick dived in and found no sign of her, an even worse possibility came to mind. Swimming to the far edge, he peered over it to the ledge below, hoping against hope that he'd see her sitting there, waiting for him to pull her up into his arms.

The most appalling dread consumed him when the dimly lit ledge proved empty as well. The thought that she had fallen down to the rocky waters below was so horrendous that he could hardly conceive of it. For no one could survive a fall like that.

'Nooooo!' he screamed into the wind.

She could not be dead. Not his Sarah. Not his wonderful, beautiful, sweet Sarah.

'Nick! Nick, are you there?'

Nick almost cried with relief. 'Yes, I'm here,' he called back, scrambling over the edge and dropping down to the ledge below. 'Where are you? I can't see you!'

His eyes were gradually becoming accustomed to the lack of direct light, but the wind was making them water like mad.

'Down here.'

'Down where?'

He leant right over as far as he dared, finally spotting her clinging to the cliff a few metres down under the ledge. No, not to the cliff but to a bush that was growing out of a crevice in the rock face—a rather straggly-looking bush.

Hopefully, the roots were tenacious.

'Have you got a foothold?' he called out to her.

'A bit of a one. But I think this bush is coming loose. Oh, God, yes, it is. Do something, Nick.'

Nick knew she was too far down for him to reach. He needed something long that she could get hold of. But what?

Panic turned his head to mush for a moment.

'Think, man,' he muttered to himself.

The umbrella in the pool. It was quite large and its supporting pole was long.

'Hold on, Sarah, I have an idea.'

Adrenaline had him leaping back up and into the pool with the agility of a monkey. He grabbed the umbrella, yanked it down, then jumped back with it to the ledge below.

'Here,' he said, and stretched it out towards her. 'Grab this.'

She did so.

'Hold on tight,' he ordered.

Her weight surprised him at first. But he felt strong, stronger than he'd ever felt. And then she was there, in his arms, weeping and shaking with shock.

Nick held her close, his lips buried in her wet hair, his eyes tightly shut.

'It's all right,' he said thickly. 'I have you now. You're safe.'

'Oh, Nick,' Sarah cried. 'I…I thought I was going to die.'

Nick held her even tighter. He'd thought she *had* died. And it was the most defining moment in his life. He knew now what Jim had felt at that hospital. Because as much as Jim loved Flora, *he* loved Sarah. Oh, yes, he loved her. There was no longer any doubt in his mind.

But did that make any difference? Wouldn't she still be better off if he let her go?

He just didn't know any more.

'I…I can't stop sh-shaking,' she said, her teeth chattering.

'You're in shock,' he told her. 'What you need is a warm bath, and a hot cup of tea with lots of sugar in it. But first, I have to get you up out of here. Very, very carefully.'

Sarah couldn't stop thinking about the moment she'd fallen off that ledge. Couldn't stop reliving the fear, and the split-second realisation that her life was about to be over.

It made one reassess things, facing death like that. Made one see what was important, and what wasn't. Made one more prepared to take a risk or two.

'Here's the tea,' Nick said as he came into the bathroom.

Sarah was lying back in a very deep, deliciously warm bath, her pink bikini still on. Nick, however, was still naked.

'Do you think you could put something on?' she said to him when he handed her the tea. Sarah knew she would find it difficult to talk to a naked Nick.

And she did want to talk to him. Sensibly and truthfully.

Nick pulled a towel off a nearby rail and tied it around his hips.

'This do?' he asked her.

'Yes, thank you. No, please don't leave. I...I have something I want to say to you.'

Nick crossed his arms and leant against the far wall whilst Sarah lifted the mug to her lips and swallowed, grimacing at the excessive sweetness. Finally, she put the mug down and locked eyes with him.

'I've decided I don't want to go home tomorrow.'

His eyes flickered momentarily. 'And why's that, Sarah?'

'I love you, Nick. I've always loved you. You were quite right about why I came here with you. I had this romantic dream that if we spent quality time together, you would discover that you loved me back. And then there was the ultimate fantasy of your asking me to marry you.'

Now he did move, his arms uncrossing as he levered himself away from the wall, his high forehead drawing into a frown. 'Sarah, I—'

'No, no, let me finish, please, Nick.'

'Very well.'

'You may have been right about my reasons for coming here with you. But you were wrong when you accused me of using sex to try to get what I wanted. Not once have I said yes to you sexually with that agenda in mind. I *love* it when you make love to me. I've never experienced anything like it before in my life. I can't describe how I feel when you're inside me. I don't want to walk away from that pleasure, Nick. So if you still want me, I'd like to stay. I…I promise I won't put on any more insanely jealous turns. I just want to be with you, Nick,' she finished, a huge lump having formed in her throat during her brave little speech. 'Please…I…'

When her eyes filled with tears, Nick couldn't stand it any longer. How could his sending her away be the best thing for her? Or him? Seeing her like this was killing him.

'Don't cry,' he choked out as he fell to his knees by the bath. 'Please don't cry.'

'I'm sorry,' she sobbed. 'It's just…I…I love you so much.'

His hands reached out to cup her lovely face. 'And I love you, my darling.'

She gasped, her eyes widening.

'I knew it tonight when I thought I'd lost you. I love you, Sarah. And I *do* want to marry you.'

Her eyes carried shock, and scepticism. 'You…you don't mean that. You can't. You always said…'

'I know what I always said. I thought I wasn't good enough for you.'

'Oh, Nick. That's just so not true.'

'Yes, it is,' he insisted. 'But if you will trust me with

your life I vow that I will do my best never to hurt you, or let you or your father down. I will be faithful only to you. I will love you and protect you. And I will love and protect our children.'

Her already shocked eyes rounded further. 'You're prepared to have children?'

'I'll have your children, my darling, because I know that any shortcomings I have as a father will be more than made up for by your brilliance as a mother.'

'You…you shouldn't say such sweet things to me,' she cried.

'Why not? I mean them.'

Her tear-filled eyes searched his. 'You do mean them, don't you?'

'I surely do.'

'I…I don't know what to say.'

'Yes to marrying me would be a good start.'

'Oh, yes,' she said, and he kissed her. When his mouth lifted she was smiling.

'I'm glad to see I was right,' she said.

'About what?' Nick asked.

'The heroine in a romance never dies.'

EPILOGUE

'Don't you think people might think it's odd,' Flora said, 'having a sixty-one-year-old bridesmaid?'

'Who cares what people think?' Sarah countered. 'Besides, you look absolutely beautiful.' She did, too. A few weeks of healthy eating and exercising had done wonders. So did her new blonde hair. Flora looked ten years younger.

'Not as beautiful as the bride,' Flora returned with a warm smile. 'I'm so happy for you and Nick, love. If ever a couple were made for each other it's you two. Ray would have been very pleased. Pleased about the baby, too.'

'I think so,' Sarah said, beaming with happiness.

She'd forgotten to take the Pill the morning after that traumatic night on Happy Island, and had fallen pregnant. At first she'd been a bit nervous about Nick's reaction, but he'd been absolutely thrilled.

It seemed mother nature knew what she was doing.

Now here she was, almost four months pregnant, about to marry the father of her baby and the only man she'd ever loved. She was not, however, a super-rich heiress. The day before her twenty-fifth birthday, she'd discussed her feelings over her inheritance with Nick and decided to do what he'd once said her father should have done in the first place: give all the money to charity.

So she had, dividing up the many millions in the estate between various charities that supported the poor and the needy.

Of course, she wasn't exactly broke. She still owned Goldmine, which was worth a conservative twenty million. Not that she would ever sell it. And then there were the royalties from *Outback Bride*, which would continue to flow in, the movie having been re-released after the worldwide success of its sequel. Nick had been so right about that tear-jerker ending.

Generally speaking, however, Nick would be the main provider for their family, an excellent source of motivation for him to keep working hard and feeling good about himself. Sarah vowed to never forget that underneath her husband's façade of confidence lay a damaged child who constantly needed the healing power of love. *Her* love.

A loud knock on her bedroom door was accompanied by a familiar voice. 'Time for the bride to make an appearance downstairs. We don't want the groom thinking things, do we?'

Sarah was smiling as she opened the door.

'Wow!' Derek said, looking her up and down. 'It's at moments like these I wish I weren't gay. And I'm not just talking about the bride.'

'Oh, go on with you,' Flora said, but with a big grin on her face.

Derek had become a frequent visitor to Goldmine, with Nick even warming to him. Derek had been delighted—and touched—when Sarah had asked him to give her away.

'OK, girls,' he said, linking arms with Sarah, 'it's showtime!'

'Goddamn!' Jim exclaimed beside Nick when an elegantly dressed blonde lady walked sedately down the steps into the rather crowded family room. 'Is that my Flora?'

'Indeed it is,' Nick informed his best man. But his own admiring eyes moved quickly to the radiant bride following Flora, his heart filling with emotion as he watched Sarah walk towards him with the most glorious smile on her face. It was a smile of total love and trust, that love and trust which had soothed his soul and brought it out from the dungeon into the light.

Nick still found it hard to believe sometimes that he was happy about becoming a husband and father. Still, anything was possible with Sarah by his side.

'You look amazing,' he said softly to her as he took her hand and they turned to face the celebrant.

'You do, too,' she whispered back.

'Ray would have been so proud of you.'

Her hand squeezed his tightly. 'You, too, my darling heart. You, too.'

THE MAGNATE'S
MISTRESS

CHAPTER ONE

THE beep-beep which signalled an incoming text message had Tara dropping her book and diving for her cellphone.

Max! It had to be Max. He was the only person who text-messaged her these days.

Arriving Mascot at 1530, she read with her heart already thudding. *QF310. Can you pick me up? Let me know.*

A glance at her bedside clock said five to twelve. If his plane was to arrive at three-thirty this afternoon, Max had to be already in the air.

She immediately texted him back.

Will be there.

She smiled wryly at the brevity and lack of sentiment in both their messages. There was no *I can't wait to see you, darling.* No *I've missed you terribly.* All very matter-of-fact.

Max was a matter-of-fact kind of man. Mostly.

Not quite so matter-of-fact in bed. A quiver rippled

down Tara's spine at the image of Max in the throes of making love to her.

No. Not at all matter-of-fact on those occasions.

Tara glanced at the clock again. Nearly noon.

Not a lot of time for her to get ready, catch a train into town, collect Max's car and drive out to the airport. She would have to hurry.

Jumping up from the bed reminded Tara of why she'd been lying back down at this late hour on a Saturday morning. A new wave of nausea rolled through her and she just made it to the bathroom in time before retching.

Darn. Why did she have to have a tummy bug today of all days? It had been almost a month since she'd seen Max, the current crisis in the travel industry having kept him on the hop overseas for ages. Hong Kong had been one of the cities worst affected. When she'd complained during his last phone call two nights ago that she'd forget what he looked like soon, Max had promised to see what he could do this weekend. He was flying to Auckland on the Friday for an important business meeting and might have time to duck over to Sydney on the weekend before returning to Hong Kong.

But Tara hadn't seriously expected anything. She never liked to get her hopes up too much. It was too depressing when she was disappointed. Still, maybe Max was finally missing her as much as she was missing him.

Which was why the last thing she needed today was to feel sick. She might only have the one night with him this time and she wanted to make the most of it. But it would be hard to enjoy his company if she felt like chucking up all the time.

A sigh reverberated through her as she flushed the toilet.

'Are you all right in there?' her mother called through the bathroom door.

'I'm fine,' Tara lied, experience warning her not to say anything. Her mother would fuss. Tara disliked being fussed over. No doubt she was only suffering from the same twenty-four-hour gastric bug which was going through Sydney's western suburbs like wildfire. Her sister's family had had it this past week, and she'd been over there last weekend for a family barbeque.

Actually, now that she'd been sick, Tara felt considerably better. A shower would make her feel even better, she reasoned, and turned on the spray.

Her arrival in the kitchen an hour later with freshly blow-dried hair, a perfectly made-up face and a new outfit on had her mother giving her a narrow-eyed once-over.

'I see his lord and master must be arriving for one of his increasingly fleeting visits,' Joyce said tartly, then went back to whatever cake she was making.

Saturday was Joyce Bond's baking day; had been for as long as Tara could remember. Such rigid routines grated on Tara's more spontaneous nature. She often wished that her mother would surprise her by doing something different on a Saturday for once. She also wished she would surprise her with a different attitude towards Max.

'Mum, please don't,' Tara said wearily, and popped a slice of bread into the toaster. Her stomach had settled enough for her to handle some Vegemite toast, but she still wasn't feeling wonderful.

Joyce spun round from the kitchen counter to glower at her daughter. Her impossibly beautiful daughter.

Tara had inherited the best of each of her parents. She had her father's height, his lovely blond hair, clear skin, good teeth and striking green eyes. Joyce had contributed a cute nose, full lips and an even fuller bust, which looked infinitely better on Tara than it ever had on her own less tall, short-waisted body.

Joyce hadn't been surprised when one of the wealthy men who patronised the exclusive jewellery boutique where Tara worked had made a beeline for her. She wasn't surprised—or even too worried—when Tara confessed that she was no longer a virgin. Joyce had always thought it a minor miracle that a girl with Tara's looks had reached twenty-four without having slept with a man. After all, her daughter's many boyfriends must have tried to get the girl into bed.

Tara had always claimed she was waiting for Prince Charming to come along. Joyce's younger daughter was somewhat of an idealist, a full-on romantic. An avid reader, she was addicted to novels which featured wonderful heroes and happy-ever-after endings.

In the beginning, Joyce had hoped that Max Richmond *was* her daughter's Prince Charming. He had most of the attributes. Wealth. Good looks. Youth.

Relative youth, anyway. He'd been thirty-five when they'd begun seeing each other.

But in the last twelve months Joyce had come to feel differently about her daughter's relationship with the handsome hotel magnate. It had finally become clear that Max Richmond was never going to marry his lovely young mistress.

For that was what Tara had swiftly become. Not a proper girlfriend, or a partner, as people sometimes called their loved ones these days. A *mistress*, expected to be there when he called and be silent when he left. Expected to give everything and receive nothing in return, except for the corrupting gifts rich men invariably gave to their mistresses.

Designer clothes. Jewellery. Perfume. Flowers.

A fresh bouquet of red roses was delivered every week when Max was away. But who ordered them? Joyce often wondered. The man himself, or his secretary?

If Tara had been the kind of good-time girl who could handle such a relationship, Joyce would have held her tongue. But Tara was nothing of the kind. Underneath her sophisticated and sexy-looking exterior lay a soft, sensitive soul. A good girl. When Max Richmond eventually dumped her, she was going to be shattered.

Joyce's thoughts had fired a slow-burning fury, along with her tongue.

'Don't what?' she snapped. 'Don't tell it like it is? I'm not going to sit by silently and say nothing, Tara. I love you too much for that. You're wasting your life on that man. He will never give you what you really want. He's just using you.'

Tara refrained from reminding her mother how often she'd been told in this house that she didn't know *what* she wanted in life. Joyce had frowned over her daughter not using her arts degree to get a job in Sydney. Instead, a restless Tara had gone tripping off to Japan to teach English for two years, at the same time using the opportunity to see as much of Asia as she could. When she'd returned to Sydney eighteen months ago her mother had expected her to look for a teaching position here. Instead, she'd taken a job as a shop assistant at Whitmore Opals, till she decided what she wanted to do next. Her announcement recently that she was going back to university next year to study psychology had been met with rolling eyes, as if to say, there she goes again.

In a way, her mother was right. She didn't know what she wanted to be, career-wise, the way some people did. But she knew what she *didn't* want. She didn't want to be tied down at home with children the way Jen was. And she didn't want to bake cakes every single Saturday.

'So what *is* it that you think I really want, Mum?' she asked, rather curious to find out what secret observation her mother had made.

'Why, what most women want deep down. A home, and a family. And a husband, of course.'

Tara shook her head. Given that her mother was rising sixty, she supposed there were excuses for holding such an old-fashioned viewpoint.

But the bit about a husband was rather ironic, considering her mother's personal background. Joyce had been widowed for over twenty years, Tara's electrician father having been killed in a work accident when Tara was just three. Her mother had raised her two daughters virtually single-handed. She'd worked hard to provide for them. She'd scrimped and saved and even bought her own house. Admittedly, it was not a flash house. But it was a house. *And,* she'd never married again. In fact, there'd never been another man in her life after Tara's father.

'It may come as a surprise to you, Mum,' Tara said as she removed the popped-up toast, 'but I don't want any of that. Not yet, anyway. I'm only twenty-four. There are plenty of years ahead for me to settle down to marriage and motherhood. I like my life the way it is. I'm looking forward to going back to uni next year. Meanwhile, I have an interesting job, some good friends and a fabulous lover.'

'Whom you rarely see. As for your supposed good friends, name one you've been out with in the last six months!'

Tara couldn't.

'See what I mean?' her mother went on accusingly. 'You never go out with your old friends any more because you're compelled to keep your weekends free, in case his lord and master deigns to drop in on your life. For pity's sake, Tara, do you honestly think your jet-setting lover is spending every weekend of his alone when he doesn't come home?'

Joyce regretted the harsh words the moment she saw her daughter's face go a sickly shade of grey.

Tara gripped the kitchen counter and willed the bile in her throat to go back down. 'You don't know what you're talking about, Mum. Max would never do that.'

'Are you sure of that?' Joyce said, but more softly this time. 'He doesn't love you, Tara. Not the way you love him.'

'Yes, he does. And even if he didn't, I'd still want him.'

Oh, yes, that was one thing she *was* sure about.

'I won't give him up for anything, or anyone,' she announced fiercely, and took a savage bite of toast.

'He's going to break your heart.'

Tara's heart contracted. Would he? She couldn't imagine it. Not her Max. Not deliberately. He wasn't like that. Her mother didn't understand. Max just didn't want marriage at this time in his life. Or kids. He'd explained all that to her right from the beginning. He'd told her up front that his life was too busy for a wife and a family. Since his father had been incapacitated by a stroke, the full responsibility of running the family firm had fallen on him. Looking after a huge chain of international hotels was a massive job, especially with the present precarious state of tourism and travel. Max spent more than half his life on a plane. All he could promise her for now was the occasional weekend.

He'd given her the opportunity to tell him to get lost, *before* she got in any deeper. But of course that had been *after* he'd taken her to bed and shown her a world she'd never envisaged, a world of incredible pleasure.

How could you give up perfection, just because everything wasn't perfect?

Tara threw the rest of her toast in the bin under the sink, then straightened with a sigh. 'If you disapprove of my relationship with Max this much, Mum,' she said unhappily, 'perhaps it's time I moved out of home.'

She could well afford to rent a place of her own on her salary. Her pay as a shop assistant at Whitmore Opals was boosted by generous commission each month. She was their top salesgirl, due to her natural affinity for people and her ability to speak fluent Japanese. A lot of the shop's customers were wealthy Japanese visitors and businessmen who appreciated being served by a pretty Australian girl who spoke their language like a native.

'And go where?' her mother threw back at her. 'To your lover's penthouse? He won't like that. You're only welcome there when *he's* there.'

'You don't know that. There again, you don't know Max. How could you? You never say more than two words to him on the phone and you've never invited him here.'

'He wouldn't want to come here,' she grumbled. 'This house isn't fancy enough for a man who lives on the top floor of Sydney's plushest hotel, and whose family owns a waterfront mansion on Point Piper. *Which*, might I point out, he's not taken you to, not even over Christmas? Have you noticed that, Tara?

You're not good enough to be taken home to meet his parents. You're to be kept a dirty little secret. That's what you are, Tara. A *kept* woman.'

Tara had had enough of this. 'Firstly, there is nothing dirty about my relationship with Max. We love each other and he treats me like a princess. Secondly, Max does not keep me a dirty little secret. We often go out together in public, as you very well know. You used to show your friends the photographs in the paper. Quite proudly, if I recall.'

'That was when I thought something would come of your relationship. When I thought he would marry you. But there have been no photographs in the paper lately, I've noticed. Maybe because he doesn't have time to take you out any more. But I'll bet he still has time to take you to bed!'

Tara clenched her jaw hard lest she say something she would later regret. She loved her mother dearly. And she supposed she could understand why the woman worried about her and Max. But modern life was very complicated when it came to personal relationships. Things weren't as cut and dried as they had been in Joyce's day.

Still, it was definitely time to find somewhere else to live. Tara could not bear to have to defend herself and Max all the time. It would sour her relationship with her mother.

She could see now that she should not have come back home to live after her return from Tokyo. Her two years away had cut the apron strings and she should have left them cut. But when her mother had met her at the airport on her return, Tara didn't have the heart to dash Joyce's presumption that her daughter was back to stay with her. And frankly, it had been rather nice to come home to her old bedroom and her old things. *And* to her mother's cooking.

But that had been several months before she'd met Max and fallen head over heels in love.

Things were different now.

Still, if she moved out of home, her mother was going to be very lonely. She often said how much she enjoyed Tara's company. Tara's board money helped make life easier for Joyce as well. Her widow's pension didn't stretch all that far.

Guilt screamed in to add to Tara's distress.

Oh, dear. What was a daughter to do?

She would talk to Max about the situation, and see what he said. Max had a wonderful way of making things seem clear and straightforward. Solutions to problems were Max's stock-in-trade. As were decisions. He spent most of his life solving problems and making decisions.

Max was a very decisive man. A little inflexible, however, Tara conceded. And opinionated. And unforgiving.

Very unforgiving, actually.

'Look, Mum, there are reasons why Max hasn't taken me home to meet his parents,' she started explaining to her mother. 'It has nothing to do with our working class background. His own father was born working-class, but he…' Tara broke off abruptly before she revealed things told to her in strict confidence. Max would not appreciate her blurting out the skeletons in his family's closet, even to her mother. 'Let's leave all this for now,' she said with a sigh. 'I don't feel up to arguing with you over Max today.'

The moment she added those last words, Tara regretted them, for her mother's eyes instantly turned from angry to worried. Her mother was a chronic worrier when it came to matters of health.

'I *thought* I heard you being sick earlier,' Joyce said.

'It's nothing. Just a tummy bug. Probably the same thing Jen and her kids had. I'm feeling better now.'

'Are you sure that's what it is?' her mother asked, still looking concerned.

'Well, I don't think I'm dying of some dreaded disease,' Tara said. 'Truly, Mum, you have to stop looking up those health websites on the internet. You're becoming a hypochondriac.'

'I meant,' her mother bit out, 'do you think you could be pregnant?'

'Pregnant!' Tara was totally taken aback. Dear heaven. Mothers! *Truly.* 'No, Mum, I am definitely *not* pregnant.' She'd had a period during the weeks Max had been away, which meant if she was pregnant, it had been because of an immaculate conception!

Besides, if there was one thing Tara was fanatical about, it was birth control. The last thing *she* wanted at this time in her life was a baby. Max wasn't the only one.

When they'd first become lovers, Max had said he'd use condoms. But after one broke one night last year and they'd spent an anxious two weeks, Tara had taken over the job of preventing a pregnancy. She even had her cell-phone programmed so that it beeped at the same time every day, a reminder to take her pill. Six pm on the dot. She also kept a spare box of pills in Max's bathroom, in case she accidentally left hers at home.

Her mother's tendency to always expect the worst to happen in life had trained Tara to be an expert in preventative action.

'There is no sure form of contraception,' Joyce pointed out firmly. 'Except saying no.'

Tara refrained from telling her mother that saying no to Max would never be on her agenda.

'I have to get going,' she said. 'The next train for the city is due in ten minutes.'

'When will you be back?' her mother called after her as she hurried from the kitchen. 'Or don't you know?'

It hit home. That last remark. Because Tara *didn't* know. She never seemed to know these days. In that, her mother was right. Max came and went like a whirlwind, often without much information or explanation. He expected her to understand how busy he was at the moment. Which she did on the whole. *Didn't* she?

'I'll let you know, Mum,' Tara called back as she scooped up her carry-all and swept out the door. 'Bye.'

CHAPTER TWO

HER wrist-watch said three-forty as Tara slid Max's silver Mercedes into an empty parking space, then yanked the car keys out of the ignition. Ten seconds later she was hurrying across the sun-drenched car park, wishing she was wearing her joggers, instead of high-heeled slip-on white sandals. They were sexy shoes but impossible to run in. She'd found that out on the way to the station back at home.

Missing the train had put her in a right quandary.

Did she wait for the next train or catch a taxi?

A taxi from Quakers Hill to the city would cost a bomb.

Unfortunately, Joyce had instilled some of her frugal ways in both her daughters, so whilst Tara could probably have afforded the fare, she couldn't bring herself to do it. Aside from the sheer extravagance, she was saving this year to pay for next year's uni fees.

She'd momentarily contemplated using the credit card Max had given her, and which she occasionally used for clothes. But only when he was with her, and only when it was for something he insisted she buy, and which she wouldn't wear during her day-to-day life. Things like evening gowns and outrageously expensive lingerie. Things she kept in Max's penthouse for her life there.

Till now, she'd never used the card for everyday expenses. When she considered it this time, her mother's earlier words about her being a kept woman made up her mind for her. Maybe if she'd been still feeling sick, she'd have surrendered to temptation and taken a taxi, but the nausea which had been plaguing her all morning had finally disappeared. So she'd bought herself some food and sat and waited for the next train, and now she was running late.

Tara increased the speed of her stride, her stiletto heels click-clacking faster on the cement path. Her heart started to beat faster as well, a mixture of agitation and anticipation. With a bit of luck, Max's plane might not have arrived yet. She'd hate him to think she didn't care enough to be on time. Still, planes rarely seemed to land on schedule. Except when you didn't want them to, of course.

The contrariness of life.

Once inside the arrivals terminal, Tara swiftly checked the overhead information screens, groaning when she saw that Max's plane *had* landed, although only ten minutes earlier. The exit gate assigned was gate B.

Surely he could not be through Customs yet, she told herself as she hurried once more, her progress slightly hampered by having to dodge groups of people. Gate B, typically, was down the other end of the building.

Most of the men she swept past turned for a second glance, but Tara was used to that. Blondes surely did get more than their fair share of male attention, especially tall, pretty ones with long, flowing hair and even longer legs.

Tara also conceded that her new white hipsters were on the eye-poppingly tight side today. She'd been doing some comfort eating lately and had put on a couple of pounds since she'd bought them at a summer sale a fortnight ago. It was as well they were made of stretch material. Still, lord knew what the view of her was like from behind. Pretty in-your-face, no doubt.

Her braless state might have stopped traffic as well, *if* she'd been wearing a T-shirt or a singlet top.

Thankfully, she wasn't wearing either. The pink shirt she'd chosen that day did a fair job of hiding her unfettered breasts.

In her everyday life, Tara always wore a bra. But Max liked her braless. Or so he'd said one night, soon after they'd starting seeing each other. And, being anxious to please him, she'd started leaving off her bra whenever she was with him.

But as time had gone by, she'd become aware of the type of stares she'd received from other men when Max had taken her out in public.

And she hadn't liked it.

Nowadays, when she was with Max, she still left her bra off, but compromised by never wearing anything too revealing. She chose evening gowns with heavily beaded bodices, or solid linings. For dressy day wear, she stuck to dresses and covering jackets. For casual wear, she wore shirts and blouses rather than tight or clingy tops. Tara liked the idea of keeping her bared breasts for her lover only.

Her nipples tightened further at the mere thought of Max touching them.

She would have to wait for that pleasure, however, till they were alone in Max's hotel suite. Although Max seemed to like her displaying her feminine curves in public, he was not a man to make love anywhere but in total privacy. And that included kissing.

The first time he'd come home after being away, she'd thrown her arms around him in public and given him a big kiss. His expression when she finally let him come up for air had been one of agitation, and distaste. He'd explained to her later that he found it embarrassing, and could she please refrain from turning him on to that degree when he could not do anything about it?

He *had* added later that he was more than happy for her to be as provocative and as assertive as she liked in private. But once stung by what she'd seen as a rejection of her overtures—and affection—Tara now never made the first move where lovemaking was concerned. She always left it up to Max.

Not that she ever had to wait long. Behind closed doors, Max's coolly controlled façade soon dropped away to reveal a hot-blooded and often insatiable lover. His visits home might have become shorter and less frequent over the last few months—as Tara's mother had observed—but whilst he was here in Sydney, he was all Tara's. They spent most of Max's visits in bed.

Her mother would see this as conclusive evidence that she was just a sex object to Max. A kept woman. In other words, a mistress.

But her mother was not there when Max took her in his arms. She didn't see the look in his eyes; didn't feel the tenderness in his touch; or the uncontrollable trembling which racked his body whenever he made love to her.

Max *loved* her. Tara was sure of it.

His not wanting to marry her at this time in his life was a matter of timing, not lack of love. Max had never said that marriage was *never* on his agenda.

And as she'd told her mother, *she* was in no hurry to get married, anyway. What she was in a hurry for was to get to gate B, collect Max and take him back to the Regency Royale Hotel, post-haste.

Fate must have been on her side, for no sooner had she ground to a breathless halt not far from gate B than Max emerged through the customs exit, striding purposefully down the ramp, carrying his laptop in one hand and wheeling a black carry-on suitcase in the other.

Tara supposed he didn't look all that much different from dozens of other well-dressed businessmen there at the airport that day. Perhaps taller than most. More broad-shouldered. And more handsome.

But just the sight of him did things to her that she could never explain to her mother. She came alive as she was never alive when she wasn't with him. Her brain bubbled with joy and the blood fizzed in her veins.

Tara conceded not every twenty-four-year-old girl's heart would flutter madly at Max's more conservative brand of handsome, or his very conservative mode of dressing. Tara rarely saw him in anything but a suit. Today's was charcoal-grey. Single-breasted, combined with a crisp white shirt and a striped blue tie.

All very understated.

But Tara liked the air of stability and security which Max's untrendy image projected. She liked the fact that he always looked a man of substance. And she very much liked his looks.

Yet till now, she'd never really analysed him feature by feature. It had been his overall appearance, and his overall aura which had initially taken her breath away. And which had kept her captivated ever since.

But as Max made his way through gate B, his eyes having not yet connected with hers, Tara found herself studying Max's looks more objectively than usual.

Now, that was one classically handsome guy, she decided. Not a pretty boy, but not a rough diamond, either.

A masculine-looking man, Max had a large but well-balanced face, surrounded by a thick head of dark brown hair, always cut with short back and sides, and always combed from a side-parting. His ears were nicely flat against his well-shaped head. His intelligent blue eyes were deeply set, bisected by a long, straight nose and accentuated with thick, dark brown brows. His mouth, despite its full bottom lip, had not a hint of femininity about it and invariably held an uncompromising expression.

Max was not a man who smiled a lot. Mostly, his lips remained firmly shut, his penetrating blue eyes glittering with a hardness which Tara found sexy, but which she imagined could be forbidding, especially when he was annoyed, or angry. Tara suspected he could be a formidable boss, if crossed. She'd heard him a few times over the phone when he'd been laying down the law to various employees.

But with her, he was never really annoyed, or angry. He *had* been frustrated that time when she'd kissed him in public. And exasperated when she refused to let him buy her a car. But that was it.

Tara knew that when he finally caught sight of her standing there, waiting for him, he *would* smile.

And suddenly, it was there, that slow curve to his lips, that softer gleam in his eyes, and it was all she could do not to run to him and throw herself into his arms. Instead, she stayed right where she was, smiling her joy back at him whilst he walked slowly towards her.

'For a few seconds, I thought you weren't here,' he said once they were standing face to face.

'I almost wasn't,' she confessed. 'I was running horribly late. You should have seen me a minute ago, trying to bolt across the car park in these shoes.'

He glanced down at the offending shoes, then slowly let his eyes run up her body. By the time his gaze reached her mouth, her lips had gone bone-dry.

'Are you sure it was the shoes, or those wicked white trousers? How on earth did you get them on? You must have had them sewn on.'

'They're stretchy.'

His eyes glittered in that sexy way she adored. 'Thank the lord for that. I had visions of spending half the night getting them off you. You know, you really shouldn't wear gear like that to greet me when we've been apart for nearly a month. It does terrible things to me.'

'I thought you liked me to dress sexily,' she said, piqued that he hadn't bothered to ask her why she was late. It occurred to her with a degree of shock that maybe he didn't care.

'That depends on how long I've been away. Thank goodness you're wearing a bra.'

'But I'm not.'

He stared at her chest, then up at her mouth. 'I wish you hadn't told me that,' he muttered.

'For pity's sake, Max, is there no pleasing you today?'

'You please me all the time,' he returned thickly, and putting his laptop down, he actually reached out to stroke a tender hand down her cheek. If that didn't stun her, his next action did.

He kissed her, his hand sliding down and around under her hair, cupping the back of her neck whilst his mouth branded hers with purpose and passion.

The kiss must have lasted a full minute, leaving Tara weak-kneed with desire and flushed with embarrassment. For people were definitely staring at them.

'Max!' she protested huskily when his hand then slid down her shirt over her right breast.

'That's what you get for meeting me in those screw-me shoes,' he whispered.

When Tara gaped at him, Max laughed.

'You little hypocrite. You deliberately dressed to tease me today, and then you pretend to be shocked when you get the reaction you wanted. Here. Give me my car keys and take this,' he ordered and handed her the laptop. 'I want one hand free to keep you in line, you bad girl.'

Tara's cheeks continued to burn as she was ushered from the terminal with Max's hand firmly clamped to her bejeaned backside. Her head was fairly whirling with mixed messages and emotions.

In all the times she had picked Max up at the airport, he had never made her feel like this. As if sex was the *only* thing on his mind, and on hers. And whilst she was flustered by this change in behaviour—could her mother have been right about Max just using her for sex?—she was also undeniably turned on.

Neither of them said a single word till they were standing by the Mercedes and Max had put his things into the boot.

'Fifteen minutes,' Max said as he slammed the boot shut and turned to her.

'What?'

By then she was hot all over, not just her cheeks.

'Fifteen minutes,' Max repeated. 'That's how long till we're alone. I suspect it's going to be the longest fifteen minutes of my life.' His eyes ran all over her again, finally lingering on her mouth. 'If I kiss you again, I won't be able to wait. I'll ravage you in the back seat of this car and to hell with everything.'

Tara wasn't sure if she liked this beastlike Max as much as the civilised one she was used to. But she suspected that if he kissed her again, she wouldn't *care* if he ravaged her on the back seat.

In fact, she was already imagining him doing just that, and it sent her head spinning.

Just then, a couple of young fellows walked by and one of them ogled her before pursing his lips in a mock kiss. When he turned to his mate and said something, they both laughed.

Tara cringed.

'Then please don't kiss me,' she choked out.

Max, who hadn't seen this exchange, shook his head at her. 'Still playing the tease? That's a new one for you, Tara. What's happened to the sweet, naive, extremely innocent virgin I met a year ago?'

'She's been sleeping with you for a year,' she countered, stung by his inference that this change today was all hers.

His eyes darkened. 'Do I detect a degree of dissatisfaction in those words? Is that why you were late today? Because you were thinking of not coming to pick me up at all?'

'So glad that you finally cared enough to ask why I was late!' she snapped. 'For your information, I had words with my mother and then I missed my train.'

Did he look relieved? She couldn't be sure. Max was not an easy man to read.

'What was the argument about?'

'You.'

That surprised him. 'What about me?'

'Mum thinks you're just using me.'

'And what do you think?'

'I told her you loved me.'

'I do.'

Tara's heart lurched at his words. *Do you, Max? Do you, really?*

'If you truly loved me,' she pointed out agitatedly, 'then you wouldn't talk about ravaging me in the back seat of a car in a public car park.'

He seemed startled, before a thoughtful frown gathered on his high forehead. 'I see the way your mind is working, but you're wrong. And so was I. You're not a tease, or a hypocrite. You're still the incurable romantic you always were. But that's all right. That's what I love about you. Come along, then, princess. Let's get you home, where we can dive into our lovely four-poster bed and make beautiful romantic love all weekend long.'

'Do we have a whole weekend this time, Max?' Tara asked eagerly, relieved that the threat of being publicly ravaged in the back seat of Max's car had been averted.

'Unfortunately, no. I have to catch a plane back to Hong Kong around one tomorrow afternoon.

'Sorry,' he added when her face fell. 'But things there

are going from bad to worse. Who knows where it will all end? Still, that's not your concern.'

'But I like to hear about your work problems,' she said truthfully, and touched his arm.

He stiffened for a second before picking up her hand and kissing her fingertips. The entire surface of Tara's skin broke out into goose-pimples.

'I haven't come home to talk about work, Tara,' he murmured. 'I've come home to relax for a night. With my beautiful girlfriend.'

Tara beamed at him. 'You called me your girlfriend.'

Max looked perplexed. 'Well, that's what you are, isn't it?'

'Yes. Yes, that's what I am. I hope,' she muttered under her breath as she turned away from him and hurried round to the passenger side.

She could feel his eyes on her as she climbed into the car. But she didn't want to see what was in them. It was enough for now that he'd called her his girlfriend. Enough that he'd declared his love. She didn't want to see the heat in his gaze and misinterpret it. Of course he desired her, as she desired him. Of course!

But he won't ever give you what you want, Tara.

Yes, he would, she reassured herself as the car sped towards the city. Till he left for the airport tomorrow, he would give her his company, and his love, and his body. Which was all that she wanted right at this moment. His body possibly most of all.

Even now, she was thinking of the hours she would

spend in bed with him, of the way she felt when he caressed and kissed her all over, when he made her melt with just a touch of his finger or a stab of his tongue. She especially liked it when he played with her endlessly, bringing her again and again to the brink of ecstasy, only to draw back at the last moment, making her wait in a state of exquisite tension till he was inside her.

Those were the best times, when they reached satisfaction together, when she held him close and she felt their hearts beating as one.

The car zoomed down into the tunnel which would take them swiftly to the city, the enveloping darkness making Tara even more aware of the man beside her. She glanced over at his strong profile, then at his hands on the wheel.

Her thighs suddenly pressed together at the thought of him taking her, her insides tightening.

When Tara sucked in sharply Max's head turned and his eyes glittered over at her. 'What are you thinking about?'

She blushed and he laughed, breaking her tension.

'Same here. But we're almost there now. It won't be long to wait.'

CHAPTER THREE

THE Regency Hotel—recently renamed the Regency Royale by Max—was situated towards the northern end of the city centre, not far from Circular Quay. Touted as one of Sydney's plushest hotels, it had a décor to suit its name. Guests could be forgiven for thinking they'd stepped back in time once they entered the reception area of the Regency, with its wood-panelled walls, velvet-covered couches and huge crystal chandeliers.

The arcade which connected the entrance of the hotel to the lobby proper was just as lavish, also resonant of England in past times, with its intricately tiled floor and stained-glass ceiling. The boutiques and bars which lined the arcade reflected a similar sense of period style and grace.

Max had once told Tara that was why he'd bought the Regency. Because of its period look.

The Royale chain specialised in hotels which weren't modern-looking in design or décor. Because modern,

Max told her, always eventually dated. History and grandeur were what he looked for in a hotel.

Tara had to agree that this made sound business sense. Of all the hotels in Sydney, the Regency Royale stood out for its style and good, old-fashioned service. But it was the look of the place which captivated guests. The day she came here for her interview at Whitmore Opals eighteen months ago, she'd spent a good while walking around the place, both amazed and admiring.

Today, however, as Max ushered her along the arcade past her place of employment, her focus was on anything but the hotel. Her thoughts were entirely on the man whose hand was clamped firmly around her elbow, and on the state of almost desperate desire he'd reduced her to.

Never, in the twelve months they'd been seeing each other, had she experienced anything quite like this. She'd always been happy for Max to make love to her. But never had she wanted him this badly.

'Afternoon, Mr Richmond,' a security guard greeted as he walked towards them.

'Afternoon, Jack,' Max replied, and actually stopped to talk to the man whilst Tara clenched her teeth in her jaw.

It was probably only a minute before they moved on but it felt like an eternity.

'Glad to see you again, Mr Richmond,' another employee chirped after a few more metres.

'Same here, Warren.'

This time Max didn't stop, thank goodness. Tara smothered a sigh of relief, even happier when Max bypassed the reception desk and headed straight for the lifts. Not that he needed to book in, for heaven's sake. But Max was a hands-on hotel owner who liked to be kept informed over the ins and outs of everything. He usually stopped by Reception for a brief chat on arrival.

In the past, Tara hadn't minded his stopping to talk to his employees. She'd always admired the way Max knew every employee by their first name, from the valet-parking attendants to the managers.

Today, however, she was extremely irritated by the delays. Which wasn't like her at all.

The alcove which housed the lifts was not empty. A man in his forties, and presumably his wife, were standing there, waiting for a lift. They didn't look like tourists. Or members of Sydney's élite. Their clothes and faces betrayed them as working-class Australians, perhaps staying here in Sydney's flashest hotel for some special event, or occasion.

'I will never stay in this hotel again,' the man grumbled. 'I'd go somewhere right now if it didn't mean losing my deposit. I couldn't believe that girl, insisting that I hadn't booked a harbour-view room. As if I would bring you here for our silver anniversary and not get the very best room I could afford.'

'It doesn't matter, Tom,' the wife placated. 'I'm sure all the rooms here are lovely.'

'That's not the point. It's the principle of the thing. And that girl behind the desk was quite rude, I thought.'

'Not really,' the woman said with a nervous glance

towards Max and Tara. 'It was just a mix-up. These things happen. Let's try not to let it spoil our night.'

Tara smothered a groan when she felt Max's fingertips tighten around her elbow. She knew, as she glanced up at his tightly drawn face, that he was going to do something about this situation.

'Excuse me, sir,' he said, just as the lift doors opened. 'But I couldn't help overhearing. I'm Max Richmond, the owner of this hotel. If you'll allow me, I'd like to accompany you back to Reception, where I will sort this out to your satisfaction.'

'Max,' Tara whispered urgently.

'You go on, darling,' he said. 'I'll be up as quick as I can. Slip into something more comfortable,' he murmured as he pecked her on the cheek.

Tara stared after him as he led the awestruck couple away, struggling to contain her bitter disappointment and understand that of course, he couldn't have done anything else. Not her Max. Hadn't she tried to tell her mother what a good man he was?

But did he have to be good right at this moment? She would have much preferred him to be bad. *Very* bad.

Again, Tara was amazed by the intensity of her craving, her sudden wish for Max to make love to her not quite so tenderly as he usually did. Maybe Max had been right after all. Maybe she *had* dressed as she had today to tease and arouse him. Yet her clothes weren't all that different from what she usually wore. This change seemed to be coming from inside her.

Now that she came to think of it, she felt more aware of her body than usual today. Her breasts. Her nipples. Her belly. She craved to have them stroked, and licked, and kissed. She craved…oh, she wasn't sure what she craved. She just craved.

Agitated, Tara fished her keycard out of her bag and hurried into the lift before anyone else could come along. She wanted to be alone with her frustrations, and her bewilderment.

But she wasn't alone in the lift. She had company. Herself, in the reflection she made in the mirrored section of the walls. Was that her, the creature looking back at her with dilated green eyes and flushed cheeks?

Yes. That was her. Tara, the suddenly sex-mad tart.

Shaking her head at herself, Tara dropped her gaze to the floor for the ride up, determined not to look up into those knowing mirrors till the lift doors opened.

The mirrors were actually a new addition, Max having had the lifts recently renovated in keeping with the rest of the hotel. The floor she was staring down at was now covered in thick red carpet which ran up the walls to waist height, at which point the mirrors took over.

Tara knew without glancing up that the ceiling overhead shone like gold. Probably not in real gold but the effect was the same. Recessed lighting was the only visible concession to the twenty-first century, along with the tiny and very discreet cameras situated in the corners.

Tight security was a must in the Regency Royale, its guest list ranging from pop stars to presidents, with the occasional prince thrown in for good measure. There was even a heliport on top of the building so that these more esteemed guests could arrive and leave with less drama and more safety. Nevertheless, Max only allowed a few helicopter movements each week, partly because of local-authority restrictions but mostly because he couldn't stand the noise himself. His penthouse apartment occupied the floor just below the heliport.

Everything was deathly quiet, however, when Tara emerged from the lift into the spacious lobby which led to the penthouse door. She used another passkey to let herself inside, where it was almost as quiet, just a small humming sound from the air-conditioning which kept all the rooms at a steady twenty-four degrees Celsius, regardless of the temperature outside.

The perfect temperature for lovers and lovemaking, came the immediate thought. For being naked and walking around naked.

This last thought startled Tara. Because that was one thing she never did. Walked around naked. The idea was theoretically exciting, but the reality made her cringe. She would feel embarrassed, and awkward.

Or would she?

Tara knew she looked good in the buff. Certainly better than most girls, though she couldn't claim this was due to any hard work on her part. Mother nature had just been kind to her. Tara suspected Max wouldn't have minded if she'd been a little less shy. He was always asking her to join him in the shower and she always refused.

Maybe this weekend might be a good place to try to overcome that particular hang-up. She doubted she would ever feel as wicked, or as driven, as she did at this moment. She could not wait to get her hands on Max. The thought of washing him all over in the shower was not unattractive, just a bit daunting.

A shudder ran through her. She would think about that later. There were other things she had to do first, such as whip around and turn some lamps on.

Max loved lamp-light, and whilst it was still bright and sunny outside—the sun wouldn't set for hours—the inside of Max's penthouse always required some lighting. Mostly this was due to the wraparound terraces and the wide eaves. On top of that, the décor of the penthouse was very much in keeping with the décor of the hotel, which meant it wasn't madly modern like some penthouses, with great open-plan living areas and huge plate-glass windows.

The décor was still period, with wallpapered walls and rich carpets on the floors. French doors lead out onto the balconies and heavy silk curtains draped over the windows. The furniture was all antique. Warm woods covered in velvet or brocade in rich colours. It was like an Edwardian English mansion set up in the sky. As big as a mansion too, with formal lounge and dining rooms, four bedrooms, three bathrooms, a study, a library, a billiard room, along with a large kitchen, laundry and utility rooms.

Everything was exquisite and *very* expensive.

Tara hadn't realised the size or extravagance of the place on the first night she'd spent with Max. She'd been overwhelmed by the events and the experience, rather than her surroundings. But the following morning, she'd soon been confronted by the extreme wealth of the man who'd just become her first lover. Initially, she'd been dumbstruck, then totally convinced that he would only want a girl like her for a one-night stand.

But Max had reassured her for the rest of that incredible weekend that a casual encounter was not what he wanted from her at all. Tara recalled thinking at the time that she had found nothing casual in letting him take her virginity less than three hours after she'd first set eyes on him. If she hadn't known she'd fallen instantly and deeply in love with the man, she would have been disgusted with herself.

Naturally, she'd been thrilled that he found her as special as she found him, and here she was, one year later, with her own private key, getting things ready for her man in the way that women in love had done so for centuries. If it fleetingly crossed Tara's mind that her role in her lover's life *was* more like a mistress than a real girlfriend, she dismissed it with the added thought that it wouldn't always be like this. One day, things would change. Max would have more time for her. Till then, she aimed to enjoy the time with him she did have and that part of him which was solely hers.

At least, she *hoped* it was solely hers.

Yes, of course it was. Her mother was wrong about

that, as she was wrong about Max all round. The man who was at this moment doing nice things for that couple downstairs was not the kind of man to be unfaithful, or a callous user. She really had to stop letting her mother undermine her faith in Max, or spoil what promised to be a very exciting night.

With a defiant toss of her head, Tara turned and hurried down the plushly carpeted corridor which led to Max's personal quarters, fiercely aware that the last few minutes away from Max's rousing presence hadn't dampened her desires in the slightest. In fact, having sex with Max was all she could think about at that moment, which was not her usual priority when Max came home these days. Mostly, she just wanted to spend time with the man she loved. His lovemaking, though wonderful, was more of a bonus than the be-all and end-all.

Today, it was not only top priority, but close to becoming an emergency!

It was Max's fault, she decided as she swept into the bedroom and starting fumbling with the tiny pearl buttons of her pink shirt. The way he'd looked at her at the airport. The things he'd said about her clothes. That kiss, and then his threat to ravage her on the back seat of the car.

Tara finally stripped off her blouse then kicked off her shoes.

'My screw-me shoes,' she said with a wicked little laugh as she bent to pick them up, carrying the shirt and the shoes into the adjoining dressing room, where she'd put her bag earlier on. There, she stripped off her jeans and undies, stuffing them into the bag's side-pocket for later washing. The shirt she hung up in her section of the walk-in wardrobe. The shoes she put into the special shoe rack before running her eyes along the clothes she kept at Max's place, looking for something more comfortable to slip into.

Her mother's *kept*-woman tag flashed into her mind at the sight of so many designer evening gowns, all paid for by Max, each worn to one of the many swanky dos Max had taken her to during the first few months of their relationship. Dinner parties at the homes of top politicians. Gala openings at the opera house. Art exhibitions. Balls. The races.

You name it, she'd been there on Max's arm.

Actually, she *had* objected the first time he'd suggested buying her a designer dress. But he'd swept aside her possibly feeble protest with what had seemed like acceptable reasoning.

He could well afford it, he'd pronounced. But possibly his most persuasive argument of all was that it gave him great pleasure to see his gorgeous girlfriend in clothes befitting her beauty.

How could she possibly say no?

The lingerie, Tara realised as her eyes shifted further along the rack, had been more recent gifts, brought home from Max's more frequent trips overseas. She had negligee sets from Paris, London, Rome, New York.

These were all she seemed to wear for him these

days, now that she came to think of it. Max hadn't taken her outside the door of this penthouse for some time. No doubt he wouldn't this evening either.

'Good!' she pronounced aloud with a dizzying rush of excitement, and pulled out a green satin wrap which she knew complemented her fair colouring and green eyes. The matching nightgown she left on the hanger. No point in wearing *too* much.

Tossing the wrap over her arm, she headed for the bathroom and was about to have a quick shower before Max arrived when she remembered she hadn't put her pills and her mobile phone on the bedside chest as she usually did. Dashing back to the dressing room, she retrieved the items from her bag and bolted into the bedroom to do just that. Then she stopped to quickly turn the bedclothes back before glancing around to see that everything was ready for a romantic interlude.

Not that Max's bedroom needed anything to enhance its already romantic décor. Everything about it was rich and sensual. The soft gold carpet was extra thick and the gold-embossed cream wallpaper extra rich, both perfect foils for the dark mahogany wood used in all the elegant furniture. The four-poster bed. The bedside chests. The dressing table and matching stool. The cheval mirror that stood in one corner and the wingbacked chairs that occupied the other corners.

The soft furnishings were rich and sensual-looking as well, all made in a satin-backed brocade which carried a gold fleur-de-lis design over an olive-green background. A huge crystal and brass chandelier hung from the centre of the ceiling, but there were also several dainty crystal wall lights dotted around the room.

Tara loved it when it was dark and all the lights were turned off except those. The room took on a magical glow which was so romantic. Much better than the bedside lamps which she thought threw too much light onto the bed. And them.

Of course, the pièce de résistance in Max's bedroom was the four-poster bed. Huge, it was, with great carved posts and bedhead. The canopy above was made of the same material as all the other soft furnishings, draped around the edges and trimmed with a gold fringe. There were side-curtains, which theoretically could be drawn to surround the bed, but were always kept pulled back and secured to the bedposts with gold tasselled cords.

Tara ran her fingers idly through one of the tassels and wondered what it would be like to be in bed with Max with the curtains drawn.

'What are you thinking now?'

'Oh!' Tara gasped, whirling to find Max standing in the doorway of the bedroom, staring at her with coldly glittering eyes.

'I... I didn't hear you come in,' she babbled, her heart pounding madly as she tried to cover herself with her hands.

With a sigh Max stalked into the room, his face now showing exasperation. 'Don't you think we've gone past that, Tara? I mean, I do know what you look like naked. Surely you must know that I'd *like* it if you walked around in front of me nude,' he finished as he took off his jacket and threw it onto the nearest chair.

She just stared at him, her heartbeat almost in suspension. But her mind was racing. Yes, yes, it was saying. I'd like to do that, too. Truly. I just can't seem to find the courage.

'And there I was,' he muttered as he yanked his tie off, 'thinking today that you might have finally decided you wanted more than for me to make love to you under the covers with the lights turned down.

'It's all right,' he added a bit wearily when she remained frozen and tongue-tied. 'I understand. You're shy. Though heaven knows why. You have the most beautiful body God ever gave to a woman. And you're passionate enough, between the sheets.'

Turning away from her, he tossed the tie on top of the jacket then started undoing the buttons on his shirt.

'Go and put something on,' he bit out, not looking at her. 'If you must.'

Tara dashed into the bathroom and shakily pulled on the green wrap, hating herself for feeling relieved. When she finally returned to the bedroom, Max was sitting on the foot of the bed, taking off his shoes and socks. His shirt was hanging open, but he hadn't taken it off.

Tara's heart sank. Did he think she was *that* modest? She *loved* his chest, with its broad shoulders, wonderfully toned muscles and smattering of curls.

'Did…did you fix up things for those people?' she asked somewhat sheepishly.

'Naturally,' he replied without looking up at her. 'I had them moved into one of the honeymoon suites, on the house. And I told them they could have a free harbour-view room for their anniversary next year.'

'Oh, Max, that was generous of you. And very smart. That man would have bad-mouthed the hotel for years, you know. To anyone who would listen. Now he'll say nothing but good things. People love getting something for free. I know I do. I can never resist those buy-one, get one-free promotions.'

'Really?' He finally looked up, but his clouded eyes indicated that he was suddenly off in another world. Max did that sometimes. Tara knew better than to ask him what he was thinking about. Whenever she did, he always said 'nothing important'.

'So which honeymoon suite are they in?' she asked instead. The hotel was famous for its four themed honeymoon suites, which Tara knew cost a bomb to stay in. Bookings showed that the Arabian Nights suite was the most popular, followed by the Naughty Nautical suite, the French Bordello suite and, lastly, the Tropical Paradise suite.

'What? Oh, there was only the one available tonight. The French Bordello. Mr Travis seemed tickled pink. Can't say the same for Mrs Travis. She seemed a little nervous. Maybe she's on the shy side. Like you.'

'I'm not all that shy,' Tara dared to say at last.

Max darted her a dry look.

'All right, I am, a bit,' she went on, swallowing when he stood up and started undoing his trouser belt.

The prospect of watching him strip down to total nakedness before he'd even kissed her was definitely daunting. But at the same time she wanted him to, wanted him to do what she wasn't bold enough to do, wanted him to force her to stop being so silly.

'Don't panic,' he said drily and, whipping out his belt, deposited it with his other clothes. 'I won't take anything more off. I'm going to have a shower, and when I come out I'll be wearing my bathrobe. Meantime, why don't you order us something from Room Service? I don't know about you but I'm starving. I nodded off on the plane so I didn't get to eat anything. I've made us a booking for dinner at eight but that's hours away.'

'We're going out to dinner?' Tara said, taken aback.

'I've only booked the restaurant here in the hotel. Is that all right with you?'

'Oh, yes. I love going to dinner with you there. It's just that…well, the last couple of times you've come home, we've eaten in.'

'Yes, I know. And I'm sorry. That was selfish of me. But, as I said earlier, you're a different girl between the sheets, so I try to keep you there as long as possible.'

She blushed. 'Don't make fun of me, Max.'

He groaned and walked round to draw her into his arms. 'I'm not making fun of you, princess. I would never do that. You're you and I love you just the way you are.'

'Kiss me, Max,' she said quite fiercely.

His eyes searched hers. 'I don't think that's a good idea. Not yet.'

'But I can't wait any longer!'

'*You* can't wait. Hell, Tara, what is it with you today? Are you punishing me for neglecting you lately?'

'I just want you to kiss me. No, I *need* you to kiss me.'

With a groan, he kissed her. Then he kissed her some more, till her knees went to water and she was clinging to him for dear life. When he swept her up and dropped her less than gently onto the bed, Tara made no protest. Neither did she turn her eyes away whilst he started ripping off the rest of his clothes.

She wanted to look. Wanted to see him wanting her.

Her breath caught at the extent of his desire.

He loomed over her, tugging the sash of her robe undone, throwing the sides back to bare her body to his blazing eyes.

For what felt like an eternity, he drank her in, leaving her breathless and blushing. Then, with a few more savage yanks, the satin robe joined his clothes on the floor.

There was no tender foreplay. No gentle kisses all over. Just immediate sex. Rough and raw. Maybe not quite ravagement but close to.

And oh, how she thrilled to the primitive urgency of his passion. And to her own.

She splintered apart in no time, rocked by the force of her orgasm, overwhelmed by the experience, and by a degree of emotional confusion.

As the last spasm died away, a huge wave of exhaustion flooded Tara's body, her limbs growing as heavy as her eyelids. She could not keep them open. She could not stay awake. With a sigh, she sank into the abyss of sleep.

CHAPTER FOUR

MAX stared down at her with a stunned look on his face.

Asleep! She'd fallen asleep!

He shook his head in utter bewilderment. Tara never fell asleep afterwards.

On top of that, she'd actually *enjoyed* his making love to her like that! Hell, no, she'd *exulted* in it! She'd dragged him over the edge with her in record time. And now she was out like a light, more peaceful than he'd ever seen her.

Relief swamped him at the realisation he didn't have to feel *too* much remorse over losing control and being less than the careful, considerate, patient lover he'd come to believe Tara wanted, and needed. *Not* losing control when he was around her this past year had been a terrible battle between the lust she evoked in him, and the love.

Max thought he'd done pretty well… until today.

If only she hadn't met him looking delicious in those skin-tight jeans and those sexy shoes. If only she hadn't told him she wasn't wearing a bra. If only he hadn't kissed her then and there.

His relationship with Tara was full of 'if only's, the main one being if only he hadn't stopped to look in the window of Whitmore Opals that Friday night, and spotted her inside.

It had been lust at first sight. When she'd agreed to have drinks with him less than ten minutes after his going in and introducing himself, he'd been sure he was in for a wild night with a woman of the world. With his impossible workload and repeated overseas trips, Max's sex life had been reduced to the occasional one-nighter with women who knew the score, and Tara seemed just the ticket to ride.

But the reality had proven so different. Her telling him shakily that she was a virgin even before he'd got her bra off had certainly put the brakes on the type of activities he'd been planning. Max had been shocked, but also entranced. Who would have believed it?

Fortunately, finding out before he'd gone too far gave him the opportunity to slow things down and make sure her first experience was pleasurable and not painful. He'd taken her to bed and really taken his time with her.

Looking back, making love to her at all had probably been a mistake. He should have cut and run. But he hadn't; that very first time had made him swiftly decide that one night with Tara would not be enough. He'd kept her in his bed all weekend, making love to her as he hadn't made love to a female in years. Sweetly. Tenderly. And totally selflessly.

Unfortunately, this was what Tara came to expect from him every time. Max soon realised he was dealing with a girl whose appearance belied her real nature. Underneath the sexy-looking blonde surface, the long legs and fabulous boobs, lay a naively romantic girl.

In *some* ways, Tara could be surprisingly mature. She was well-educated, well-read and well-travelled. And she certainly had a way with people, exuding a charm and social grace far beyond her years.

But when it came to sex she was like a hothouse flower, gorgeous to look at but incredibly soft and fragile.

Or so he'd thought, up till now.

Max sat back on his haunches and stared down at her beautiful but unconscious body, lying in shameless abandonment in front of his eyes.

If only she would lie like that for him when she was awake…

Max almost laughed at this new 'if only'.

But maybe she would in the near future, came the exciting thought. She'd said she wasn't totally shy and maybe she wasn't. Maybe she just lacked the confidence to do what she really wanted to do. All she needed was some masterful persuasion at the right time, and a whole new world would open for her.

Up till this moment, Max had reluctantly accepted that Tara didn't seem the raunchy type of girl. He'd reasoned it was worth sacrificing some more exotic experiences to feel what Tara could make him feel, what she'd made him feel from their very first night together.

But tonight had shown him that maybe, they could share more erotic lovemaking together in future.

Max became aroused just thinking of the things he'd like to do with her, and her with him. Not a good idea when it looked as if she would be asleep for some time. A shower was definitely called for. A cold one.

Wincing at his discomfort, he climbed off the bed and carefully eased the bedclothes from underneath Tara's luscious derriere, rolling her gently onto the bottom sheet before pulling the other one up to her shoulders. She stirred but didn't wake, though the sheet did slip down to reveal one of her incredible breasts.

Max bent and pressed his lips softly to the exposed nipple before whirling away and heading straight for the bathroom.

CHAPTER FIVE

'WHAT?'

The startled word shot from Tara's lips as she sat bolt upright in bed. She blinked, then glanced somewhat glazedly around before realising what had woken her so abruptly.

It was the alarm on her mobile phone, telling her it was six o'clock, reminding her it was time to take her pill.

With a groan, she leant over and picked up the small pink handset, pressing the button which turned off the alarm. The sudden silence in the room highlighted Max's absence. She wondered where he was, then wished she hadn't. She didn't want to think about Max at that moment.

Tara retrieved her packet of pills from the bedside chest, popped today's pill through the foil then swallowed it promptly without bothering about getting any water. The doctor had warned her that you had to take the mini Pill around the same time every day or risk getting pregnant. Tara didn't take hers *around* the same time. She took it at *exactly* the same time every day.

That done, she threw back the sheet and—after checking that Max wasn't lurking in the doorway watching her—Tara rose to her feet. She winced at the wetness between her legs.

Impossible to pretend any longer that she didn't remember what had happened before she fell asleep.

Why she was even trying to forget suddenly annoyed her. She hadn't done anything to be ashamed of. Neither had Max, for that matter.

So he'd made love to her more forcefully than usual. So what? He'd delivered exactly what she'd been subconsciously wanting since he'd threatened to ravage her at the airport. And how she'd loved it!

Tara quivered all over at the memory. Had she ever experienced anything with Max quite so powerful before? She didn't think so.

The sight of her green wrap lying tidily across the foot of the bed brought a frown to her forehead. Max must have picked it up off the floor whilst she was asleep. His own clothes as well. They were now draped over one of the chairs.

He hadn't dressed again, she realised with a tightening of her stomach. He was somewhere in the penthouse, probably wearing nothing but his favourite bathrobe. Tara hurried into the bathroom to check, and yes, his bathrobe was missing from where it usually hung on the back of the bathroom door. And his towels were still damp. Obviously, he'd showered whilst she'd been asleep.

Swallowing, Tara hung her wrap up on the empty hook behind the door, wound her hair into a knot on top of her head, then stepped into the spacious, marble-lined shower cubicle.

She wasn't yet sure what she was going to do after she'd showered. All she knew was that her body was already rebuilding a head of steam far hotter than the water which was currently cascading over her body.

She didn't spend much time in the shower. Just long enough to ensure that she was freshly washed and nicely perfumed. She was careful not to wet her hair. She didn't want to present herself to Max like some bedraggled kitten come in from a storm. Her hair was not at its best when wet. And she wanted to look her *very* best.

No, Tara amended mentally as she towelled herself down then slipped her arms into the silky wrap. She didn't want to look her best, but her sexiest. She wanted to tempt Max into stopping doing whatever he was doing and take her back to bed. Right now.

For a second she almost left the wrap hanging open, but in the end decided that was tacky. So she tied it just as tightly as usual. Actually, even a bit tighter, so that her small waist was emphasised, as well as the rest of her curvy figure.

Swallowing, Tara took one final glance in the huge mirror which stretched along above the double vanity basins. On another day, at another time, she would have taken the time to make her face up all over again. There was little of her pink lipstick left, and her mascara had smudged all around her eyes. But she rather liked her slightly dishevelled look. She even liked the way her hair was up. Roughly, with some escaping strands hanging around her face. She looked like a woman who'd just come from her lover's bed. She looked... wanton.

Spinning on her bare heels, Tara headed for the bedroom door.

The hallway that led from the master bedroom to the main body of the penthouse seemed to go on forever. By the time she reached the main living room, she wasn't sure if she was terrified or over-excited. Her heart was going like a jack-hammer and her mouth was drier than the Simpson Desert.

But Max was not there.

Disappointment rather than relief showed her that nerves were not the most dominating force in her body at that moment. Desire was much stronger.

Whirling, she hurried down the hallway which led to Max's den, his favourite area of the penthouse when he was up and about. It was actually two rooms, connected by concertina doors which were always kept open. The first room you entered was a study-cum-library, a very masculine room with no windows, book-lined walls, a desk in one corner and several oversized, leather-studded chairs in which to sit and read. The next room was the billiard room, which had a huge, green-felted billiard table, a pub-like bar in one corner, complete with stools, and lots of French doors which opened onto the balcony.

Max was an excellent snooker player and had tried to teach Tara in their early days together, when they had time for more than bed. But she was never much good and they hadn't played in ages.

Tara wasn't about to suggest a game today. She had other games in mind, a thought which both shocked and stirred her. She'd never thought of making love as a game before.

Her hand shook as it reached for the brass door knob but no way was she going to back out now. But she didn't barge straight in. Tara had been brought up with better manners than that. She tapped on the door before she opened it, then popped her head inside.

Max, she swiftly saw, was sitting in his favourite chair, bathed in a circle of soft light from the lamp which stood behind the chair. Yes, he was wearing the white towelling bathrobe, she noted. And yes, nothing else, not even on his feet.

But he wasn't exactly sitting around, impatiently waiting for her to wake up so that he could make love to her again. He was working. *And* drinking. His laptop was open and balanced across his thighs, he was sipping a very large Scotch and chatting to someone on the phone at the same time.

Max was one of those rare men who could actually do more than one thing at a time.

'Ah, there you are,' she said, containing her irritation with difficulty.

Instead of asking him if it was all right if she interrupted him, as she usually would have, Tara walked straight in and shut the door behind her.

He was taken aback, she could see. But that was just too bad. This was *her* time with him, no one else's.

When he put up his hand towards her in a stopping gesture and kept on talking—something about a website—rebellion overcame Tara's usually automatic tendency to obey him. Slowly, she moved towards him across the expanse of dark green carpet, her hips swaying seductively, her breasts moving underneath the wrap. The act of walking parted the silky material around her knees, giving tantalising glimpses of her bare legs.

One of his brows arched as he eyed her up and down. 'I'll have to speak to you later, Pierce,' he said into the phone. 'Something's just come up.'

'*Much* later,' Tara said as he clicked off the call. Pierce was only Max's PA, after all. He could wait.

Max smiled an odd smile before dropping his eyes back to the laptop screen. 'I have something I have to finish up here first, Tara,' he said without looking up at her again. 'Why don't you toddle off back to bed and I'll join you there as soon as I can?'

Pique fired her tongue before she could think better of it. 'What if I don't want to go back to bed? What if I want to stay here? What if I want you to stop working right here and now?'

Slowly, his eyes rose. Hard and glittering, they were, just as she liked them. He sipped some more of his drink whilst he studied her over the rim of the glass.

His gaze was knowing. He was mentally stripping her, making her face flush and her nipples tighten.

'*Make* me,' he said at last, his voice soft and low and dark.

His challenging words sent a bolt of electricity zig-zagging through her, firing her blood *and* her resolve not to weaken. Because she knew what he wanted. He wanted to see her, *all* of her. Not lying in a bed, but standing upright, in front of him. Facing him.

Her heartbeat quickened whilst her hands went to the sash on her wrap. She might have fumbled if the knot had been difficult, but she only had to tug the ends of the ties to make the bow unravel. In a split-second, the sides of the wrap fell apart.

But he showed no reaction whatsoever, just went back to sipping his drink.

Shock at his low level of interest held her frozen, and finally, his eyes dropped back to the screen in his lap.

'Go back to bed, Tara,' he said. 'Clearly, you're not cut out for the role of seductress just yet.'

Stung, she stripped the robe off and dropped it to the floor. When he still didn't pay her any attention, she went right up to him and banged the lid of the laptop down.

'*Look* at me,' she hissed.

He looked at her, his narrow-eyed gaze now travelling with exquisitely exciting slowness over every inch of her nakedness.

'Very nice,' he murmured. 'But it's nothing I haven't seen before.'

'You might see something new,' she threw at him, 'if you put that drink down. And that infernal computer.'

He closed the laptop and placed it beside the chair, but kept the drink. He looked her over again as he leant back into the chair and took another mouthful of whisky.

Now fear did return. The fear of making a fool of herself.

'I'm waiting,' he said, and finally placed the near-empty glass on the small round side-table next to the chair.

Tara swallowed.

'Come, come, Tara. This is *your* show. I'm curious to see how far you'll go before you turn tail and run. I'm not going to help you one little bit.'

Tara gaped at him as the realisation struck that he didn't just want her to parade herself in front of him. He wanted *her* to make love to *him*.

If he'd issued this type of challenge on any other day before today, she probably *would* have turned tail and run. But today was a different day in more ways than one. Today, a new and exciting dimension had entered their relationship and she refused to retreat from it.

Don't think, she told herself as she stepped forward to stand between his stretched-out legs. Just do what he thinks you don't dare to do.

She heard his sharp intake of breath when she knelt down and reached for the sash on his robe.

Don't look up at his face, she warned herself shakily.

She didn't want to see any undermining shock, or surprise, in his eyes. He'd told her once he didn't mind how provocative or assertive she was in private. Well, he was just about to get a dose of provocative assertiveness, even if she was quaking inside.

The sash on his robe was as easy to undo as her own, being only looped over. Pushing the sides of the robe back was not so easy, because she knew what would confront her when she did so.

Her eyes widened at the sight of him.

So his apparent uninterest had all been a lie! He was already aroused. Fiercely so.

Tara resisted the urge to close her eyes and put her mind elsewhere. Her days of cowardice were over. She *would* look at him there, and touch him there, and kiss him there.

Yet oddly, once she started stroking the velvety length of him, once she felt Max quiver and grow even harder beneath her hands, any reluctance or revulsion melted away. Tara found herself consumed by the intense desire to make the beast emerge in him again, to drive him wild with pleasure and need, to love him as she had never loved him before.

Max could not believe it when she took him into her mouth, making the blood roar through his veins, his flesh expand even further, threatening to make him lose all control.

Surely she would not want that. Surely not!

Max groaned his worry that he might not be able to stop himself. Then groaned again when her head lifted, showing him that he had wanted her to continue more than anything he had wanted in a long time.

But any disappointment was swiftly allayed by her crawling up onto the chair onto his lap. She was even at that moment straddling his tautly held thighs, her knees fitting into the far corners of the chair.

He gasped when she took him in her hands again and directed him up into her body. Her hot, wet, delicious body. She sank downwards and suddenly he was there, totally inside her. Her face lifted and their eyes met, hers dilated, his stunned.

'Max,' was all she said before she bent down to kiss his mouth, her hands cupping his face, her tongue sliding deep into his mouth.

How often had he hoped for a Tara like this?

Then she began to ride him. Slowly at first, but then with more passion. The wilder rise and fall of her hips wrenched her mouth away from his. Her hands fell to his shoulders to steady herself, her fingernails biting into his flesh till suddenly her back arched, her flesh gripping his like a vice.

'Oooh,' she cried out.

The power of her climax was mind-blowing. He exploded in erotic response, the pleasure blinding as, all the while, she kept moving upon him, rocking back and forth, her eyes shut, her breathing ragged.

Afterwards, she sank down against his chest, her head nestling into the base of his throat. His arms encircled her back and he held her like that for quite a while, both of them silent and content.

But inevitably, the significance of what had just happened came home to him. His gorgeous Tara had finally abandoned her inhibitions.

Suddenly, he wanted her in every way a man and a woman could make love.

Tara sat up straight, her startled eyes searching his.

'Too soon?' he said, his hands sliding down her back to cup her bottom.

She shook her head.

He kept on caressing her bottom, and soon her lips fell apart on a sensual sigh of surrender. Max had never felt such love for her. Or such desire.

He was glad that their dinner reservation wasn't till eight o'clock. He had plans for the hour and a half till then, and none of them had anything to do with going back to bed.

CHAPTER SIX

'THAT gold colour looks fabulous on you,' Max said as they waited for the lift to take them down to the restaurant. 'So does the dress. I'm glad you took my suggestion to wear it tonight.'

Tara almost laughed. *Suggestion!* He hadn't suggested. He'd insisted.

The dress was a cheong-san, brought home by Max after an earlier trip to Hong Kong. Made in gold satin, it might have looked demure with its knee-length hem and high Chinese collar, except for the fact it was skintight, with slits up the sides which exposed a good deal of thigh. It was an extremely sensual garment.

Not that Tara needed help in feeling sensual at that moment. The last couple of hours had left all her senses heightened and her body humming. She'd certainly aroused the beast in Max with her provocative behaviour, along with another couple of Maxes. Max, the insatiable. And Max, the rather ruthless.

She shivered at the memory of the interlude on the billiard table.

Tara had briefly thought of sex as a game before going into Max's den. She hadn't realised at the time that Max was far ahead of her in the playing of erotic games, making her now wonder how many other women he'd entertained in the past in such a fashion.

At least, she *hoped* they'd been in the past.

A long and more objective look at Max—so resplendent tonight in black tie—confirmed what Tara had always subconsciously known. That women would throw themselves at him in droves. *She* had, hadn't she?

'Max,' she said with sudden worry in her voice and in her eyes.

'What, my darling?'

When he took her hand and raised it to his lips, she looked deep into *his* eyes.

'Have you ever been unfaithful to me?'

'Never,' he returned, so swiftly and so strongly that she had to believe him.

And yet…

'Why do you ask?' he went on, clearly perturbed by her question.

'I can see by tonight,' she said carefully, 'that I haven't exactly…satisfied you these past twelve months.'

'That's not true, Tara. I've been very happy with you,' he claimed.

A flicker in his eyes, however, showed otherwise.

'I don't believe you, Max. Tell me the truth.'

'Look, I admit there have been moments when I wished you were more comfortable with your body, and your sexuality. But I was not discontented. I love *you*, Tara, not just making love to you. Still, I'm glad you've finally realised that sex can be enjoyed in lots of different ways. It doesn't always have to be slow and serious. It can be fast and furious. Or it can just be fun. You had fun tonight, didn't you?'

Fun. Had it been fun? It had certainly been exciting, and compelling.

'I…I guess so.'

His smile was wry. 'Come, now, Tara. You loved it. All of it. Don't deny it.'

'I guess I'm just not used to being so wicked.'

'Wicked!' Max exclaimed, laughing. 'We weren't wicked. A little naughty perhaps. But not wicked. I could show you wicked later tonight, if you'd like.'

'What…what do you mean? Doing what?'

'I've always wanted to put those cords around my bed to far better use than tying back the curtains.'

Tara tried to feel scandalised. Instead, curiosity claimed her. What would it feel like for Max to tie her to the bed, to render her incapable of stopping him from looking at her all over, and touching her all over?

Just thinking about it gave her a hint as to what it would actually feel like. *Wicked.*

Heat filled her face. And the rest of her.

'I can see that's a bit of a leap for you,' Max said wryly. 'Forget I mentioned it.'

But how *could* she forget? He'd put the image into her mind. She would never be able to look at that bed now without thinking of herself bound to the bedposts!

The lift doors opened. When she stood there, still in a daze, Max took her hand and pulled her into the lift.

'Come along, princess, stop the daydreaming. We have to go down and eat. We're already a quarter of an hour late, courtesy of your keeping me in the shower longer than I intended.'

'*Me* keeping *you* in the shower!' she gasped. 'You liar! It was *you*. You wouldn't let me get out till I…till I…'

'Till you'd finished what you started. Yes, I know. Sorry. You're right. I got a bit carried away. But I didn't hear you objecting.'

'I could hardly speak at the time,' she countered with a defiant glower.

He laughed. 'That's the girl. Give it back to me. That's what I want from you always, Tara. Lots of fire and spirit. I'm never at my best around yes people.'

'That's rubbish, Max, and you know it. You love yes people. I hear you on the phone all the time, giving orders and expecting to be instantly obeyed. You like being the boss, in the bedroom as well as everywhere else! You expect all your lackeys to do exactly what they're told, when they're told.'

'Aah, yes, but you're not one of my lackeys.'

'I'm not so sure,' she snapped. 'Isn't a mistress another form of lackey?'

'Mistress! Good lord, what a delightfully old-fashioned word. But I like it. Mistress,' he repeated thought-fully. 'Yes, you would make me a perfect mistress. *Now.*' And with a wicked gleam in his eye, he put her fingers to his lips once more.

Tara pulled her hand away. She might have hit him if the lift doors hadn't opened at that moment.

A brunette was standing there, waiting for the lift. A strikingly attractive brunette with big brown eyes, eyes which grew bigger when they saw Max, then narrowed as they shifted over to Tara.

Max's fingers tightened around Tara's.

'Hello, Max,' the brunette said first. 'Long time, no see.'

'Indeed,' Max replied, but said no more.

Tara could feel the tension gripping all of Max's body through his hand. No, not tension. Hostility. He hated this woman, for whatever reason. Why? Had he loved her once?

Tara stared at the brunette more closely, trying to guess her age for one thing. Impossible to tell accurately. Maybe mid-to late-twenties. She had the sleek look of the very rich, which meant she might be older. Weekly visits to beauty salons could hold back the hands of time. Her face was clear of wrinkles and superbly made up. But her shoulder-length, shiny dark-brown hair was her crowning glory, framing her face in a layered bob with not a single strand out of place.

She made Tara conscious of her own hair, which was scraped back from her face and pulled up high on her head into a tight knot, the only style she could manage in the small amount of time Max had given her to get ready. Less than fifteen minutes earlier, her whole head had been sopping wet.

'You're looking well,' the brunette addressed to Max.

'If you'll excuse us, Alicia,' Max said. 'We are already late for our dinner reservation.' And he ushered Tara away, stunning Tara with his rudeness. Ever since she'd met Max, she'd never known him to act like that with anyone.

Tara did not glance back, or say a word during the short walk from the lift to the restaurant. She remained discretely silent whilst the *maître d'* greeted them, then instructed their personal waiter—a good-looking young guy named Jarod—to show them to their table.

It was a very special table, reserved for special occasions and people who wanted total privacy from the other diners. Set in a back corner of the restaurant, the candlelit table was housed in a tiny room, which was dimly lit and very atmospheric.

The first time Max had brought her here, she'd thought it was so romantic. Subsequent visits had been just as romantic. Tonight, however, the encounter with the brunette had turned Tara's mind away from romance. Unless one could consider jealousy an element of romance. Max could say what he liked but the way that woman had looked at him—just for a moment—had been with the eyes of a woman who'd been more than a passing acquaintance, or an employee.

As the minutes dragged on—Max was spending an inordinate amount of time studying the drinks menu—her agitation increased. By the time the waiter departed and the opportunity presented itself to ask him about the infernal woman, Tara feared she was going to put her questions all wrong. She dithered over what to actually say.

'There's no need to be jealous,' Max pronounced abruptly. 'Alicia was Stevie's girlfriend, not mine.'

'I wasn't jealous,' Tara lied with a lift of her chin. 'Just bewildered by your rudeness. So what did this Alicia do to Stevie to make you hate her so much?'

'The moment my brother was diagnosed with testicular cancer, Alicia dumped him like a shot. Said she couldn't cope.'

Tara was stunned to see Max's hands tremble as he raked them through his hair.

'My God, *she* couldn't cope,' he growled. 'How did she think Stevie was going to cope when the girl he loved—and who he *thought* loved him—didn't stand by him through his illness? I blame her entirely for his treatment being unsuccessful. When she left him, he lost the will to live.'

'But I thought…'

'Yes, yes, I blame my father, too. But Alicia even more so. At least Dad never pretended a devotion to Stevie. When he didn't come home to be by his dying son's bedside, it wasn't such a shock. Not to Stevie, anyway. He told me just days before he died that Dad didn't love him the way he loved me.' Max's deeply set blue eyes looked haunted. 'God, Tara, do you know how I felt when he said that? Stevie, who was such a good boy, who'd never hurt anyone in his life. How could any father not love him more than me? I wasn't a patch on my little brother.'

Tara frowned. Max had told her ages ago about the circumstances surrounding his younger brother's tragic death. Yet he'd never mentioned Stevie's girlfriend's part in it.

'Why didn't you tell me about Alicia, Max? You told me what your father did.'

'I don't like to talk about Stevie. I told you as much as I had to, to explain why I didn't invite you home to visit my parents, especially last Christmas. Alicia was irrelevant to that explanation,' he finished brusquely. 'Aah, here's the champagne.'

Tara wasn't totally satisfied with Max's explanation but stayed silent whilst the waiter opened the bottle, poured them both a glass then finally departed after Max told him to return in ten minutes for their meal order.

'It's not like you to order champagne,' she said as she took a sip. Max usually ordered red wine.

'I thought we would share a bottle. To celebrate the anniversary of our meeting. It was a year ago today that I walked into Whitmore's. Of course, it was a Friday not a Saturday, but the date's spot-on.'

'Oh, Max, how sweet of you to remember!'

'I'm a sweet guy.'

Tara smiled. 'You can be. Obviously. But I wouldn't say sweetness is one of your best-known attributes.'

'No?' He smiled across the table, reminding her for the second time that night how very handsome he was. 'So what *is* my best-known attribute?'

She couldn't help it. She blushed.

Max laughed. 'I will take that as a compliment. Although you've hardly been able to compare, since I'm your one and only lover. At least, I presume I am. Though maybe not for long, after today.'

'What on earth do you mean by that?'

'Maybe you'll want to fly to other places. Experience other men.'

Tara stared at him. 'You don't know me very well if you think that. What happened earlier, Max, is because I love you deeply and trust you totally. I could never be like that with some other man. I would just die of embarrassment and shame.'

His eyes softened on her. 'You really mean that, don't you?'

'Of course I do!'

He shook his head. 'You're one in a million, Tara. There truly aren't many women like you out there for men like me. True love is a luxury not often enjoyed by the rich and famous. Our attractiveness lies in our bank balances, not our selves.'

'I don't believe that. You're far too cynical, Max.'

'I've met far too many Alicias not to be cynical. Do you know that within six months of telling Stevie she loved him but couldn't cope, she'd married another heir to a fortune? Then, when she'd divorced that sucker twelve months later, she even had the temerity to make a line for me one night when our paths crossed.'

'And?'

'And what?'

'Don't take me for a total fool, Max. Something happened between you two. I felt it.'

He sighed. 'You feel too much sometimes. OK, so I was in a vengeful mood that night. When Alicia started coming on to me, I played along with it. When I suggested leaving the party we were attending she jumped at the chance, even though she'd come with someone else. I took her to a club, where we drank and danced.'

Danced! Tara's stomach crunched down hard at the mere thought of another woman in her Max's arms. She knew it was before they'd met, but still…

'I waited for her to make her excuses about Stevie,' Max continued as he twisted his champagne glass round and round. 'I knew she would. But what she said really floored me. She told me that she'd only dated Stevie to be near me. She told me that she'd never really loved my brother. It was me she'd loved all along. She claimed she only married that other man because she thought she had no chance with me. I told her what I thought of her and her so-called love and walked out.'

Tara never said a word, because she suspected that what the woman had said might be true. She'd seen a photograph of Stevie and whilst he had been a nice-looking boy, his face had lacked Max's strength and charisma.

'Love is just a weapon to such women,' Max added testily. 'My own mother pretends she still loves my father, despite his having been a neglectful husband, as well as a neglectful father. Why? Because it would probably cost too much money to divorce him. I over-heard her tell a lady friend once that she knew about Dad's womanising ways, but turned a blind eye. Even now that he's in a wheelchair, a wretched wreck of a man, she stays with him, catering to his every need. They're as bad as each other, bound together by their greed and their lack of moral fibre. That's why I have as little as possible to do with them these days. Both of them make me sick.'

Tara was stunned by his outburst, and the depth of his bitterness. Bitterness was never good for anyone's soul. Neither was revenge. It was very self-destructive.

'But you could be wrong, Max,' she ventured quietly. 'Your mother might very well love your father. There might be things you don't know. We rarely know what goes on inside a marriage. I found that out last weekend. I always thought my sister was unhappy in her marriage. She fell pregnant, you see, during her last year at school. Dale wasn't much older, and still doing his plumbing apprenticeship. They got married, with Jen thinking she could finish her schooling. But she was too sick during her pregnancy to study. Then, when her first baby was barely six months old, she fell pregnant again. She's always complaining about her life, and her husband. She says he spends too much time and money drinking with his mates. But when I asked her why she didn't leave him and get a divorce, she looked at me as though I was mad. Told me she was *very* happy with Dale and would never dream of getting a divorce. So maybe you're wrong, Max. It *is* possible, you know,' she added with a wry little smile.

He smiled back. 'Possible. But not probable. Look, let's not spoil tonight with such talk. Let's just eat some wonderful food together and drink this wonderful champagne. I want to get you delightfully tipsy so that I can take you back upstairs and have my truly wicked way with you.'

Although Tara's stomach flipped at the prospect, she stayed calm on the surface, suspecting that Max was watching her for her reaction. As much as she was curious, she wasn't sure if the reality would be as exciting as the fantasy. And even if it was, what about the consequences? Did she really want Max thinking she would do *anything* he asked? What next?

'You think that's the answer to my co-operation?' she asked coolly. 'Getting me drunk?'

'Is it?'

'I hope not.'

'Then how about this?' And he extracted a small gold velvet box from his pocket.

Tara stared at the ring-sized box.

An engagement ring. He'd bought her an engagement ring. He was going to ask her to marry him!

The shot of adrenalin which instantly charged through her bloodstream made a mockery of her denial to her mother that marriage to Max was not what she wanted at this moment in her life.

Clearly, her body knew things which her brain did not.

'Go on,' he said, and reached over to put the gold box on the white tablecloth in front of her. 'Open it.'

Something about the scenario suddenly didn't fit Tara's image of how a man like Max would ask her to marry him. It was all far too casual. *He* was far too casual.

She sucked in a deep breath, then let it out slowly, gathering herself before opening the box. When she did, and her eyes fell upon a huge topaz dress ring, she was ready to react as she was sure Max expected her to react, with seeming pleasure and gratitude.

'Oh, Max, it's lovely! Thank you so much.'

'I knew it would match that dress. That's why I wanted you to wear it tonight. Go on,' he said eagerly. 'Put it on. See if it fits.'

She slipped it on the middle finger of her right hand.

'Perfect,' she said, and held it out to show him. The diamond-cut stone sparkled under the candlelight. 'But you really shouldn't have, Max. You make me feel guilty that I didn't buy you anything. I had no idea you were such a romantic.'

'I think I'm catching the disease from you.'

'I don't know why you keep calling me a romantic.'

'When a girl of your looks reaches twenty-four still a virgin then I know she's a romantic.'

'Maybe. Maybe not. I consider myself more of an idealist. I didn't want to have sex till I *really* wanted it.

I wasn't waiting for love to strike so much as passion. Which it did. With you. I didn't realise I was in love with you till the following morning. How long did it take till you realised you loved me?'

'The moment you smiled at me in that shop I was a goner.'

'Oh, Max, now who's being the romantic?'

He smiled. 'Aah, here comes Jarod to take our order. Let me order for you tonight, darling. Now that you're breaking out in other ways, I think it's time you tried some different foods.'

'If you insist.'

He grinned. 'I insist.'

Tara sat back and sipped her champagne whilst Max went to town with their meal order. He'd always liked ordering the rarest and most exotic foods on the menu for himself.

Clearly, Max was happier now with her than ever. Tara glanced down at the topaz ring and told herself it had been silly of her to want it to be an engagement ring.

Max was right. She *was* a romantic.

'You don't like it,' Max said.

Tara glanced up to see that Jarod had departed and Max was looking at her with a worried frown.

'Of course I do,' she said with a quick smile. 'It's gorgeous.'

'So what were you thinking about that made you look so wistful?'

She shrugged. 'I guess I'd like to spend more time with the wonderful man who gave it to me.'

'Your wish is my command, my darling. How would you like to quit that job of yours and come with me when I go overseas?'

Tara's mouth dropped open.

'I take it that stunned look on your face means a yes?'

'I... I... Yes. Yes, of course. But Max, are you sure?'

'I wouldn't have asked you if I wasn't sure.'

So why haven't you asked me this before now?

The question zoomed into her mind like an annoying bee, buzzing around in her brain, searching for the truth. What had changed in their relationship that he suddenly wanted her with him all the time?

Tara hated the answer that would not be denied.

The sex. The sex between them had changed.

'Why now, Max?' she couldn't stop herself asking whilst her stomach had tightened into a knot.

He shrugged. 'Do you want the truth? Or romantic bulldust?'

'Romantic bulldust, of course.'

He laughed. 'OK. I love you. I love you so much that I can no longer stand leaving you behind when I go away. I want you with me, every day. I want you in my bed, every night. How's that?'

'Pretty good. Now how about the truth?'

Max looked at her and knew he would never tell her the truth, which was that he was afraid of losing her if he left her behind. He suspected she had never felt anything like she'd felt with him today. How, now, could he expect her to patiently wait for him to come home? She might not actively look for other lovers, but men would always pursue Tara…

'The truth,' he repeated, doing his best to look in command of the situation. 'The truth is I love you, Tara. I love you so much I can't stand the thought of leaving you behind when I go away. I want you with me, every day. I want you in my bed, every night.'

And wasn't *that* the truth!

Tara tried not to burst into tears. She had a feeling that sobbing all over the place was not what Max wanted in a mistress. Because of course, if she did this, if she quit her job and let Max pay for everything whilst she travelled with him, that was what she would be. Possibly, that was all she would ever be. There was no guarantee their relationship would end in marriage, no matter how much Max said he loved her.

Still, there'd never been any guarantees of that. He'd never given her any. And he wasn't giving her any now.

Tara thought of what her mother had said about how he would *never* give her what she wanted. Once again, she tried to pin down in her mind what she actually wanted from Max at this stage in her life. That ring business had rocked her a bit. Suddenly, she wasn't at all sure. The only thing she *was* sure of was that she didn't want to lose Max. Now more than ever.

'I'll have to give Whitmore's two weeks' notice,' she said, her voice on the suddenly breathless side. Her heart was racing madly and her mouth had gone dry. 'I can't just leave them in the lurch. February is top tourist season for the Japanese.'

'Fine. But what about next weekend? I have to go back to Auckland, negotiate with some owners there about a hotel. If I arrange plane tickets for you, would you join me there?'

'I wouldn't be able to leave till the Saturday morning. We'd only have the one night together.'

'Better than nothing,' he said, blue eyes gleaming in the candlelight.

'Yes,' she agreed, a tremor ripping down her spine. By next Saturday, her body would be screaming for him.

She picked up her glass and took a decent swallow, aware that he was watching her closely.

'Are you all right, Tara?' he asked, softly but knowingly, she thought.

'No,' she returned sharply. 'No, I'm not. And it's all your fault. I feel like a cat on a hot tin roof.'

'Aaah.'

There was a wealth of satisfaction—and knowledge—in that aaah.

'Would you like me to have our meals sent up to the penthouse?'

Tara blinked, then stared at him. If she blindly said yes, it would be the end of her. She would be his in whatever way he wanted her. There would be no further questioning over what *she* wanted, because what she wanted would be what *he* wanted.

But how could she say no when she wanted it too? To be his. To let him take her back into that world he had shown her today, that dizzying, dazzling world where sensation was heaped upon sensation, where giving pleasure was as satisfying as receiving it, where the mind was set free of worry and all its focus was centred on the physical.

'Can we take the champagne too?' she heard herself saying, shocked to the core at how cool her voice sounded.

'Absolutely.' Max was already on his feet.

'Will you still respect me in the morning?' she said with a degree of self-mockery as he walked round the table towards her.

Placing one hand under her chin, he tipped up her face for a kiss which was cruel in its restraint.

He's teasing me, she realised. Giving me a taste of what's to come.

'Tell me you love me,' he murmured when his mouth lifted.

'I love you.'

'Let's go.'

CHAPTER SEVEN

'I'M BEING punished for last night,' Tara groaned.

'You've just got a hangover,' Max reassured her, sitting down on the side of the bed and stroking her hair back from her forehead. 'You must have had too much champagne.'

'I'll never touch the stuff again,' Tara said, not sure which was worse. Her headache or her swirling stomach.

'Pity,' Max said with a wry smile. 'You really were *very* cooperative.'

'Don't remind me.'

Max laughed. 'I'll get you a couple of painkillers and a glass of water.'

Max disappeared into the bathroom, leaving Tara with her misery and her memories of the night before. Impossible to forget what she had allowed. Ridiculous to pretend that she hadn't thrilled to it all.

Tara groaned, then groaned again. She was going to be sick.

Her dash to the bathroom was desperate, shoving

Max out of the way. She just had time to hold her hair back and out of the way before everything came up that she'd eaten the night before. It came up and came up till she was left exhausted and shaken.

It's just a hangover, she told herself as Max helped her over to the basin, where she rinsed out her mouth and washed her face. Or the same virus I had yesterday morning. I couldn't possibly be pregnant. Mum put that silly thought into my head. And it *is* silly. I had a period, for pity's sake.

'Poor darling,' Max comforted as he carried her back to bed and placed her still naked body gently inside the sheets. When she started shivering he covered her up with a quilt and tucked it around her. 'No point taking any tablets if you're throwing up. I'll go get you that glass of water. And a cool washer to put on your forehead. That helps sometimes. Take it from one who knows. I've had a few dreadful hangovers in my time. Still, you must be extra-susceptible to champagne, because you didn't have *that* much. I think I had the major share. And we wasted a bit. On you.'

'Don't remind me about that, either,' she said wretchedly. 'Could you dispose of that disgusting champagne bottle? I don't want to look at it.'

'Come, now, Tara, you loved it last night. *All* of it,' he said as he swept the empty bottle off the bedside table and headed for the doorway. 'But I will tolerate your morning-after sensitivities,' he tossed over his shoulder, 'in view of your fragile condition.'

Her fragile condition…

Tara bit her bottom lip as the question over her being sick for a second morning in a row returned to haunt her. Max was right. She hadn't had that much champagne. Hard to pin her hopes on the gastric virus going around, either. With that, Jen and her kids had been running to use the loo all the time. Then there was her sudden recovery yesterday afternoon and evening, only for her to become nauseous again this morning.

If she hadn't had a period recently then she would have presumed she was pregnant, as her mother had. Was it possible to have a period and still be pregnant? Tara had read of a few such cases. They weren't proper periods, just breakthrough bleeding, mostly related to women who'd fallen pregnant whilst on the Pill. Nothing was a hundred per cent safe, except abstinence. Her mother had told her *that,* too.

'Oh, God,' she sobbed, and stuffed a hand into her mouth.

'That bad, huh?' Max said as he strode back into the bedroom, carrying a glass of water with some ice in it. 'Do you want me to ring the house medico? I have one on call here at the weekends.'

'No! No doctor.'

'OK, OK,' Max soothed, coming round to place the glass on the bedside table. 'No doctor. I'm just trying to help. I don't like seeing you this sick.'

'What you don't like is not having your new little sex slave on tap this morning!'

The horrible words were out of her mouth before she could stop them. She saw Max's head jerk back. Saw the shock in his eyes.

Tara was truly appalled at herself. 'I'm sorry,' she cried. 'I didn't mean that. Truly. I'm not myself this morning. I'm a terrible person when I'm sick.' And when I'm petrified I might be pregnant.

The very thought sent her head whirling some more. She didn't want to be pregnant. Not now. Not when Max had just asked her to travel with him. Not when her life had just become so exciting.

'It's all right, Tara. I understand.'

'No, no, you don't.'

'I think I do. What happened yesterday. And last night. It was a case of too much too soon. I became greedy. I should have taken things more slowly with you. You might have enjoyed yourself at the time, but hindsight has a way of bringing doubts and worries. It's good, in a way, that this morning has given us both a breather. Even if it's not under pleasant circumstances for you.'

'You don't mind?'

His smile was wry. 'Mind? Of course I mind. I'd love to be making love to you right at this moment. But I'm a patient man. I can wait till next weekend. And next time, I promise I won't frighten you with my demands.'

'You…you didn't frighten me, Max.'

He stared into her eyes. 'No? Are you sure?'

'I'm sure. I liked everything we did together.'

He let out a sigh of relief. 'I'm so glad to hear that.

I have to confess I was a bit worried that I might have gone too far last night. Not at the time. But when I woke, this morning.'

Not as worried as *she* was this morning.

Max sat down beside her on the bed and started stroking her head again. 'Still, I don't want you to ever think you have to do anything you don't want to do, Tara. I love *you*, not just having sex with you. All right?'

She nodded, but tears threatened. Max might say that now, but what if she *was* pregnant? Would he be so noble when faced with her having his baby? Or would he do and say things which might threaten their relationship for good?

Endless complications flooded into her mind, almost overwhelming her with fear, and feelings of impending doom.

But you don't *know* you're pregnant, she tried telling herself. You could very well be wrong.

Yes, yes, she would cling to that thought. At least till Max left. She couldn't continue thinking and acting this way or she would surely break down and blurt out what was bothering her. And she really didn't want to do that. Max had enough things on his mind these days without burdening him with premature news of an unconfirmed pregnancy.

No, she had to pull herself together and stop being such a panic artist. Max had a couple of hours yet before he left for the airport. Surely she could stay calm for that length of time. Why spoil the rest of his stay with negativity and pessimism? What would that achieve? He was being so sweet and understanding this morning. It wasn't fair to take her secret fears out on him, especially when it was only a guess, and based on nothing but her feeling nauseous two mornings in a row.

Hardly conclusive proof.

'Max…'

'Yes?'

'I'm feeling a bit better now. My stomach is much more settled. Do you think I should try something to eat? Maybe some toast?'

'I think that would be an excellent idea. Eating is another good cure for a hangover. I'll have Room Service send some up.' And he stood up to walk round to the extension that sat on his bedside chest. 'I'll order myself a decent breakfast at the same time. Just coffee won't cut it this morning. Not with airline food beckoning me later today. I need something far more substantial.'

Tara pulled herself up into a sitting position, dragging the sheet up with her over her breasts and tucking it modestly around her. As much as she might have discovered a new abandon when she was turned on, she was still not an exhibitionist.

'You know, Max,' she said when he'd finished ordering, 'you should keep some staple foods in your kitchen. Cereals last for weeks. So does long-life milk and juice. And bread freezes. It's rather extravagant to order everything you eat from Room Service.'

'Maybe, but I intend to keep on doing it. I work incredibly long hours and I have no intention of spending my precious leisure time in the kitchen. I have far more enjoyable things to do when I'm on R & R.' And he gave her a wickedly knowing smile.

Tara was taken aback. Maybe she was extra-sensitive this morning, but she didn't like Max describing the time he spent with her as R & R—rest and recreation.

She dropped her eyes to her lap to stop his noting her negative reaction and found herself staring at the huge topaz ring which was still on her finger. His gift was the only thing he hadn't removed from her last night.

Suddenly, she saw it not as an anniversary present, but the beginning of many such gifts, given to her for services rendered; rewards for travelling with him and filling his rest and recreation hours in the way he liked most.

She pictured their sex games being played out in lavish hotel rooms all over the world, Max's demands becoming more and more outrageous in line with the extravagance of his gifts. Soon, she'd be dripping in diamonds and designer clothes. But underneath, she wouldn't be wearing *any* underwear. In the end, she would become his sex slave for real, bought and paid for, fashioned to fulfil his every desire. She would cease to be her own person. She'd just be a possession. A toy, to be taken out and played with during Max's leisure time, and ignored when he went back to his real life. His work.

Of course, such a sex toy had to be perfect, physically. It could never be allowed to get fat. Or pregnant.

Pregnant sex slaves had two choices. They either

got rid of their babies. Or they themselves were dispensed with.

Both scenarios horrified Tara.

'Max!' she exclaimed, her eyes flying upwards.

But Max was no longer in the bedroom. Tara had been so consumed with her thoughts—and her imaginary future—that she hadn't noticed his leaving.

'Max!' she called out and the door of his dressing room opened. He emerged, dressed in one of his conservative grey business suits, though not teamed with his usual white shirt today. His shirt was a blue, the same blue as his eyes. And his tie was a sleek, shiny silver, a change from his usual choice. His hair was still damp from a recent shower and slicked straight back from his head.

He looked dashing, she thought. And very sexy.

But then, Max *was* very sexy.

An image flashed into her mind of his tipping champagne from the bottle over her breasts, then bending to lick it off. Slowly. So very slowly. She'd pleaded with him to stop teasing her.

But he'd ignored her pleas.

That was part of the game, wasn't it?

The best part. The most exciting part.

'What?' he asked, frowning over at her.

'I… I didn't know where you were,' she said lamely, hating herself for her sudden weakness. She'd been going to tell him that she'd changed her mind about travelling with him; that she didn't really like the way things were heading.

But the words had died in her throat at the sight of him. It was so true what they said. The mind could be willing but the flesh was very weak.

'Thought I might as well get dressed before Room Service called,' he explained. 'I know how you don't like the butler coming in when you're in bed. Besides, no point in staying in my bathrobe with you feeling under the weather, is there?'

The front door bell rang right at that moment. Max hurried from the room, returning in no time, wheeling a traymobile. By then, Tara had decided she was being a drama queen. Max loved her and she loved him. It was only natural that he would ask her to travel with him. And it was only natural that she would go.

As for her pregnancy…

That was as far-fetched an idea as her becoming some kind of mindless sex slave. She had always had a strong sense of her own self. Her mother called her wilful and her sister said she was incredibly stubborn. If Max started crossing the line where she was concerned, she would simply tell him so and come home. Nothing could be simpler.

'Now, that's what I like to see,' Max said as he tossed her one of the Sunday papers. 'Almost a happy face.'

She smiled at him. 'Nothing like feeling better to make you feel better.'

He scowled. 'Now she tells me, *after* I'm dressed.'

'That was not an invitation for more sex, Max Richmond. I think we've indulged enough for one weekend. I would hate to think that all I'd be if and when I travel with you is a means of rest and relaxation.'

He frowned at her. 'If and when? Did I hear correctly? I thought you'd agreed to come with me. It was just a matter of giving your notice.'

'Yes, well, I've been having some second thoughts.'

Tara knew how to play that game. The hard-to-get game.

For years before she'd met Max, she'd played it to the hilt. Whilst she'd not been so successful with Max, she suspected that it would do him good to be a little less sure of her.

'Aah,' he said. 'I see. Hence, the sex-slave accusation.'

'Yes…'

Max sighed, then came over to sit on the bed once more.

'I don't know how many times I have to tell you this weekend, Tara, but I love you. Deeply. I want you with me for more than just sex. I enjoy just being with you, even when we're not making love. I enjoy your company and your conversation. I enjoy your wit and your charm with other people. Taking you out is a delight. *You* are a delight. When you're not sick, that is,' he added drily, dampening her pleasure in his compliments.

'Charming,' she said. 'So if I ever get sick, I will be tossed aside, like a toy whose batteries have run low?'

'No more of this nonsense!' he pronounced, and rose to his feet. 'You're coming with me and that's that. So what would you like on your toast? There is a choice of honey, Vegemite and jam. Strawberry jam, by the look of it.'

'Vegemite.'

'Vegemite toast coming up, then.'

Tara raised no further objections to travelling with him.

But she resolved not to ever let him take away her much valued sense of independence. She'd always been her own person and would hate to think that her love for Max would eventually turn her into some kind of puppet.

She munched away on her toast and watched him tuck into his huge breakfast, which he ate whilst sitting with her on the bed. He chatted away when he could, pleasing her with the news that the comment she'd made yesterday about never being able to resist a buy-one, get-one-free sale had inspired him to make such an offer with his hotel in Hong Kong.

Stay one week, get one free was now posted on its website and was already bringing in results with scads of bookings.

'We won't make a great profit on the accommodation,' he told her. 'But empty rooms don't return a cent. Hopefully, the type of guest this promotion attracts will spend all the money they think they've saved in other places in the hotel. Pierce thought I was crazy, but that was yesterday. This morning he's singing my praises. Says I'm a genius. Forgive me for not telling him that my little genius is my girlfriend. Male ego is a terrible thing.'

Tara suspected that it was.

But it was also an attractive thing. It gave Max his

competitiveness, and his drive. It made him the man he was, the man she loved.

'Isn't it unusual to have a male PA?' she remarked, somewhat idly.

'Unusual maybe. But wise, given the amount of time we spend overseas together.'

Tara blinked as the meaning behind Max's words sank in. 'Did you hire Pierce *because* he's a man?'

'You mean because I didn't want to risk becoming involved with a female secretary?'

'Yes.'

'Absolutely. Been there, done that, and it was messy.'

'How long ago?'

'A good year or so before I met you.'

'Did you sleep with her?'

Max pulled a face. 'I wish you hadn't asked me that.'

'Did you sleep with her?'

'Once or twice.'

'Was it once, or twice?'

'More than that, actually. Look, it was messy, as I said.'

'Tell me about it.'

He sighed. 'I'd rather not.'

'I want to know. You know all about my past.'

'Tara, you don't *have* a past.'

'Yes, I do. I might not have slept with guys but I made out with quite a few. I told you all about them that first night. I want to know, Max. Tell me.'

'OK, but it isn't pretty.'

'Was *she* pretty?'

'Pretty? No, Grace was not pretty. Not plain, either. Very slim. Nicely groomed. With red hair. Out of a bottle. She was already my personal assistant when Dad had his stroke. Up till then I'd taken care of the money side of things in the firm, here at home in Sydney. Suddenly, I had to go overseas. A lot. I took her with me. The man she was living with at the time didn't like it and broke up with her. We'd never been involved before but all of a sudden, we were together every day of the week. We were both lonely, and stressed out. One night, over too many drinks, she made a pass at me and it just happened. It wasn't love on my part. And she said it wasn't on hers. It was more a matter of mutual convenience. I should have stopped it. I still feel guilty that I didn't. Finally, when I tried to, she told me she was pregnant.'

Tara sucked in sharply.

'She wasn't,' he went on. 'It was just a ploy to get me to marry her. Frankly, I was suspicious right from the start. I'd always used condoms and there'd never been an accident, not like that one I had with you last year. When I insisted on accompanying her to a doctor to find out how far pregnant she was, she broke down and confessed she wasn't at all.'

'And if she had been, Max? What then? What would you have done?'

He shrugged. 'I honestly don't know. But she wasn't, so I didn't have to face that dilemma. Thank God. But it made me wary, I can tell you. Hence, Pierce.'

'I see. And what happened to her?'

'I'm pleased to say she went back home to the man she'd been living with before. I had a note from her some months later to say they were getting married, and this time she really was having a baby. I was happy for her because I suspect she thought she was past having a child. She wasn't all that young, you see. She was forty by then.'

'An older woman,' Tara said with an edge to her voice. 'And an experienced one, I'll bet. Did you learn some of those kinky games from her, Max? Was that why you couldn't stop? Because she never had to be persuaded to finish anything she started?'

'Stop it, Tara,' Max snapped. 'Stop it right now. You have no reason to be jealous of Grace. I'm sorry my past is not as pure as yours but I won't be cross-questioned on it. And I won't apologise for it. I'm a mortal man. I've made mistakes in my life, but hopefully I have learned from them.'

Putting aside his breakfast tray, he stood up. 'I think perhaps I should get going before you find something else to argue about. I can see you're out of sorts this morning in more ways than one. When you do feel well enough to go home, for pity's sake use the credit card I gave you to take a taxi this time. I noticed in the statements I receive that you never use the darned thing these days.'

'Fine,' she said, wanting him to just go so that she could cry.

His eyes narrowed on her. 'I wish I knew what was going on in that pretty head of yours.'

'Not much. Blonde-bimbo mistresses aren't known for their brains.'

'Tara…'

'I know. I'm acting like a fool. Forgive me.' Tears pricked at her eyes.

'Oh, Tara…' And he started walking towards her.

She knew, without his saying a word, that he was going to take her into his arms. If he did that, she was going to disintegrate and say even more stupid things.

'Please don't come near me,' she said sharply. 'I smell of sick.'

He stopped, his eyes tormented. 'I don't want to leave you on this note.'

'You can make it up to me next weekend in Auckland, when I feel better.'

'That's a week away.'

'Ring me from Hong Kong, then. But not tonight. Tonight I want to go to bed early and sleep. I'm wrecked.'

He smiled. 'Same here. I'll be sleeping on that plane. All right, I'll ring you tomorrow night. Can I peck you on the forehead?'

'If you must.'

'Oh, I must,' he said softly as his lips brushed over her forehead. 'I must…'

Tara waited till he was definitely gone before she dissolved into some very noisy weeping.

CHAPTER EIGHT

TARA stared at the blue line, all her fears crystallised.

She was pregnant.

Stumbling back from the vanity basin, she sank down onto the toilet seat, her head dropping into her hands.

But somehow, she was beyond tears. She'd cried for ages after Max left. Cried and cried.

It had been close to two o'clock by the time she'd pulled herself together enough to get dressed and go downstairs to buy a pregnancy-testing kit from the chemist shop in the foyer.

And now there was no longer any doubt. Or guessing. She was going to have Max's baby.

Tara shook her head from side to side. It wasn't fair. She'd taken every precaution. This shouldn't be happening to her. What on earth was she going to do?

Tara sucked in deeply as she lifted her head. What *could* she do?

Nothing. The same way Jen had done nothing when

Dale had got her pregnant. The Bond sisters hadn't been brought up to have abortions.

Not that Tara wanted to get rid of Max's baby. If she could just get past her fear over what Max would say and do when he found out, she might even feel happy about it.

But that was her biggest problem, wasn't it?

Telling Max.

What if he accused her of deliberately getting pregnant? Even worse, what if he demanded she get a termination?

That would be the death knell of their relationship, she knew. Because it would prove to her once and for all that he didn't really love her.

A huge wave of depression washed through her, taking Tara lower than she'd ever been in her life before. If she discovered Max didn't really love her, how could she stand it? How would she cope?

You'll have to cope, girl, came back the stern answer. You're going to become a mother. You're going to be needed. Having some kind of breakdown is simply not on.

Tara squared her shoulders as her self-lecture had some effect. But when she thought of having to tell her own mother about the baby she wilted again.

Not yet, Tara decided with a shudder. She couldn't tell her yet. Maybe she wouldn't tell Max yet, either. First babies didn't show for quite a while. Maybe she could delay the confrontation with Max till she was over four months, past the safe time for a termination. As much as Tara was confident he couldn't succeed in talking her into an abortion, she didn't want him to even try.

Unfortunately, she had no idea just how far pregnant she actually was. That was her first job. To find out.

Jen, Tara thought with a lifting of spirit. Jen had a nice doctor that she'd gone to when she was having her babies. Tara had gone with her a couple of times and had really liked him. On top of that, Jen wouldn't be too shocked, or read her the Riot Act. How could she when she'd got pregnant herself when she'd only been seventeen?

Yes, she would tell Jen, then ask her to arrange an appointment with her doctor. Preferably for this week, *before* her supposed trip to New Zealand. Tara need to know where things stood. Though really, unless her morning sickness went away, she couldn't see herself going anywhere overseas for ages.

Tara stood up and returned to the bedroom, where she sat down on Max's side of the bed and picked up the phone. After pressing the number for an outside line, she was about to punch in Jen's number when she realised she hadn't called her mother at all this weekend. Yet she'd promised to let her know when she'd be back.

Tara sighed. Really, once Max was on the scene, she couldn't think about anything or anyone else. The man had obsessed her these last twelve months. He probably would have obsessed her more after this incredible weekend, if his baby hadn't come along to put a halt to the proceedings. As much as she had thrilled to his forceful lovemaking—and it didn't seem to have hurt the baby—she really couldn't let him continue to make love to her in such a wild fashion.

Which meant her idea of keeping the baby secret for weeks wouldn't work. Max wouldn't understand why she wanted him to go back to his former style of slow, gentle lovemaking all of a sudden.

No. She would have to tell him the truth. And soon.

Now Tara wasn't sure whether to view this pregnancy as a saviour, or one huge sacrifice all round. No travelling overseas. No adventurous sex. Possibly, no Max at all!

Her chin trembled at this last thought.

Oh, life was cruel. Too cruel.

Tara slumped down on the bed and burst into tears again, the phone clutched in her hands. This time, her crying jag was considerably shorter than the last. Only ten minutes or so.

I'm definitely getting it together, she told herself as she dabbed at her eyes with the sheet, then took several gathering breaths.

'Time to ring Mum,' she said aloud, proud of her firm voice, and her firm finger. The number entered, she waited for her mother to answer.

'Hi there.'

'Oh. Oh, Jen. It's *you*!'

'Hi, Tara. Yep. It's me. I came over to visit Mum. She seemed a bit down. Dale's minding the kids. We're playing Scrabble and eating far too much cake. I presume his lord and master is in town?'

'Er— *Was*. He's gone now.'

'Brother, he doesn't stay long these days, does he?'

'Jen, can we talk? I mean…can Mum hear what you're saying?'

'Hold it a sec. Mum, it's Tara… Tara, Mum wants to know when you're coming home.'

'Shortly.'

'Shortly, Mum,' Tara heard Jen say. 'Why don't you go make us a cuppa while I have a chat with my little sister? I haven't talked to Tara in ages. Great. I'm alone now, Tara,' she said more quietly. 'What's up?'

'I… I'm pregnant.'

Jen stayed silent for a second, then just said, 'Bummer.'

'Is that it? Just *bummer*? I was hoping for some words of sympathy and wisdom.'

'Sorry. It was the shock. So how did this happen? I mean, I know how it *happened*. You had sex. I meant…did you forget the Pill one day or something?'

'Nope. Took it right on the dot every day.'

'Now, that is a real bummer. I was at least stupid and careless when I fell pregnant. Oh, Tara, what are you going to do?'

'Have my baby. The same way you did.'

'Yeah. We're suckers for doing the right thing, aren't we? So does Max know yet? I presume not.'

'No. I only found out myself a few minutes ago. The test went bluer than blue.'

'What do you think he'll say?'

'My head goes round and round every time I think about that. He's not going to be happy.'

'Men are never happy over unexpected pregnancies. But if he loves you, he'll stick by you. Dale went ballistic at first but after a while he calmed down, and really he was like a rock after that. Much better than me, actually. I cried for weeks and weeks.'

'I remember.'

'Do you think Max might ask you to marry him?'

'He's made it clear that marriage and kids are definitely not on his agenda, so your guess is as good as mine.'

'No, it isn't, Tara. You know the man. I don't. Does he love you?'

'He says he does.'

'You don't sound convinced.'

Tara sighed. 'I'm a bit mixed up about Max at the moment.'

'Is the pregnancy causing that, or what's going on in your relationship right now? Mum told me he's hardly ever around any more.'

Tara resented having to defend Max but, in fairness to the man, she felt she should. 'He's been very busy with all the world crises in the tourist industry. On the plus side, he did ask me just this weekend to quit my job and travel with him in future.' Tara didn't add that she was more qualified for the role of travelling companion since finding her sexual wings.

'Wow! And what did you say to that? Silly question. Yes, of course. I know you're crazy about the man.'

'I can't see myself travelling at all in the near future. I'm sick as a dog every morning. I need to see a doctor,

Jen. Do you think you could get an appointment with your doctor this week?'

'He might be able to fit you in. But he won't be able to cure you of morning sickness. You'll just have to ride that out. Have a packet of dry biscuits by your bed and eat a couple before you get up. That helps. So, how far gone are you?'

'That's another thing. I don't know. Before this weekend, I hadn't seen Max in almost a month. Yet I had a period whilst he was away. At least, I thought I did. There was some bleeding when my period was due.'

'Yeah, that can happen. You're probably about six weeks gone if you're chucking up. But you need to have it checked out. Don't worry. I'll explain to the reception-ist that it's an emergency. Now, when are you going to tell lover-boy?'

'Max,' Tara corrected firmly. 'Call him Max.'

'I'd like to call him lots of things, actually. But Max isn't one of them. Look, once you've been to the doctor and had things properly confirmed, you *have* to tell him. Even if he doesn't want to marry you, he's legally required to support this baby. You have no idea how much having children costs these days. Do you have private health cover?'

'For pity's sake, Jen, do you have to be so…so… pragmatic? I've just found out I'm having a baby. It's a very emotional time for me.'

'You can be emotional later. First things first, which

is your welfare and the welfare of your child. Trust me. I know better than you in this.'

'I wish I hadn't told you at all!'

'Don't be ridiculous. You need all the support you can get. Which reminds me. You really should tell Mum.'

'Are you kidding? I'm going to delay that disaster area for as long as possible. Promise me you won't tell her, Jen. Right now. *Promise.*'

'OK. I think you're wrong, but it's your call. Speaking of calls, I'll ring the surgery first thing tomorrow morning. Then I'll ring you at work to let you know. I'll come with you, of course.'

'Would you? Oh, Jen, that would be great. I…I feel kind of… Oh, I don't know. I just can't seem to get my head around all this. A baby, for heaven's sake. I'm going to have a baby!' Tears threatened again.

'A beautiful baby, I'll warrant. And you'll love it to pieces.'

Tara gulped down the lump in her throat. 'Will I? I've never thought of myself as good mother material. I'm too…restless.'

'You just didn't know what you wanted. Having a baby will bring your life into focus. Er—we'd better sign off now before Mum comes back.'

'Yes, I really couldn't cope with the third degree she'd give me. You won't forget to call me tomorrow?'

'I won't forget.'

'OK. Bye for now.'

Jen hung up, then grimaced up at her mother, who was standing there, mugs in hand.

'You heard that last bit, didn't you?'

Joyce nodded.

'She…she's too scared to tell you,' Jen said quietly, knowing by the look on her mother's face that she was about to have a hissy fit.

'But why?' Joyce wailed, putting the mugs down on the coffee-table next to the Scrabble board and flopping down into her chair.

'You know why, Mum. It's the same reason I didn't want to tell you when *I* was pregnant. Daughters want their mothers to be proud of them, not ashamed.'

'But Jen, I was never ashamed of you. Just disappointed for you. And worried. You were so young. And neither of you had any money.'

'What's age or money got to do with it? Love's what matters, Mum, when it comes to kids and marriage. Dale loved me and I loved him. We've had some tough times but we're going to make it. Unfortunately, I'm not so sure Max Richmond loves our Tara. Certainly not enough to give up his jet-setting lifestyle. That's why she's in such a tizz, because she knows it too. She's going to need a lot of support through this, Mum.'

'But how can I support her when I'm not supposed to even know?'

'She'll tell you. Just give her a little time.'

'From the sounds of things, she hasn't told Max Richmond.'

'Not yet. She's just found out herself, I gather, and he's not there.'

'He's never going to be there for her.'

'Probably. But he can be forced to support her financially. At least she won't be poor.'

'Yes, that's true. But Tara never wanted his money. You know she's not that kind of girl. She just wanted him to love her.'

'Yeah, I do know. She's always been a real romantic. She's been living in a fantasy world with her fantasy lover and now the real world has come up and bitten her, big time.'

Joyce was shaking her head. 'I've been afraid of something like this for a long time. If that man lets her down, I'm not sure she'll be able to cope.'

'She'll be upset, but she'll cope, Mum. You brought us up to be survivors. We're a stubborn pair. Trust me on that.'

'You're both good girls.'

'More's the pity. If Tara wasn't so damned good, she wouldn't have a problem.'

'Jen, you don't think she'd ever…'

'No. Never in a million years. She's going to have this baby whether lover-boy wants her to or not.'

Joyce looked shocked. 'You mean he might try to persuade her to get rid of it?'

'It's highly likely, don't you think?'

'She does love him a lot, Jen. If he puts the pressure on, she might do what he wants. Women in love can sometimes do things they regret later.'

'If he does that, *he'll* be the one to regret it,' Jen said fiercely. 'Tara would never forgive him, *or* herself. Look, I'd better drink this tea and get on home, Mum. Don't worry too much about Tara. Max can't put any pressure on her yet, because she doesn't intend telling him yet. OK?'

Joyce nodded, but inside she was beside herself with worry. Yet she could do nothing to help, because she wasn't supposed to know!

She glanced over at Jen and tried to work out why it was that daughters always misunderstood their mothers. All she wanted was for them to be happy.

Fancy Jen thinking she'd been ashamed of her when she fell pregnant. How could she possibly be ashamed of her daughters for doing exactly what she had done herself? Fallen madly in love. Maybe she would tell them one day that she had been pregnant when she'd married her beloved Bill.

Tears filled Joyce's eyes as she thought of the handsome man who'd swept her off her feet and into his bed before she could blink. How she'd loved that man. When he'd died, she could not bear to ever have another man touch her, though there'd been plenty who'd tried. Her daughters might be surprised to know that. But she'd only ever wanted her Bill.

'Please don't cry, Mum,' Jen said, reaching over to touch her mother's hand. 'Tara will be fine. You'll see.'

Joyce found a watery smile from somewhere. 'I hope so, love.'

'She's strong, is our Tara. And stubborn. Max won't find it easy to make her do anything she doesn't want to do. And she doesn't want to get rid of her baby. Come on, give me a hug and dry those tears. If you're all puffy-eyed when Tara gets home, she'll think I told you and then there'll be hell to pay. Promise me now that you won't let on.'

Joyce gave her daughter a hug and a promise. But it was difficult not to worry once she was alone, so she did the one thing she always did when she started to stress over one of her daughters. She took out the photo albums which contained the visual memories of all the good times they'd had as a family before her Bill died.

It always soothed her fears, looking at the man she'd loved so much and whom she still loved. She liked to talk to him; ask his advice.

He told her to hang in there, the way he always did. And to be patient. Some things took time. Time. And work. And faith.

She frowned over this last piece of advice. She had faith in Tara. The trouble was she had no faith in Max Richmond.

CHAPTER NINE

MAX replaced the receiver, a deep frown drawing his brows together. Something was wrong. He could feel it. He'd been feeling it all week.

Tara was different. Each night she'd cut his calls off after only a few minutes with some pitiful excuse. Her hair was wet. She wanted to watch some TV show. Tonight she'd said she had to go because she'd forgotten to feed her mother's cat and her mother was out playing bingo.

As if that couldn't have waited!

Then there was her definite lack of enthusiasm over their meeting up in Auckland. Tonight she'd even said she might not be able to make it. They were short-handed at Whitmore's this weekend and she felt obliged to help out. Would he mind terribly if she didn't come?

When he'd said that he definitely would, she'd sighed and said she would see what she could do, but not to count on her coming. She hadn't said she loved him before she ended the call, the way she usually did. Just a rather strained goodbye.

Last weekend had been a mistake, Max realised. He'd frightened her.

He shook his head. Hell, didn't she realise he didn't really care about that kind of sex? All he wanted was to be with *her*.

He would ring her back, reassure her. It wasn't late. Only eight o'clock, her time.

When Mrs Bond answered the phone, he was startled. But not for long. Hadn't he subconsciously known Tara was lying to him?

'Max Richmond here, Mrs Bond. Can I speak to Tara, please?'

'No, you may not!' the woman snapped. 'I'm not going to let you upset her any more tonight. She's been through enough today.'

'What? But I didn't upset her tonight. And what do you mean she's been through enough today? What's going on that I don't know about?'

'Oh, Mum,' he heard Tara say in the background. 'How could you? You promised. I should never have told you.'

'He has to know, Tara. And the sooner the better. Why should you shoulder this burden all on your own?'

Max was taken aback. 'Burden? What burden? Speak to *me*, woman. Tell me what's going on.'

But she didn't answer him. All he heard was muffled sounds. His blood pressure soared as a most dreadful feeling of helplessness overwhelmed him. He wanted to be there, not here, hanging on the end of a phone thousands of miles away. If he was there, he'd make them both look at him and talk to him.

'Hey!' he shouted down the line. 'Is anyone there? Mrs Bond. Answer me, damn it!'

More sounds. A door slamming. A sigh.

'It's me,' Tara said with another sigh.

'Thank heaven. Tara, tell me what's going on.'

'I suppose there's no point in keeping it a secret any longer. I'm pregnant, Max.'

'Pregnant!' He was floored. 'But how c—?'

'Before you go off on one,' she swept on rather impatiently, '*no*, I didn't do this on purpose and *no*, I didn't even do it by accident. I took that darned Pill at the same time every day. I even had what I thought was a period a few weeks back. The doctor I saw today said that can happen. It's rare but not unheard-of. I'm about six or seven weeks gone, according to the ultrasound.'

A baby. Tara was going to have his baby. She wasn't tired of him, or frightened of him. She was just pregnant.

'Say something, for pity's sake!' she snapped.

'I was thinking.'

'I'll bet you were. Look, if you think I'm *happy* about this, then you're dead wrong. I'm not. The last thing I wanted at this time in my life was to have a baby. If being pregnant feels the way I've been feeling every morning then maybe I'll *never* want to have one.'

'So that's why you were sick the other morning!' Max exclaimed. 'It wasn't the champagne.'

'No, it wasn't the champagne,' she reiterated tetchily. 'It was *your* baby.'

'Yes, I understand, Tara. And your mother's right. This is my responsibility as much as it is yours. So how long have you known? You didn't know last weekend, did you?' Surely she wouldn't have encouraged him to act the way he had if she knew she was pregnant!

'No, of course I didn't. But when I woke up on the Sunday morning, chucking up two mornings in a row, I began to suspect.'

'Aah, so that's why you were so irritable with me that morning. I understand now. Poor baby.'

'Yes, it is a poor baby, to not be wanted by its parents.'

'You really *don't* want this baby?' His heart sank. When Grace had told him she was having a baby, he hadn't felt anything like what he was feeling now. He really wanted this child. It was his, and Tara's. A true love-child.

Tara's silence at the other end of the phone was more than telling. *He* might want their baby, but she didn't. She'd already raced off to a doctor to find out how far pregnant she was. Why? To see if it wasn't too late to have a termination?

Panic filled his heart.

'This is not the end of the world, Tara,' he said carefully. 'I don't want you making any hasty decisions. We should work this out together. Look, I won't go to New Zealand tomorrow. Pierce can handle that. I'll catch an overnight flight to Sydney. I should be able to get a seat. I'll catch a taxi straight out to your place as soon as I land and we'll sit down and work things out together. OK?'

Again, she didn't say a word.

'Tara…'

'What?'

The word was sharp. Sour, even. Max tried to understand how she felt, falling pregnant like that when she'd taken every precaution against it. She was only young, and just beginning to blossom, sexually speaking. She'd definitely been very excited about travelling with him. She probably felt her whole life was ruined with her being condemned to domestic boredom whilst he continued to jet-set around the world.

But having a termination was not the answer. Not for Tara. It would haunt her forever.

'Promise me you'll be there when I arrive,' he said. 'Even if the plane is late, promise me you won't go to work tomorrow.'

'Why should I make promises to you when you haven't made any to me? Go to hell, Max.' And she slammed the phone down in his ear.

Max gaped, then groaned once he saw what he'd done wrong. He should have told her again that he loved her. He should have reassured her straight away that he would be there for her, physically, emotionally and financially. Maybe he should have even asked her to marry her as a demonstration of his commitment to her and the child.

Of course, it wasn't an ideal situation, marrying because of a baby. He'd shunned marriage and children so far because he'd never wanted to neglect a family the way his father had. But the baby was a *fait accompli* and he truly loved Tara. Compromises could be made.

Yes, marriage was the answer. He would ring her back and ask her to marry him.

He swiftly pressed redial.

'Damn and blast!' he roared when the number was engaged.

Max tried her mobile but it was turned off. Clearly, she didn't want to speak to him. She was too angry. And she had every right to be. He was a complete idiot.

Max paced the hotel room for about thirty agitated seconds before returning to the phone and pressing redial once more. Again, nothing but the engaged tone. He immediately rang Pierce in the next room and asked him to get on to the airlines and find him a seat on an overnight flight to Sydney, money no object. He was to beg or bribe his way onto a plane.

'But what about New Zealand?' Pierce asked, obviously confused by these orders.

'You'll have to go there in my place,' Max said. 'Do you think you can handle that situation on your own?'

'Do I have complete authority? Or will I have to keep you in touch by phone during negotiations?'

'You have a free hand. You decide if the hotel is a good buy, and if it is, buy it. At a bargain price, of course.'

'You kidding me?'

'No.'

'Wow. This is fantastic. To what do I owe this honour?'

'To my impending marriage.'

'Your what?'

'Tara's pregnant.'

'Good lord.'

Max could understand Pierce's surprise. Max was not the sort of man to make such mistakes. But he wasn't in the mood to explain the circumstances surrounding Tara's unexpected pregnancy.

'Just get on to the airlines, Pierce. Pronto. Then ring me back.'

'Will do. And boss?'

'Yes?'

'Thanks.'

'If you do a good job, there'll be a permanent pro-motion for you. And a lot more travelling. I'm planning on cutting down on my overseas trips in future. But first things first. Get me on a plane for Sydney. Tonight!'

Max didn't sleep much on the plane. Pierce had managed to get him a first-class seat on a QANTAS flight. He spent most of the time thinking, and planning. By the time the jumbo landed at Mascot soon after dawn, he had all his actions and arguments ready to convince Tara that marriage was the best and only option.

'A brief stop at the Regency Royale,' he told the taxi driver. 'Then I'm going on to Quakers Hill.'

The driver looked pleased. Quakers Hill was quite a considerable fare, being one of the outer western suburbs.

Max hadn't been out that way in ages, and what he saw amazed him. Where farms had once dotted the surrounding hillsides, there now sat rows and rows of new houses. Not small houses, either. Large, double-storeyed homes.

Tara's place, however, was not one of those. Her address was in the older section of Quakers Hill, near the railway station, a very modest fibro cottage with no garage and little garden to speak of. The small squares of lawn on either side of the front path were brown after the summer and what shrubs there were looked bedraggled and tired. In fact the whole house looked tired. It could surely do with a makeover. Or at least a lick of paint. But of course, Tara's mum was a widow, had been for a long time. She'd had no sons to physically help her maintain her home.

It suddenly struck Max as he opened the squeaky iron gate and walked up onto the small front porch that Tara's upbringing would not have been filled with luxuries. He recalled how awestruck she'd been the morning after the first night they'd spent together, when she'd walked through the penthouse and oohed and aahed at everything.

For the first time, a small doubt entered his mind about her falling pregnant. Could she be lying about it having been a rare accident? Could she have planned it? Was it a ploy to *get* him to marry her?

If it was, she would have to be the cleverest, most devious female he had ever known.

No, he decided as he rang the doorbell. The Tara he knew and loved was no gold-digger. She had a delightfully transparent character. She wasn't capable of that kind of manipulative behaviour. She was as different from the Alicias of this world as chalk was to cheese.

That was why he loved her so much.

The door opened and Max peered down into eyes which were nothing like Tara's. In fact, the short, plump, dark-haired woman glowering up at him was nothing like Tara at all, except perhaps for her nose. She had the same cute little upturned nose.

'You've wasted your time coming here, Mr Richmond,' she said sharply. 'You should have rung first.'

'I thought it best to speak to Tara in person. I did try to ring last night from the airport, but Tara must have taken the phone off the hook. She wasn't answering her mobile, either. Look, Mrs Bond, I can understand your feelings where I'm concerned. You think I'm one of those rich guys who prey on beautiful young girls, but you're wrong. I love your daughter and I would never do anything to hurt her. Now, could you tell her that I'm here, please?'

His words seemed to have taken some of the anger out of the woman's face. But she still looked concerned. 'That's what I'm trying to tell you. She's not here.'

'What? You mean she's gone to work, even after she knew I was coming?'

'No. She left here last night. Packed a bag and took a taxi to I don't know where.'

Max's astonishment was soon overtaken by frustration. The woman *had* to be lying. 'What do you mean you don't know where? That's crazy. You're her mother. She would have told you where she was going.'

A guilty colour zoomed into the woman's cheeks. 'We had an argument. She was angry with me for making her tell you about the baby. And I was angry with her for hanging up on you, then taking the phone off the hook. I thought she was being silly. And stubborn. I... I...'

Joyce bit her bottom lip to stop herself from crying. If only she could go back to yesterday. She'd handled the situation terribly from the moment Tara had told her about the baby. After the initial shock had worn off, she'd begun badgering the girl about telling Max and demanding that he marry her. When Tara threw back at her that men these days didn't marry girls just because they were pregnant, Joyce had been less than complimentary over the morals of men like Max Richmond, *and* the silly girls who became involved with them. By the time the man himself had rung last night, Joyce had been determined to somehow let him know that Tara was having his baby.

She'd thought she was doing the right thing. But she'd been wrong. It had not been her decision to make. Tara was a grown woman, even if Joyce had difficulty seeing her daughter as that. To her, she would always be *her* baby.

'I don't know where she's gone. Honestly, Mr

Richmond,' she said, her head drooping as tears pricked at her eyes.

'Max,' he said gently, feeling genuinely sorry for the woman. 'I think it's about time you called me Max, don't you? Especially since I'm going to be your son-in-law.'

Joyce's moist eyes shot back up to his. 'You...you mean that? You're going to marry my Tara?'

'If she'll have me.'

'If she'll *have* you. The girl *adores* you.'

'Not enough to stay here when I asked her to.'

'I was partly to blame for that. I...I didn't handle the news of her pregnancy very well.'

'Don't worry, neither did I. Did she say something before she left?'

'She said to tell you she had to have some time by herself. Away from everyone telling her what to do. She said it was her body and her life and she needed some space to come to terms with the situation and work out what she was going to do. I spoke to Jen after she left. Jen's her older sister, by the way...'

'Yes, I know all about Jen.'

'You *do*?' Joyce was surprised.

Max's smile was wry. 'We do talk sometimes, Tara and I.'

The implication sent some pink into Joyce's cheeks. But truly, now that she'd met the man in the flesh, she couldn't blame Tara for losing her head over him. He was just so handsome. And impressive, with an aura of power and success about him. A wonderful dresser too. That black suit must have cost a small fortune.

'You were saying?' he prompted. 'Something about Tara's sister.'

'Oh, yes, well, I thought at first that Tara might have gone there, so I called Jen. I was probably on the phone when you rang from the airport. Tara had taken it off the hook but I put it back on later. Much later, I guess,' she added sheepishly. 'Anyway, she wasn't there and Jen didn't know where she might have gone. I was feeling awful because I thought I'd made her run away. But Jen said it was also because she was frightened you might try to talk her into getting rid of the baby when you got here.'

Max was appalled. But he could see that it wasn't an unreasonable assumption.

'And there I was,' he said wearily, 'worrying that *she* might do that.'

'Oh, no. Tara would never have an abortion. Never!'

'I'm glad to hear that. Because she'd never get over it, if she did. She's far too sweet and sensitive a soul.'

Joyce was touched that he knew Tara so well. This was not a man who wanted her daughter for her beauty alone. 'You...you really love Tara, don't you?'

'With all my heart. Clearly, however, she doesn't believe that. And I have only myself to blame. I've been thinking about our relationship all night on the plane and I can see I've been incredibly selfish and arrogant. People say actions speak louder than words, but not once did I stop to think what my actions were shouting to Tara. No wonder she had no faith in my committing to her and the baby. All I've ever given her were words. And words are so damned cheap. I have to show her now that I mean what I say. But first, I have to find her. Do you think you might invite me in for a cup of coffee, Mrs Bond, and we'll try to work out where she might have gone?'

'Joyce, Max,' she said with a smile which did remind him of Tara. 'If I'm going to be your mother-in-law, then I think you should call me Joyce.'

CHAPTER TEN

MAX waved Joyce goodbye through the taxi window, feeling pleased that he'd been able to make the woman believe that his intentions towards Tara were, at last, honourable. Not an easy task, given the way he'd treated her daughter this past year.

Joyce had not been backward in coming forward over his misdeeds. He was accused of having taken Tara for granted. Of neglecting her shamefully. But worst of all, of not caring enough to see how a girl like Tara would feel with his not making a definite commitment to her a lot sooner.

She'd poo-poohed Max's counter-arguments that Tara hadn't wanted marriage and children up till this point any more than he had.

'Tara needs security and commitment more than most girls,' she'd explained. 'She was more upset at losing her father than her older sister, yet Tara was only three at the time. She cried herself to sleep every night for months after the funeral. Having met you, I think, in a way, you are more than a lover to her. You are a father figure as well.'

Max hadn't been too pleased with this theory. It had made him feel old. He didn't entirely agree with it, either. Maybe Joyce didn't know her daughter as well as she thought she did. The grown-up Tara was a highly independent creature, not some cling-on. Yes, she was sensitive. And yes, she probably needed reassurance at this time in her life. But he didn't believe she thought of him as a father figure. Hell, she didn't even think of him as a father figure for their baby! If she had, she wouldn't have run away like this.

'Where in heaven's name *are* you, Tara?' he muttered under his breath.

'You say somethin', mate?' the taxi driver asked.

'Just having a grumble,' Max replied.

'Nothin' to grumble about, mate. The sun's out. We're winnin' the cricket. Life's good.'

Max thought about that simple philosophy and decided he could embrace it, if only he knew where Tara was.

He and Joyce decided she probably hadn't gone too far at night. Probably to a friend's house. The trouble was he'd discovered Tara had dropped all of her friends during the year she'd spent being his lady friend.

That was the term Joyce had tactfully used, although he had a feeling she was dying to use some other derogatory term, like mistress. Tara's mother hadn't missed an opportunity to put the knife in and twist it a little. Guilt gnawed away at him, alongside some growing frustration.

If Tara thought she could punish him this way indefinitely, then she was very much mistaken. He had ways and means at his disposal to find his missing girlfriend, especially one as good-looking and noticeable as Tara. In fact, he had one of two choices. He could hire a private investigator to find her, or he could spend a small fortune another way and hopefully come up with a quicker solution.

Max decided on this latter way.

Leaning forward, he gave the taxi driver a different address from the Regency Royale, after which he settled back and started working out what he would say to Tara when they finally came face to face.

Two hours later—they'd hit plenty of traffic on the way back to the city—Max was in his penthouse at the hotel. Snatching up some casual clothes, he headed straight for the shower. Once refreshed and dressed in crisp cream trousers and a blue yachting top, he headed for the lift again. Thankfully, Joyce had fed him as they'd talked, so he didn't need to order any food from Room Service. It crossed his mind to make himself some coffee, but decided he didn't want to wait. Having made up his mind what other things he had to do that day, Max wasn't about to dilly-dally. If he had one virtue—Joyce didn't seem to think he had too many—it was decisiveness.

This time he called for his own car, and within minutes was driving east of the city. Thankfully, by then, the traffic was lighter. It was just after eleven-thirty, the sun was well up in the summer sky and Max would have rather gone anywhere than where he was going.

His stomach knotted as he approached his parents' home. He hadn't been to see them since Christmas, a token visit which he felt he couldn't avoid. Ever since Stevie's death, he'd kept his visits to a minimum. They were always a strain, even more so since his father's stroke. The accusing, angry words he might have once spoken—and which might have cleared the air between father and son—were always held back. He could hardly bear to watch his mother, either. He resented the way she tended to his father. So patiently, with never a cross word.

Maybe Tara was right. Maybe she really did love the man. She'd certainly been prepared to forgive him for lots of things.

Max wondered if he could ever really forgive his father. He doubted it. But he'd have to pretend to, if he was to have any chance of convincing Tara he was man enough to be a good father to their baby.

Max parked his car at the kerb outside his parents' Point Piper mansion and just sat there for a minute or two, looking at the place. It was certainly a far cry from Tara's house. Aside from the house, which ran over three levels, there were the perfectly manicured gardens at the front, a huge solar-heated pool out the back and magnificent harbour views from most of the rooms.

It was a home fit for a king. Or a prince.

He'd been brought up here, taking it all for granted. The perfect house. The private schools. Membership of the nearby yacht club.

And then there were the women. The ones who'd targeted him from the moment he'd been old enough to have sex. The ones who'd done anything and every thing to get him to fall in love with them.

But he hadn't loved any of them.

The only woman he'd ever fallen for was Tara.

And she was in danger of slipping away from him, if he wasn't careful.

With his stomach still in knots, Max climbed out from behind the wheel and went inside. He still had keys. He hadn't moved out of home till after the episode with Stevie.

His mother was sitting out on the top terrace, reading the newspaper to his father, who was in his wheelchair beside her. Dressed in pale blue trousers and a pretty floral top, she was immaculately groomed as usual. Her streaked blonde hair was cut short in a modern style and she was wearing make-up and pearl earrings.

For as long as Max could remember, she'd looked much younger than her age, but today, in the harsh sunlight, she looked every one of her fifty-nine years. And then some.

Her father's appearance, however, shocked him more than his mother's. Before his stroke he'd been a vibrant, handsome man with a fit, powerful body and thick head of dark hair. Now his hair was white, his muscles withered, his skin deeply lined. He looked eighty, yet he was only sixty-two.

For the first time, some sympathy stirred in Max's soul. Plus a measure of guilt. How come he hadn't noticed the extent of his father's deterioration at Christmas? It had only been a couple of months ago.

Maybe he hadn't noticed because he hadn't wanted to. It was easier to cling to old resentments rather than see that his father was going downhill at a rate of knots, or that his mother might need some hands-on help. Much easier to hate than to love.

Max realised in that defining moment that he didn't really hate his parents. He never had. He just didn't understand them. Tara was right when she'd said people never knew what went on in a marriage.

One thing Max did know, however, as he watched his mother reach out to tenderly touch his father's arm. She did love the man. And if the way his father looked back was any judge, then that love was returned.

Max's heart turned over as he hoped that Tara would always look at him like that.

Neither of them had seen him yet, standing there just inside the sliding glass doors which led out onto the terrace. When he slid one back, his mother's head jerked up and around, her blue eyes widening with surprise, and then pleasure.

'Max!' she exclaimed. 'Ronald, it's Max.'

'Max…' His father's hands fumbled as they reached to swivel his chair around. His eyes, too, mirrored surprise. But they were tired eyes, Max thought. Dead eyes.

All the life had gone out of him.

'Max,' the old man repeated as though he could still not believe his son had come to visit.

'Hi there, Mum. Dad,' he said as he came forward and bent to kiss his mother on the cheek. 'You're both looking well,' he added as he pulled up a chair.

His father croaked out a dry laugh. 'I look terrible and I know it.'

Max smiled a wry smile. The old man wasn't quite dead yet.

'You know, Dad, when I was a boy you told me that God helps those who help themselves. You obviously practised what you preached all your life. After all, you worked your way up from a valet-parking attendant to being one of Australia's most successful hotel owners.'

Max generously refrained from reminding his father that marrying the daughter of an established hotel baron had been a leg-up, especially when Max's maternal grand-father was already at death's door. Within weeks of Max's grandfather dying, Ronald Richmond had sold off the hotels that didn't live up to his ideals and started up the Royale chain. He hadn't looked back, till three years ago, when his stroke had forced his premature retirement.

'I have to say I'm a bit disappointed,' Max went on, 'that you seem to have thrown in the towel this time. Frankly, I expected more from you than this.'

Some more fire sparked in the old man's eyes, which was exactly what Max had intended.

'What would you know about it, boy? My whole right side is virtually useless.'

'Something which could be remedied with therapy. You should be thankful that your speech wasn't affected. Some people can't talk after a stroke.'

'My eyes are bad,' he grumbled. 'Your mother has to read to me.'

'But you're not blind. Look, how about I line up a top physiotherapist to come in every day and work with you? He'll have you up and out of that wheelchair in no time.'

'That would be wonderful, Max,' his mother said. 'Wouldn't it, Ronald?'

'It's too late,' his father muttered. 'I'm done for.'

'Rubbish!' Max countered. 'Never too late. That's another of your own philosophies, might I remind you? Besides, I need you up and about in time for my wedding.'

'Your wedding!' they chorused, their expressions shocked.

'Yep. I'm getting married.'

After that, Max was regaled with questions. He thought he lied very well, telling them all about Tara and the baby, but nothing about her disappearance. He made it sound like a done deal that he and Tara would walk down the aisle in the near future. He also promised to bring her over to meet them by the end of the weekend. He made some excuse that she was away visiting friends for the next couple of days.

Talk about optimism!

Over lunch he also told his father that he planned to stay in Australia more in future and delegate some of the overseas travelling to his assistant.

'Good idea,' his father said, nodding. 'When a man has a family, he should not be away from home too much. I was away from home too much. Far too much.'

When tears suddenly welled up in his father's eyes, his mother immediately jumped up. 'I think it's time for your afternoon nap, dear,' she said. 'He gets tired very easily these days,' she directed at a shocked Max as she wheeled his father off. 'I won't be long. Have another cup of coffee.'

Max did just that, sitting there, sipping some coffee and doing some serious thinking till his mother returned.

She threw Max an odd look as she sat down. 'I'm so glad you stayed. Usually, you bolt out the door as soon as you can. Your becoming a father yourself has changed you, Max. You're different today. Softer. And more compassionate. Perhaps the time is right for me to tell you the truth about Stevie.'

Max stiffened. 'What…what do you mean…the truth?'

His mother heaved a deep sigh, her eyes not quite meeting his. 'Stevie was not your father's child.'

Max gaped.

'I thought you might have guessed,' she went on when he said nothing. 'After all, Stevie was very different from you. And from your father. He also had brown eyes. Two blue-eyed parents can't have a brown-eyed child, you know.'

Max shook his head. 'I didn't know that. Did Stevie?'

'Thankfully, no. At least…he never said he did.'

'So that's why Dad didn't love him.'

'You're wrong, Max. Your father did love Stevie. The trouble was every time he looked at him, he was reminded of the fact that I had slept with another man.'

'But I thought Dad was the unfaithful one!'

His mother stared at him. 'Why do you say that?'

'Years ago, I overheard you telling a friend that you knew Dad had other women, but you just turned a blind eye.'

His mother looked so sad. 'I'm so sorry you heard that. You must have thought me very weak. Or very wicked.'

'I didn't know what to think. I've never known what to think about you two. At least I can now understand why Dad treated Stevie differently from me.'

'He did try, Max. But it was very hard on him. He never seemed to know what to say to Stevie. Or how to act with him. It was much easier with you, because you were like two peas in a pod. But that didn't mean he didn't care about Stevie. When he was diagnosed with cancer, your father was terribly upset. His way of coping with his grief was to work harder. He couldn't bear to see the boy in pain. He knows now that he should have come home to be with Stevie. He understands what it's like when the people you love aren't there for you when you're ill.'

She didn't look at him directly. Neither were her words said in an accusing tone. But Max felt guilty all the same. He hadn't been any better than his father, had he? He'd let both his parents down by not being here to help.

'Your father feels his stroke was a punishment for his letting Stevie down,' his mother choked out.

Max could not deny that he had entertained similar thoughts himself over the past three years. Suddenly, however, they seemed terribly mean-spirited, and very immature. But he could not find the right words to say and was sitting there in an awkward silence, when his mother spoke once more.

'Do you want to know about Stevie's real father, or not?'

'Yes,' Max said sincerely. 'Yes, I do.'

'I have to go back to the beginning of my relationship with your father so that you can get the full picture.'

'OK.'

She smiled a wry smile. 'I hope you won't be too shocked at me.'

Max could not imagine that anything more his mother could say today would shock him.

'I'm no saint myself, Mum,' he reassured, and so she began her story.

She'd first met his father when he parked her car for her one day at one of her own father's hotels. She'd fallen in love with him at first sight, and had pursued him shamelessly as only a spoiled and beautiful rich woman could do. She confessed to seducing him with sex and playing to his ambitious nature with her money and her contacts. Not to mention her potential fortune. She was her wealthy father's only child.

The trouble was she'd never believed he truly loved her when he married her, and was always besieged by doubts. The arrival of their first-born son—Max himself—calmed her for a while. Her husband seemed besotted, if not with her then definitely with his child. She began to feel more secure in her marriage. But after her father died and her husband started travelling overseas more and more often, all her doubts over his love increased. There was a photograph in a newspaper of him with some gorgeous socialite in London. She flew into a jealous rage when her husband finally came home, accusing him of being unfaithful. He claimed he wasn't but she didn't believe him.

Their marriage entered one of those dangerous phases. Ronald started staying away even more and she started going out on her own. She met Stevie's father at an art exhibition. *His* art exhibition. He was an up-and-coming artist. She'd argued with her husband over the phone earlier in the evening over his delaying his return home yet again and was in a reckless mood. She drank too much and the rest, as they said, was history.

Perversely, Ronald arrived home the next night, and when she discovered she was pregnant a month later she didn't know whose baby she was having. When the baby was born with blue eyes, she thought Stevie was Max's full brother. But by six months his eyes had changed to brown and he looked nothing like Max's father.

When Ronald confronted her with his suspicions, she confessed her indiscretion and her husband went crazy, showing her at last that he did love her. But the marriage had been irreparably damaged. After that, she suspected her husband was no longer faithful to her when he went away. A few times, she found evidence of other women on his clothes. Lipstick and perfume. She turned a blind eye for fear that he might actually divorce her. She tried to make a life for herself with charity work and society functions but she was very unhappy.

She reiterated that when Stevie was diagnosed with cancer, Ronald *had* been genuinely upset. Unfortunately, his way of handling such an emotional crisis was to go into his cave, so to speak, and work harder than ever.

'Stevie might have survived his sickness,' his mother added, 'if it hadn't been for his girlfriend dumping him. That was what depressed him far more than his father not being around. Trust me on that. Stevie and I were very close and he told me everything he felt.'

Max nodded. 'I can imagine. I've never known a boy like Stevie. The way he could express his feelings. I wish I could be like that sometimes.'

'His biological father was like that,' his mother said. 'A real talker. And a deep thinker. A sweet, soft, sensitive man whom you couldn't help liking. He made me feel so special that night. He didn't know I was married, of course. He was shocked when I told him afterwards. Didn't want anything more to do with me. As I said, a nice man.'

'I see. So he never knew about Stevie?'

'God, no. No, I never saw him again. Sadly, he died a few years later. Cancer. And they say it's not hereditary…'

Tears glistened in her eyes as she looked straight at Max. 'Your father finally forgave me. But can you?'

Not ever being at his best with words, Max stood up and came round to bend and kiss his mother on the cheek.

Her hands lifted to cover his, which had come to rest on her shoulders. She patted them, then glanced up at him. 'Thank you. You're a good boy, Max. But a terrible liar. Now, why don't you sit back down and tell *me* the total truth about this girl of yours? I'd especially like to know how someone as clever as you could have made the mistake of making her pregnant in the first place. Or was that *her* idea? You are a very rich man, after all.'

Max walked back to settle in his chair before answering.

'I have to confess that idea did briefly occur to me. But only briefly. You'll see when you meet Tara that she does not have a greedy, or a manipulative bone in her body.'

'Tara,' his mother said. 'Such a lovely name.'

'She's a lovely girl.'

'And was it her idea for you to come here today?'

'Not directly. But she would have approved. The fact is, Mum, I don't know where Tara is. She's run away.'

'Run away! Max, whatever did you do?'

'It's what I *didn't* do which caused the problem. When she told me she was having a baby, I didn't tell her I loved her. And I didn't ask her to marry me.'

'Oh, Max… No wonder she ran away. She must be heartbroken.'

'Don't say that, Mum,' he said with a tightening in

his chest. 'I don't want to hear that. I'm just hanging in here as it is, waiting for tomorrow.'

'What's going to happen tomorrow?'

He told her.

CHAPTER ELEVEN

TARA lay in bed, slowly nibbling on one of the dry biscuits she'd put beside the bed the night before. Hopefully, they would make her feel well enough to rise shortly and go for a walk on the beach.

Yesterday, she'd stayed in bed most of the day before going for a walk. But then yesterday she'd been desperately tired.

Today she'd woken more refreshed, but still nauseous. Hence the biscuits.

It had been good of Kate to give her some, no questions asked. Although there'd been a slight speculative gleam in her eyes as she'd handed Tara the plate of biscuits after dinner last night.

But that was Kate all over. The woman was kind and accommodating without being a sticky-beak, all good qualities for anyone who ran a bed and breakfast establishment. Tara had met her a few years ago when she'd stayed here at Kate's Place with some of her uni friends. It was popular with students because it had been chcap and conveniently located, only a short stroll to Wamberal Beach.

When she'd been thinking of where she could go and be by herself for a while, Tara had immediately thought of Kate's Place. Wamberal was not far away from Sydney—an hour and a half's drive north—but far enough away that she would feel secure that she wouldn't run into Max, or anyone who knew Max.

So on Thursday night she'd taken a taxi to Hornsby railway station, then a train to Gosford, then another taxi to Wamberal Beach. Rather naively, in a way. What would she have done if Kate had sold the place in the years since she'd stayed there? Or if she didn't have any spare rooms to rent?

Fate had been on her side this time and whilst Kate had gone more upmarket—renaming her refurbished home Kate's Beachside B & B—she had still been in the room-renting business, although the number of rooms available had been reduced to three.

Fortunately, all of them were vacant. The end of February, whilst still summer, was not peak tourist season. On top of that she'd stopped advertising, not wanting to be full all of the time.

'I'm getting old,' she'd complained as she showed Tara upstairs. 'But I'd be bored if I stopped having people to stay altogether. And terribly lonely. Still, I might have to give it away when I turn seventy next year. Or give in and hire a cleaner.'

Tara had selected the bedroom at the front of the

two-storeyed home, which had a lovely view of the beach as well as an *en suite* bathroom. No way did she want to have to race down hallways to a communal bathroom first thing in the morning.

True to form, Kate hadn't asked her any questions on her arrival, although Tara had spotted some concern in the elderly woman's eyes. She supposed it was rare for a guest to show up, unannounced and unbooked, at ten-thirty at night. Tara's excuse that it was a spur-of-the-moment impulse had probably not been believed.

But Kate at least appreciated that she was an adult with the right to come and go as she pleased, something Tara wished other people recognised. She was not a child who had to be directed. She did have a mind of her own and she was quite capable of making decisions, provided she was given the time to work out what was best for herself, and the baby.

Impossible to even think at home at the moment with her mother criticising and nagging all the time. Jen wasn't much better. She seemed to have forgotten how emotional and irrational *she* was when she found out she was pregnant.

Of course, Tara would not have bolted quite so melo-dramatically if Max hadn't been on his way. Max of the 'we should work this out together' mode.

Huh! Tara knew what that meant. Max, taking total control and telling her what to do.

From what she'd seen, Max had no idea how to truly

work together with anyone or anything. Max ordered and people obeyed.

She'd been obeying him for twelve months.

But not any more.

The time had come for mutiny.

Her first step had been to put herself beyond his reach. Which she had. And, to be honest, taking that action had felt darned good. Clearly, she'd been harbouring more resentment than she realised over Max's dominant role in their relationship.

Not so good was the niggling remorse she felt over her mother. By last night guilt had begun to override her desperate need for peace and privacy. She would have to ring her mother today. It wasn't fair to leave her worrying.

And she would be worrying. Tara had no doubt of that.

A firm tap-tap on her bedroom door had Tara calling out that she was coming before gingerly swinging her feet onto the floor and standing up. As she reached for the silky housecoat she'd brought with her, she was pleased to find her stomach hadn't heaved at all when she got to her feet. Those biscuits seemed to have done the trick.

But still, she didn't hurry, taking her time as she padded across the floral rug which covered most of the polished floorboards. Kate's décor leant towards old world, but Tara liked it.

She opened the door to find Kate standing there with a newspaper in her hands and a worried look on her face.

'Yes?' Tara asked.

Kate didn't say a word. She just handed the newspaper to Tara. It was opened and folded back at page three.

Tara went cold all over as she stared down at the full-page photograph of herself, an enlargement of the one she knew Max kept in his wallet. It had been taken on one of their first dinner dates, at a restaurant where a photographer went around and snapped photos of people who were likely to buy them as mementos. Targeted were groups partying there for special occasions, plus romantic couples possibly celebrating their engagements, or just their love for each other.

Tara could see the happiness shining out of her eyes in that photograph. She doubted her eyes would reflect the same emotion at that moment.

Her teeth clenched hard in her jaw as she glared down at the words written across the bottom of the photograph. *Tara, your loved ones are worried about you. Please call home. If anyone knows Tara's whereabouts, contact the following number for a substantial reward.*

Tara's head shot up. 'Please don't tell me you rang it. That's not my home phone number. It belongs to my boyfriend.'

'Not me, love. But Milly Jenson did. My busybody neighbour. She must have had a good look at you when you went out walking yesterday afternoon. I think her conscience finally got the better of her and she came and told me what she'd done. Either that, or she was indulging in more mischief-making. Either way, I thought you'd want to know.'

'I certainly do. Thanks, Kate,' she said, her head whirling with the news Max was on his way up here.

'Boyfriend, eh? Not one you'll be wanting to see again, I'll warrant. Do you want me to drive you anywhere, love? I can get you away from here before he arrives. Milly gave him this address over an hour ago, so he could be arriving any time soon.'

Tara thought about running away again, then decided there was little point. Wherever she went, someone would spot her and call Max and that would be that. Her stand-out looks had always been a curse. Oh, how she would have preferred to be less striking. Less tall. Less blonde!

She shook her head as she stared down again at the photograph in the paper.

'Thank you, Kate, but no. I'll talk to him when he arrives. But not here. I have no intention of meekly staying here till he arrives. I'll get dressed right now and go for a walk on the beach. You can point him in that direction when he arrives. OK?'

'Only OK if he's no danger to you, love. He hasn't been beating you up, has he?'

'Good lord, no! Max would never do anything like that. But as you might have gathered he's very rich. And used to getting his own way. He's also the father of my baby. I'm pregnant, Kate.'

'Yes, so I gathered, love. That's a popular old remedy,

eating dry biscuits when you're suffering from morning sickness. As soon as you asked me for them, I guessed.'

'You didn't say anything.'

'Not my place. I keep my nose out of other people's private business. Except when it comes to arrogant members of the opposite sex. One of the reasons I never married was because I couldn't stand it when men thought they could run my life. Oh, yes, I had quite a few suitors when I was younger. All wanting me to marry them, especially the ones I slept with. One became very insistent once he found out I was having his baby. More than insistent. Violent, actually. As if I would ever marry a man who hit me. Or inflict such a father on an innocent child.'

Tara's mouth had dropped open slightly at these astonishing revelations. But it seemed Kate was not yet finished baring her soul, or her rather adventurous past.

'If it had been more acceptable back in my day, I would have chosen to be a single mother. But I didn't. I did something else, love, something I've always bitterly regretted. Girls these days have so many options. So don't do what I did, love. You have your baby and to hell with what this man says or wants. He can't be much of a man if you ran away from him like that.'

'He's not a bad man,' Tara said. 'Or a violent one. He's just…domineering.'

'Does he want you to have an abortion?'

'I don't know.'

'Mmm… Does he love you?'

She frowned down at the photograph, then nodded. 'Yes. I think he does. As much as he is capable of loving.'

'He sounds a bit mixed up.'

'You know what, Kate, I think he is. Yet he's very successful. And filthy rich.'

'And wickedly handsome, no doubt,' Kate said drily.

'Oh, yes. That too.'

Kate pulled a face. 'They always are. I'll see what I think of him when he arrives, then I'll put him through the third degree before I tell him where you've gone. Would you mind if I did that?'

Tara had to laugh. 'Not at all. Do him good.'

'Right. You hurry and get yourself dressed now. And take one of the sunhats from off the pegs by the front door. Put your hair up under it. And pop some sunglasses on. Otherwise you'll have everyone on the beach who's seen this photograph in this morning's paper running home to call that number.'

'I'll do that. And Kate…'

'Yes?'

'Thank you. You've been very kind. And wonderfully understanding.'

Kate smiled a surprisingly mischievous smile. 'We girls have to stick together.'

Max stomped over the sand, disbelieving of what that woman had just put him through before telling him where Tara was. Anyone would think he was a murderer instead of a man in love, trying to do the right thing!

His gaze scanned the various semi-naked bodies sprawled over the warm sand. None of them was Tara. He would recognise her in a heartbeat. He headed for the water's edge and stood there, searching for her tell-tale head of fair hair amongst the swimmers. Not there, either.

A rogue wave suddenly washed further up the beach than the others, totally soaking his expensive Italian loafers.

Max swore.

Still, ruining a pair of shoes was the least of his worries at that moment. Where was Tara? Had that old tartar lied to him? Was Tara at this very moment on her way somewhere else?

Max's stomach began to churn. And then he saw her, further down the wide arch of beach, paddling along the water's edge, coming towards him.

It wasn't her hair which revealed her identity. Her long blonde mane was out of sight underneath a large straw hat. It was her legs which gave her away. Not many girls had legs like Tara's.

She was wearing shorts. Denim, with frayed edges. And a red singlet top. No bra, he noticed as she drew closer.

The automatic stirring of his body annoyed him. This was not why he had come. Tara already knew he wanted her sexually. He had to convince her that he wanted her for much more than that.

Willing his flesh back under control, he marched towards her, determined not to let desire distract him.

For he suspected if it did, he was doomed to failure. And failure was not something Max could cope with today. His mission was to win Tara back, not lose her. Instinct warned him that making love to her in any way, shape or form would lose her for sure. His job was to convince her that he would make a good husband and father, not just a good lover.

Tara had spotted Max some time back, but she gave no signal to him, watching surreptitiously as he'd made his way with some difficulty across the soft sand. He was hardly dressed for the beach in grey dress trousers and a long-sleeved white silk shirt, even though the shirt *was* rolled up at the sleeves and left open at the neck.

It had amused her when the wave washed over his shoes. She wasn't so amused now as he hurried towards her. Most annoying was the way her body went into full foreplay mode at his approach. Her heartbeat quickened. Her nipples hardened. Her belly tightened. All in anticipation of his touch.

Disgusting, she thought. Deplorable!

Delicious, another darker, more devilish part of her brain whispered.

She sighed. Clearly, she still had to be careful with him. Her sexual vulnerability remained high.

Of course, if this was a romantic movie, both of them would suddenly break into a run and throw themselves into each other's arms. They would kiss, the music would soar and THE END would come up on the screen.

But this was not a movie. It was real life with real people and real issues. Serious relationship problems were never solved with one kiss. Making love was a masking agent, not a lasting solution.

No way was she going to let him touch her. Not today, anyway.

'Max,' she said drily when he was close enough.

Thankfully, he ground to a halt outside of grabbing and kissing distance. Though was it Max doing that which worried her the most? Or her own silly self?

'So you found me,' she added, and crossed her arms. Not only did the action demonstrate he wasn't all that welcome, but it also hid her infernal nipples.

'With some difficulty,' came his sharp return.

Clearly, he was not in a good mood. Kate must have given him heaps. But not as much as *she* was going to give him.

'I don't know how you can say that. One little—or should I say not so little?—photograph in the paper, with the added incentive of a reward, and Bob's your uncle, you had your man.'

His gaze ran down her body then up again. 'No one in their wildest dreams, Tara, would call you a man.'

Tara pulled a face at him. 'You know, it must be wonderful to have enough money to buy anything you want.'

His eyes searched hers, as though he was weighing up her attitude. Her sarcastic tone had to be telling him something.

'You're still angry with me,' he said. 'And you have

every right to be. I didn't handle your news the other night at all well.'

'No. You certainly didn't.'

'There again, you didn't give me much opportunity to make things right by hanging up on me and then running away. That was hardly fair, Tara. Even you have to agree your news was a shock. I was not prepared for it.'

'Tough. I did what I had to do. For me.'

'And have you come to any decisions during your time alone?'

'Would you mind if we walk while we talk?'

Tara just started walking, forcing him to fall into step beside her.

'I'd prefer to go sit somewhere private together.'

I'll just bet you would, she thought ruefully. Before she knew it he would be kissing her and she'd either go to mush, or hit him. Neither prospect pleased her. This was her chance to show him that she would not live her life on *his* terms. Seeing him in the flesh again, however, had brought home to her that he still wielded great power over her. She had to be very careful. And very strong.

'I'm hardly dressed for the beach, Tara,' he pointed out. 'I'm ruining my shoes for starters.'

'You chose to come up here, Max. I didn't make you. Take off your shoes, if you're worried about them. And roll up your trousers.'

To her astonishment, he did just that. Unfortunately,

it made her even more physically aware of him. Being pregnant didn't seem to have dampened her desires one iota. If anything, she craved Max's lovemaking even more. How contrary could you get?

'I called your mother,' he said when they started walking again. 'Told her I'd found you. Joyce said to tell you to believe me when I say that I would never have tried to talk you into an abortion.'

Any relief Tara felt over this news was overshadowed by shock, and anger. She ground to a halt and spun in the sand to face him.

'*Joyce?* Since when did you call my mother *Joyce?* And since when has she started taking *your* side?'

'Since we had a good chat yesterday morning.'

Tara laughed. A dry, knowing laugh. 'I get it. You told Mum you were prepared to marry me and she melted. That's the be-all and end-all with Mum. Marriage.'

'You make it sound like a crime.'

'It is if you marry for all the wrong reasons.'

'You think my loving you is a wrong reason?'

Tara found it increasingly difficult to hold her temper. 'You've told me you love me. But not one mention of marriage. So why now? As if I don't know. You've decided you want your child. You're getting older and it's suddenly come home to you that maybe an heir in your image and likeness would be a very nice thing to have, along with a silly, besotted wife who thinks the sun shines out of your bum and who'll wait around for you for weeks at a time, no questions asked.'

'Now wait a minute!'

'No, *you* wait a minute. It's your turn to do the waiting, buster.'

An angry colour slanted across his cheekbones, and his hands tightened their grip on his shoes.

But he stayed tactfully silent, allowing her the opportunity to say what was on her mind. And there was plenty!

'You must have thought you were on to a good thing this past year. You never explained and I never complained. Of course, things weren't absolutely perfect for you. Whilst I'm sure it was exciting and ego-stroking at first to have a virgin in your bed—something tells me you hadn't had the pleasure of one of *those* before!—I didn't quite have the confidence you would have liked. Till last weekend. After which, suddenly, I was being invited to travel with you.'

'That's not true!' he protested.

'Of course it's true! I've finally grown up, Max. I don't see you through rose-coloured glasses any more. I can even appreciate your reasoning. Why go to the trouble of finding suitable one-night stands in whatever city you were in, when you could take the new me with you for the price of a plane ticket?'

She saw his eyes darken, but she hadn't finished.

'Even better was the fact that I had the makings of such a *cheap* mistress. A dress here and there. The odd outing. Some champagne and you'd be In Like Flynn.'

'Now, hold it right there!' he ground out. 'Firstly, I was never unfaithful to you. Not once. Secondly, I never thought of you as my mistress. I always meant to marry you, Tara. When the time was right.'

'Really? And when would that have been?'

'When I was less busy and you were older. My asking you to travel with me was a compromise. I was afraid of losing you. Just as I'm afraid of losing you now. Losing you and our baby.'

It shocked Tara, his admitting to such emotions. Max, the macho man, was not given to admitting that he was afraid of losing anything. But then she realised his confessing such fears was his way of *not* losing. His words were designed to weaken her resolve, to make her do what *he* wanted, as usual.

'I love you, Tara,' he went on. 'I've loved you from the beginning. I know I told you I didn't want marriage and children, and I meant it at the time. But things have changed. You're going to have my baby.'

'Yes, Max, I am. And yes, things have changed. But you haven't. You're still the same Max I met. The same exciting, successful, ambitious, ruthless man. Just look at what you did to find me. What kind of man does something like that?'

'The kind you fell in love with. But you're wrong, Tara. I *can* change. I've already started.'

'How? I see no evidence of it.'

'Come back to Sydney with me and I'll show you.'

'No.'

His head jerked back, blue eyes shocked. 'No?'

'No. That's part of your problem, Max. People jump to

do your bidding far too much. I've been way too accommodating where you're concerned. I've always done what you wanted. Now you can do what *I* want for a change.'

'Tell me and I'll do it,' he stated boldly.

And rather recklessly, Tara thought. No way would he agree to what she was about to demand. But it would be interesting to see how he tried to wriggle out of it.

'All right. Go home, collect some beach clothes and come back up here. Kate will rent you a room. Stay here, with me, for a week. Separate rooms. No sex. We'll spend quality time together, but we'll just talk.'

Tara was quietly confident he would never just drop his business commitments like that.

'It's a deal,' he said.

Tara blinked in shock, but reserved her judgement till he actually followed through.

'What happens at the end of the week?' he asked.

'I'll let you know…at the end of the week.'

'That doesn't seem fair.'

'I'm not going to explain and you're not to complain. You are just to do what I want, when I want.'

'But no sex.'

'Absolutely no sex.'

'Mmm. Are you sure you can handle that?'

Her chin lifted. 'No trouble,' she lied.

'I will only agree to those conditions if, at the end of the week, I get to take you out to dinner, then back to bed for the night. The whole night. In the same bed.'

'Why does there have to be a catch?'

'Darling, there's always a catch. There's no such thing as a free lunch, or a free week of total slavery and submission. Which is what you're asking for. I know you want me to prove to you that I love you. That I don't want you just for sex. Fine. I'm happy to do that. But then I want the chance to show you that I do love you. *My* way.'

Tara's heart turned over. She knew, once she was in his arms again, that all her new resolves would weaken. She had one week to achieve all she wanted to achieve. One week to make Max see that the only way they could be truly happy was if he offered her a genuine partnership, not just a ring on her finger.

'You sure have developed a way with words all of a sudden,' she tossed back at him. 'We'll see if you can keep it up for a week.'

He laughed. 'I'll have no trouble keeping it up. Especially if you go round looking like that all the time.'

Tara flushed. 'If you try to seduce me, Max, you'll be sorry.'

'You don't know who you're talking to, honey. This is the boy who went for three days without food. Going without sex couldn't be as hard as that. Oops. Scratch that word hard and replace it with difficult.'

Tara frowned at him. This was the first time he'd spoken of himself when he was a boy. That was something she would get him to do during the next week. Open up to her about his childhood. Intimacy was not just about sex, but also about knowing all there was to know about your partner.

'Why did you go without food?'

'Mum was raising funds for some charity. She spent half her life doing that. This time, she got us kids involved. Stevie found sponsors who paid various amounts for his reading books. I think he read eighty-five books. I chose to starve. Got paid a fortune for every day I went without food. Much easier than reading. I hate reading.'

'Nothing's changed in that regard,' Tara said drily. 'You don't have any decent books at the penthouse. Just boring stuff about business and sport. You don't know what you're missing, Max. Reading is a fabulous past-time. I'll read you some good books this week whilst we lie on the beach. Kate has a wonderful selection of best-sellers.'

Max winced.

'Having second thoughts already?' Tara said in a challenging tone.

'Definitely not,' he replied. And smiled.

Tara wasn't sure she liked that smile. There was something sneaky about it.

'I'd better get going if I'm to get back today,' he said.

'You only have to pack a few clothes.'

'And make a few phone calls. I have to let Pierce know where I'll be, for one thing.'

'If you take or make one business phone call during your week up here, Max, the deal's off.'

Max suspected she was bluffing, but he had to admire her stance. Tara didn't realise it but he would never marry a mealy-mouthed woman, or one who kowtowed to him all the time. Most of his life, he'd been pursued by women who indulged his every desire, in bed and out of it. He liked it that Tara was finally standing up to him; that she was so strong. She was going to make a wonderful wife and mother.

His eyes softened on her. 'Fair enough. I'll leave my mobile at home.' With his father. Do the old man good to have to make some business decisions. Probably perk him up no end. But not as much as that physio he'd hired yesterday to come in every day and work those atrophied muscles. Max had stayed with his parents all day Friday, inspiring both of them with their new role as grandparents-to-be, leaving them looking younger than when he arrived. 'I'll be back before you can say Jack Robinson.'

'Don't speed,' she warned him. 'I'd like our child to have a live father, not a memorial in some cemetery.'

'Right. No speeding. Any other instructions? Or rules?'

Her head tipped to one side and her lips pursed.

God, how he would love to just slide his hands around that lovely long neck of hers and kiss that luscious mouth till it was soft and malleable. Till *she* was soft and malleable.

Instead, he had to stand there and play at being a sensitive, new-age guy. Not a role Max aspired to. He had definite ideas about male roles in life, and wishy-washy wimp was not one of them. He could not wait for this week to be over. Already he was looking forward to the following Saturday night.

'None that I can think of at the moment,' she said. 'But I'll have a written list by the time you return.'

Max blinked. My God, she meant it. Maybe he shouldn't marry her at all. Strong, he liked. But a bossy-boots nag was another story.

What she needed, of course, was a night in bed. With him. Those rock-like nipples said something else to the words coming out of her mouth. By the time this week was up, he wouldn't be the only one having cold showers.

But he could be patient, if the rewards were worth it. What better reward could there be than to have Tara back in his arms once more, right where she belonged?

CHAPTER TWELVE

A WEEK was a long time in politics. Or so they said. Probably because of the great changes which could happen in such a relatively short space of time.

When Max looked back over the past seven days he marvelled at the changes which had taken place, mostly within himself.

The tanned man jogging down to the beach at dawn this morning with a surfboard tucked under his arm was not the same man who'd arrogantly thought of his deal with Tara as an endurance test, to be tolerated but not enjoyed. A means to an end. A pain in the neck, as well as in other parts of his body.

Max had not anticipated the delights, or the discoveries he had made during the past week.

Tara had been so right in forbidding all business calls, for starters. He hadn't realised just how much of every day he spent on work and work-related issues. He'd actually suffered withdrawal symptoms at first. But soon, he wasn't giving a thought to whether profits were up or down. Neither did he worry over what new worldwide crisis might happen which would impact on the hotel industry.

No news was definitely good news.

After a few days he'd even revised his earlier decision to just delegate more in future so that he would have more time for Tara and their child. Now he was thinking of downsizing the Royale chain of hotels altogether. Travelling all over the world and spending every day in meetings or having business dinners no longer held such an attraction for him.

Max plunged into the surf, deftly sliding his body face-down onto the board as he hand-paddled out across the waves. The sun had just broken over the horizon, the blue-green sea sparkling under its rays. Once out into deeper water, Max sat up and straddled the board, watching and waiting for just the right wave to ride in.

This was good!

He'd forgotten how much he'd liked surfing. He hadn't done any in years. But when Kate offered him use of the spare surfboards and wetsuits she kept in the garage, he couldn't resist. And, after a few minor disasters, he'd regained his balance, his confidence and his natural athletic skill. Max had been born good at all sports.

Each morning since, he'd spent a few hours in the surf whilst Tara languished in bed. She was still not feeling tippy-top in the mornings. By eleven she would be up and he would return for a shower and a leisurely brunch. Kate was an excellent if old-fashioned cook, paying no mind to the modern dictates of low-fat food. Max might have put on quite a few pounds if he hadn't been using up a few thousand calories each day in the water. Tara was saved by her delicate stomach, keeping to tea and toast.

After brunch, he and Tara would take a beach umbrella and a book, find a nice spot on the side of one of the sand dunes which overlooked the ocean and settle down to read. The first time they'd done this, Max had thought he would have to pretend to enjoy being read to. But Tara was such an expressive reader, and the bestseller she chose to read obviously hadn't been a bestseller for nothing. It was one of those legal thrillers which twisted and turned on every page. The murder trial itself had been riveting. He'd changed his mind on who the killer was several times but finally settled on the wife, and had been tickled pink when he was proved right.

His remark to Tara during one of these early reading sessions that his mother read to his father these days had led to his finally telling her about his reconciliation with his parents. He'd talked to Tara for ages over dinner that night about his parents' marriage and all their misunderstandings. In fact, this past week, he'd talked more about his parents and his growing-up years than he ever had in his life.

Admittedly, there wasn't much else he could do but talk to Tara. She hadn't wavered from her strictly hands-off rule the whole week. Not an easy situation to bear with her going round in an itsy-bitsy bikini most of the time. In the end, he'd ordered that she cover up when she wasn't swimming, mostly for his own frustration's sake but partly because he was sick to death of the ogling of other males on the beach. She'd given him a droll look and totally ignored him.

Max realised at that point that she might never obey any of his orders ever again. The jury was still out on whether he liked that idea, or not.

Still, she'd had some jealousy of her own to contend with. His own ego had been benefiting from some serious stroking with the looks he'd been getting from the local ladies, the mirror telling him that his less hectic and more outdoor lifestyle was suiting him.

He was going to hate having to give it up.

But why would you *have* to? his brain piped up. You're a very wealthy man. And a smart one. Surely you can work something out. If you downsize the hotel chain the way you're going to, the demands on your personal time will be lessened. With all the modern communication technology around, you can keep in touch with the world from anywhere. You don't even have to be in Sydney. You could be up here, in one of those houses right over there...

His gaze scanned the various buildings fronting Wamberal Beach. Some were holiday apartment blocks. Some were large homes. But some were simple and rather small beach houses, built decades ago. Surely one of those owners could be persuaded to sell. He could have it pulled down and build the home of Tara's dream, with a granny flat for Joyce.

No, no, that wouldn't work. Joyce wouldn't like to be that far away from Jen and her children. She was needed to look after the children after school on the days when Tara's sister was at work.

Max hadn't been the only one to talk this past week. Tara had told him things about her family that she hadn't told him before, possibly because he'd never asked. It was no wonder she thought he was only interested in her body.

Actions *were* louder than words.

Max's brain started ticking away. What time was it? Around seven was his best guess. He had twelve hours before he took Tara out to dinner tonight. Twelve hours before he asked her to marry him again.

He had to have more armoury than romantic words and a two-carat diamond. Flashy gifts and verbal promises wouldn't cut it with Tara. Not any more. He needed proof that he meant what he said. When he took her to bed tonight, he wanted more than his ring on her finger. He wanted her to have faith in their marriage. He wanted her trust that he would be a good husband and father.

Max's heart flipped over when he thought of that last part. He was going to become a father. An enormous responsibility. But also, hopefully, a joyful and satisfying experience. But there would be no true joy or satisfaction unless he could be a hands-on father, not a long-distance one, as his own father had been.

No, this was the place to live and bring up his son or daughter. Max resolved to make it happen, come hell or high water. The trouble was, he had to start making it happen in the next twelve hours.

So much to do, yet so little time.

It would be a challenge all right. But Max liked a challenge more than anything else.

Putting his head down, he caught the next wave to shore and started running towards Kate's place.

Tara rose earlier than usual, courtesy of the wonderful discovery that she didn't feel sick that morning. Not even a small swirl of nausea as she made her way from the bed to the bathroom.

It was a good omen, she believed.

The agreed week was over and Max was not planning to sweep her back to Sydney today, as she had feared he might. Yesterday afternoon he'd said he was happy to stay on till Sunday.

Of course, possibly that was because Kate had announced earlier at brunch that she herself was off to Sydney today for a family reunion at her niece's home, and would not be returning till Sunday morning.

Tara had no doubt Max would claim his reward tonight, either in his bed or in hers. No doubt also that once she was in his arms and vulnerable to his will, he was sure to ask her to marry him again. After a week of being with him and not being able to touch him, Tara suspected she would be extra vulnerable tonight. Her forbidding any physical contact this past week had been hard on her as well. Jen had always complained that when she was pregnant, she couldn't stand sex. It seemed with Tara it was just the opposite.

She stepped into the shower and began to lather up her hair with shampoo. But her mind was still on tonight, not her ablutions.

What would she say to Max when he proposed again? What *could* she say? He was the father of her baby, the man she loved. Her answer was probably a foregone conclusion. She knew that. She'd always known that. Her escape up here was just a temporary gesture of defiance.

Yet it had been worth it. She'd regained some control over her life and shown Max she was not a pushover, or weak. And she'd seen a side to Max which had surprised and pleased her. He *was* capable of not living and breathing his work. He was even capable of enjoying life like an ordinary, everyday person.

He loved surfing. And was surprisingly good at it. He was also learning to love books. Soon, he'd be as addicted to reading as she was. She'd also shown him that you didn't have to eat cordon bleu cuisine at five-star restaurants to enjoy eating out. Each evening, she'd insisted they go to one of the local community-based clubs where the meals were quite cheap, often buffet-style for a set price. At one place, they'd had a roast dinner—with a free glass of beer thrown in—for eight dollars each. Max had been amazed, both at the price and the reasonable quality of the food.

But had his pleasure and co-operation this past week been real, or a con?

The truth was Tara still did not totally trust Max to be the kind of husband she wanted. Or the kind of father for their baby. In the past week, her baby had become very real to her. She loved him or her already and refused to subject her precious child to a life full of neglect and insecurity. Money alone did not bring happiness.

If Max couldn't provide the kind of secure family life she wanted for her child, then she just might have to say no to any proposal of marriage. *If* she could find the courage.

It was nine o'clock before Tara made it downstairs, taking time to blow-dry her hair and put some make-up on. She found Kate in her large, cosy kitchen, sitting at her country-style wooden table, having a cup of tea.

'You're up early today,' Kate said on seeing her. 'Feeling better? I'll get you a cuppa.'

'No, don't get up,' Tara returned swiftly. 'I can get it for myself. And yes, I'm feeling much better today. Max still surfing, I presume?'

'Actually, no, he's gone.'

Tara spun round from where she'd already crossed to the kitchen counter. 'Gone? Gone where?'

'To Sydney, he said. On business. But don't worry. He promised he'd be back in plenty of time to take you out for dinner this evening.'

A huge wave of disappointment swamped Tara. 'And there I was,' she muttered, 'thinking he'd been genuinely enjoying himself surfing every morning. But I was fooling myself. And he was fooling me.'

'No, I don't think that's the case, Tara. He did go surfing early, as usual. But he came racing back here shortly after seven, saying he had some urgent things he had to do in Sydney before tonight.'

'Such as what?' she snapped.

'He didn't say.'

'No. No, he wouldn't have. That's the old Max I grew to know and love,' she said sarcastically. 'Some business brainstorm probably struck out of the blue and he was off.'

'It might not have been *business* business, Tara, but personal business. He's probably gone to Sydney to buy you an engagement ring. How could he ask you to marry him over dinner tonight without a ring?'

'Now, why didn't I think of that?' Tara said, still with a bitter edge to her voice. 'I'm sure you're right, Kate. But trust me, he'll do business business as well whilst he's there.'

'And is that so very wrong? He is responsible for running a huge chain of international hotels, Tara. It could not have been easy for him to drop everything as you asked for a whole week. I'm sure the main thing on Max's mind today is tonight. Just before he left, he asked me to book a table for two at the best restaurant around. I chose Jardines. Very romantic place overlooking Terrigal.'

Tara sighed and shook her head at Kate. 'He's won you over too, hasn't he? Charmed you, as he did my mother. And now you're doing his bidding, as he expects all women to do. God, but we're both fools.'

'I have never been a fool where men are concerned, my dear,' Kate said with steel in her voice. 'I can always see them for what they are, once I have had the time to observe them properly. I have to confess that my first impression of Max was not too favourable. But then, I had been biased by the fact that you had run away from him. I had been ready to think poorly of him. He didn't help his cause, either, by being a tad arrogant and impatient with me that first day. But I now see your Max for what he really is. Basically, a good man. A decent man. A man willing to do anything to win back the woman he loves. That is a man in a million, my dear. A man to be treasured, not hastily condemned. Wait and see what it is he's up to today before you pass judgement. I think you might be pleasantly surprised.'

Tara decided not to argue with Kate any more. No point. Kate could never know Max as well as she did. Clearly, he'd been on his best behaviour this past week, all with a purpose. Max had a mission, which was to pull the wool over both Kate's and Tara's eyes and get what he wanted. Her, back being his *yes* girl.

Max might not realise it but he'd just made a huge tactical error in going back to Sydney without even speaking to her. By falling back into his old patterns of behaviour, he'd shown her that he hadn't really changed. He was just as selfish and inconsiderate as ever.

Kate stood up and carried her cup and saucer over to load it into the dishwasher. 'I have to get going, love,' she said as she poured in some dishwashing powder then set the machine in motion. 'I'm sure Max will ring you later and explain. You wait and see.'

Tara nodded and smiled, but the moment Kate was gone she marched over to where Kate kept her phone on the wall in the kitchen and took it off the hook. If and when Max did ring, he would not get the satisfaction of a reply. He would be the one who would have to wait and see. Then, when he eventually arrived back, he was in for a big surprise!

CHAPTER THIRTEEN

MAX had been frustrated by his inability to ring Tara all day. The phone company said Kate's phone was off the hook. He tried telling himself this was probably accidental. Kate was an older lady after all. Some older ladies did things like that.

Still, it worried him. And so he hurried. As much as he could. But visiting everyone concerned and selling them on his ideas was not a quick or easy task. It took him most of the day.

Between times, he rang every real-estate agency on the central coast, making enquiries about properties for sale in Wamberal. By four that afternoon, he was back at the penthouse to freshen up and have a quick bite to eat. By four-thirty he was on the road again, heading north towards Wamberal Beach.

The tightness in his stomach became more pronounced the closer he got. Perhaps if Kate had been there with Tara, he might not have felt so agitated. Kate was on his side now. He could see that. But the dear old thing had gone to a family do, leaving Tara alone.

The possibility that Tara had deliberately taken the phone off the hook gnawed away at him. She'd done it once before, hadn't she, when she'd run away? The thought haunted him that she might not be there when he got back.

He should have knocked on her bedroom door this morning and spoken to her personally. But he hadn't wanted to disturb her. Still, he'd left a message for her with Kate, hadn't he?

Hadn't he?

Max tried to recall what he'd actually said.

Not much, he finally realised. Not *enough*.

When would he ever learn? He should have at least written her a personal note.

'Damn and blast,' he muttered, and put his foot down.

But then he remembered what Tara had said about speeding and he slowed down to the limit again.

It was just on six as he turned into Kate's place. There was no gate to open and he followed the gravel driveway round the back of the house, where there were several guest parking bays. The sun was low in the sky and the house looked quiet. Too quiet.

But the back door wasn't locked. Max heaved a huge sigh of relief...till he saw Tara's bag sitting in the front hallway.

A black pit opened up in his stomach. She was leaving.

'Tara?' he called out.

No answer. He checked the downstairs rooms, but she wasn't in any of them. He took the stairs two at a time, his heart thudding behind his ribs. She wasn't in her bedroom, or in the nearby common room, which was a combination television-sitting room with sliding glass doors that led out onto a wide upper deck.

It was there that he found her, standing at the railing, staring out towards the ocean horizon. His heart caught at how beautiful she looked, with her long blonde hair blowing back in the sea breeze and her skin a warm golden colour from their week up here. She was wearing a simple floral sun-dress with tiny straps and very little back. Fawn sandals covered her bare feet.

'Tara,' he said softly.

She turned and his heart caught again. Never had he seen such sadness in her lovely eyes. Such despair.

'I was going to go before you got back,' she said brokenly. 'I wanted to. Oh, how I wanted to! But in the end, I couldn't. I love you too much, Max. I've always loved you too much.'

When her head dropped into her hands and she began to sob, Max just stood there, appalled. Guilt consumed him that he had brought her to this. But then he stepped forward and put his arms around her shaking shoulders, buoyed by the thought that she would feel happier about loving him once she knew what he had done.

She sagged against him, still weeping.

His heart filled to overflowing as he held her close. Maybe she *did* love him too much. But he loved her just as much. Hell, he was willing to change his whole life for her.

'There, there,' he soothed, and began stroking her hair down her back.

She shuddered, then wrenched herself away from him. Her face jerked up to his, tear-stained but defiant.

'Oh, no, Max. You don't get away with things as easily as that. For once, I want you to explain yourself. I want to know exactly what you've been doing today, every single moment. And don't think you can con your way out of things by telling me you went shopping for an engagement ring. That's what Kate thought, the poor deluded woman. And it might even be true. But that would have taken you all of ten minutes. I can see it now. You'd stride into a jewellery shop and tell the fawning female shop assistant to give you the biggest and the best diamond ring they had.'

Max was ruefully amused by her description of his shopping excursion for a ring. It was startlingly accurate. If the situation wasn't so serious, he might even have laughed.

'You're right and you're wrong, Tara. I did do that,' he confessed. 'But not today. I bought a two-carat rock a week ago. It's been up here in my room all week, waiting to be produced on cue tonight. But I took it back to Sydney today and left it there.'

She blinked, then just stared at him.

'I'm not the same man who bought that ring, Tara. During this past week I realised I didn't want to play lord and master with you any more. That is what Joyce and Jen used to call me, isn't it? For one thing, I want to take you shopping for a ring and let you pick something *you* like. If you'll still have me, that is.'

'That depends, doesn't it?' she said with a proud toss of her head. 'So what *were* you doing all day today?' she demanded to know. 'As if I don't know. You're back to wearing a business suit. That speaks for itself.'

'I'm wearing a business suit because I spent most of the day in serious negotiations. With your family.'

Tara's mouth fell open.

'You would have already known this if you hadn't taken the phone off the hook. I've been trying to ring you all afternoon. Your mother tried to ring you as well. When the number was engaged, I told her Kate was a real chatterbox to stop her from worrying. But I already suspected what you'd done. I promised to get you to ring her once you knew the good news.'

Tara looked perplexed. 'And what good news would that be?'

'Firstly, I've decided to downsize the Royale chain of hotels. The hotels in Europe will be sold as soon as I can get a reasonable price. But I will go through with the purchase of the hotel in Auckland. I'll also keep our three Asian hotels for now. We'd lose too much if we sold those at this point in time. On top of that, it doesn't take as long to fly over to them. Not that I intend doing as much travelling as I once did. I will be delegating more in future. Naturally, I'll keep the Regency Royale in Sydney, and the penthouse. It's always wise to have a Sydney base. And it will make a good place for breaks away.'

'Breaks away from where?' Tara was looking even more perplexed.

'I'm going to buy a house up here for us to live in. *If* you agree to marry me, of course,' he swiftly added, having to remind himself all the time to keep consulting her feelings. This was the most difficult change for him to embrace. He was too used to being the boss, in not having to consult anyone when making decisions.

'It all came to me when I was out surfing this morning,' he charged on. 'What better place to raise a family, I thought, than Wamberal? Of course, I realised straight away that living up here could cause some logistical problems. You'd be a long way from your mother, and your sister. I, too, would be a long way from *my* parents, who I was surprised to find I really want as part of my life again. Poor old things need my help. Hands-on help. I visited them again this morning and realised my mother could not cope alone much longer. There was only one logical solution. They would all have to move up here, lock, stock and barrel.'

'*All* of them? Move up here?'

'Yep. That's what I've been doing today. Putting that plan into action. Not an easy task to accomplish in so short a time, but I managed to at least get it off the ground.'

'You're not joking, are you?'

'Not at all. Would I joke about something like that?

You know, I was surprised just how many places there are on the market up here. We have oodles to choose from. We might not even have to do too much renovating. I was suitably impressed, I can tell you. So what do you think? Are you happy with that idea?'

'What? Why, yes, yes, it's a wonderful idea. But Max…' She reached out to touch his arm. 'Are you really sure that this is what you want?' As her eyes searched his, her surprise changed to wariness, and her hand dropped away. 'You're not just doing this to get me to marry you, are you? I won't wake up after the wedding to find you've changed your mind about all this, will I?'

'Come, now, Tara. Would I be foolish enough to do that? No, my darling, this is what I want, too,' he reassured, taking both her hands in his. 'This last week up here with you has taught me so much. You've made me see how much I've been missing with my crazy, jet-setting lifestyle. I don't want to end up like my father. That's something I vowed I would never do. I want to be an integral part of my family's life, not just living on the fringes of it. I want to be a good husband and father. I don't want to just give lip-service to the roles.'

A strange little smile played around her lips. 'Some lip-service wouldn't go astray at this point in time,' she murmured.

Max stared into her glittering green eyes, the sexual message in her words distracting him from any further verbal persuasion. Instead, he lifted her hands to his mouth, his eyes never leaving hers as he kissed each knuckle in turn.

'Your wish,' he whispered between kisses, 'is my command.'

'No, your wish is *my* command today. Remember?'

'I'm so glad you reminded me.' He placed her arms up around his neck then bent to scoop her up into his arms. 'Your room or mine?'

She smiled. 'Surprise me.'

'No, don't leave me yet,' Tara pleaded, and pulled Max back down into her arms.

They were in the room where Max had slept alone all week, in the bed where she'd wanted to be every single night.

Oh, how she'd missed him; how she'd missed this.

Her arms tightened around him.

'But I'm heavy,' Max protested. 'Are you sure this won't hurt the baby?'

'Of course not. He's only tiny yet.'

Max levered himself up onto his elbows. '*He?* It might be a girl.'

'No. It's a boy.'

He smiled. 'You could be wrong.'

'I could be. But I'm not.'

He shook his head. 'Your mother said you were stubborn. Which reminds me. I haven't called her yet. Don't go away, now.'

Tara moaned in soft protest when he withdrew.

He bent down to kiss her on the lips, then on each breast before straightening. 'Now, don't you dare cover up. I want you to stay exactly as you are.'

She lay there, happily compliant, whilst Max scrambled off the bed.

'Who dropped all these clothes on the floor?' he complained as he swept up his trousers.

'You did,' she told him, ogling him shamelessly as he stood there in the buff, rifling through his pockets.

There was no doubt that the week up here had done him good in more ways than one. He was looking great.

'I put your mum's number in the memory,' he explained as he whisked out his cellphone and pressed a few buttons.

'Joyce? It's Max. Yes, I'm with Tara and she's thrilled to pieces... What? Oh, yes, she said yes... You did say yes to marrying me, darling, didn't you?' he asked as he lay back down beside her on the bed, making her gasp when his free hand slid between her still-parted legs. 'Yes, she can't wait till you're all living up here... Yes, you're so right... Would you like to talk to her, Joyce? Yep, she's right here. Champing at the bit.'

Tara flushed all over as he handed over the phone.

'Mum,' she said somewhat breathlessly. Max was right. She *was* champing at the bit. But not for conversation with her mother.

'Isn't Max marvellous?' her mother was saying whilst Tara struggled to ignore the sensations Max was evoking. 'He's going to get me a little house close to yours. And he's going to back Dale in a plumbing business. *And* he's going to give them an interest-free loan for a house. He wanted to buy them one outright but Jen and Dale didn't want that. They want to pay their own way.'

Tara did her best to make all the right remarks whilst her mother rattled on. But it was difficult to concentrate on her mother's revelations about Max's generosity whilst the man himself was doing what he did oh, so well.

OK, so Kate had been right. Max was basically a good man. But he could also be downright wicked.

She had to bite her tongue to stop herself from crying out on one occasion. But she was doing some serious squirming. In the end, she couldn't stand it any more. She had to get her mother off the phone.

'Mum, I hate to cut and run but Max made an early reservation for dinner and I haven't even started getting dressed yet.' And wasn't *that* the truth!

'I understand,' Joyce trilled. 'You'll want to make yourself look extra-nice tonight. Ring me tomorrow, would you, and we'll have a nice long talk?'

'Will do, Mum. And tell Jen I'll ring her, too.'

'Oh, yes. Do that. She's very excited. And so are the kids. They just love the idea of living near a beach.'

'Must go, Mum,' she said through gritted teeth.

She pressed the phone off just as Max's head lifted.

'Don't you mean you must come?' he quipped when she clicked the phone shut and tossed it away.

'You're a sadist,' she threw at him. 'Oh, God, don't stop.'

He grinned down at her. 'This is my night, remember? Don't go telling me what to do and what not to do.'

'Yes, Max,' she said with a sigh.

'Now, first things first. You do agree to marry me, don't you?'

'Yes, Max.'

'And you agree to all my plans.'

'Yes, Max. Except...'

His eyes narrowed on her. 'Except what?'

'Do you think before I have this baby and before you sell all those lovely hotels in Europe, we could go on a trip together and stay in some of them? I have this fantasy about making love in Paris.'

'Are you sure you're well enough to travel?'

'Absolutely. When I woke this morning, there wasn't a trace of morning sickness.'

'In that case, I would love to take you on an overseas trip. We could make it our honeymoon. My fantasies include making love to you in every big city in the world, not just Paris. But first, I think I need to make love to you right here and now.'

Tara sighed when he rolled her onto her side and slid into her from behind, filling her heart as well as her body.

'Oh, Max,' she cried.

He caressed her breasts whilst he kissed her hair, her ear, her shoulder. 'Have I made you truly happy today at long last, my love?'

'Oh, yes.'

'You will tell me in future if and when I'm doing something wrong. I want to make you happy, Tara.'

'I'm very happy,' she choked out. 'Ooh. I really like making love this way. I think it's my favourite.'

'That's good, because we'll be doing it a lot like this in future. I looked up all the websites on pregnancy last Friday night and came across this really interesting one which listed all the safest and most comfortable positions for making love during a pregnancy. This was number one. We can do it like this till well into the last trimester.'

'There are others?' she said, her voice having taken on a faraway sound.

'There's something for every occasion, and every stage of your pregnancy.' His hands dropped down to caress her belly. 'Frankly, I can't wait till this is all big with my baby.'

'You won't find it unattractive?'

'Are you kidding? It's a real turn-on, touching you like this, knowing my child is inside there. And then there's your breasts. They're already larger, you know.'

'Yes. And very sensitive.'

'So I noticed.'

She gasped when he gave the distended tips a gentle tug.

'I… I seem to be more sensitive all round,' she said. 'My body as well as my emotions. I'm going to need a lot of loving, Max.'

'Don't worry. You'll be loved. But slowly, my love.

And gently. We don't want to do anything which might put the baby at risk.'

'No, of course not,' she said, still slightly amazed at how much he wanted this child. 'Do you want more children after this, Max?'

'If this pregnancy is anything to go by, I think I'll keep you having babies for quite a few years. I've never seen you look more beautiful or more sexy than you looked today when I saw you out on that veranda.' He didn't add that he'd never seen her look sadder.

Max vowed that he would never let her look that sad again.

'What about names?' he said. 'Have you picked out any names?'

'No. I thought I'd wait and see what he looks like first.'

'Or what *she* looks like.'

'I told you. It's a boy. Only a boy would cause so much trouble.'

'True.'

'Max…you've stopped moving.'

'If I move, I'll be history. I got myself over-excited.'

Tara laughed. 'In that case, we'll just talk for a while till you calm down.'

'Good idea.'

'Max…'

'Mmm?'

'I want to thank you…for all you did today. I can't tell you how much it means to me that you would go to so much trouble to make me happy.'

'My pleasure, princess.'

'Mum sounded ecstatic as well. I'm sure Jen and Dale are, too. You've been very generous. And I think it's really sweet that you're getting along so well with your folks now. I'll have to go and meet them soon.'

'How about tomorrow?'

'Tomorrow would be fine. What time is it now? We're supposed to be going out to dinner tonight, remember?'

'It's only five to seven,' Max said with a quick glance at his watch. 'How long will it take you to get dressed?'

'Not long.'

'In that case, I think we've talked long enough, don't you think?'

'Absolutely.'

Everyone was relocated to Wamberal before the wedding, which took place on Wamberal Beach in August. Tara was an unashamedly pregnant bride, wearing an original gown that Max had bought her in Paris. They'd enjoyed a two-month pre-wedding holiday travelling all around Europe. Their actual honeymoon was spent at home, decorating the nursery in their comparatively modest new house. Max and Tara had decided together that they wanted a simple lifestyle for their family.

Their son was born a week late. A beautiful, placid, happy baby. They named him Stevie.

Celebrating Our Authors

MORE ABOUT THE BOOKS

MORE ABOUT THE AUTHOR

WE RECOMMEND

Celebrating Our Authors

MIRANDA LEE ON
The Guardian's Forbidden Mistress and *The Magnate's Mistress*

When I first started reading Mills & Boon® romances, there were certain themes which appealed to me more than others. I always enjoyed what I called "Guardian plots", where an older, more experienced man-of-the-world had a beautiful young ward whom he was supposed to care for and protect, but whom he secretly desired. I loved reading about his doomed struggle to keep his hands off the girl, all the while wanting to reassure him that it was all right because she already loved him. It is a story-line which creates great sexual tension, as well as highly charged sex scenes. I have only ever written this theme once before, in a book called *Mistress of Deception*, so felt it was high time for a second go, this time incorporating another pet love of mine, which is the bad-boy-made-good hero. I thoroughly enjoyed writing *The Guardian's Forbidden Mistress*, and hope you enjoy reading it.

The Magnate's Mistress was written a couple of years ago, shortly after my mother died. I came to that book with a heavy heart and escaped into the pages of a story which I thought at the time was wickedly sexy and highly entertaining. I still think that. But when I re-read this book recently, I discovered that some of my subconscious feelings at the time had snuck in. The hero-ine's mother, I noticed, was misunderstood by her daughter, who could not see that her mother only ever had her best interests at heart. The hero also judged his parents

> "...It is a story-line which creates great sexual tension..."

harshly, as children so often do. But everything ended very happily, unlike real life. Maybe that's why romances are so popular. Because there are no sad endings.

Celebrating Our Authors

AUTHOR BIOGRAPHY

I was born in Port Macquarie, which is a lovely seaside town on the mid North Coast of New South Wales, Australia. My father was a school-teacher and brilliant sportsman, my mother a beautiful woman and a marvellous dressmaker. When my mother asked the midwife what I looked like, she said, "Well, she'd make a good boy." Very encouraging for a future romance writer! I nevertheless grew up into an attractive enough girl with blue eyes, and thick, dark wavy hair. I suspect I do have a few too many male hormones, however, as I have a very competitive streak and what my sister calls a killer instinct. As a child, I was very much into outdoor activity and excelled in most sports.

I didn't discover the joy of reading till I was fifteen. But it wasn't romance which turned me on. I devoured every action thriller and murder mystery I could get my hands on. After leaving school – a convent boarding school which shall remain nameless – I briefly tried a career as a cellist before a personality clash with my teacher had me turning my back on a musical life, and embracing the world of computers. I joined IBM in Sydney where my two brothers and older sister already worked. I married my own personal hero when I was only twenty and was a mother by twenty-three. By thirty I had three daughters and had left work to become a stay-at-home housewife, living on a semi-rural property with several dogs, many angora goats and a horse or two.

" … I married my own personal hero when I was only twenty … "

The desire to earn some money of my own, plus my sister's success at writing romances

– you will know her as Emma Darcy – led me to try this same career. Unfortunately, I didn't have my sister's natural writing skill. Neither did I know enough about what was required in a romance. I had read only a few and naively thought they lacked action. I intended to change the genre. Alas, I was in for a long and difficult journey to success. Several years, and many rejections, later I was finally accepted by Harlequin Mills & Boon and my first book, *After the Affair,* was published in 1990. Since then I have had over seventy books published.

During these years, my daughters grew up and left home. But I am proud to say that I am still happily married to my hero. We have three beautiful grandchildren and lots to be grateful for. Hopefully, I will continue to write romances for many years to come. It is a rewarding and satisfying career, especially when you hear from the readers you have given pleasure to.

MIRANDA LEE ON WRITING

What do you love most about being a writer?

Being able to go to work in my dressing-gown. Being paid for doing something I enjoy. Being my own boss. Being told by a twelve-year-old fan once that I was the "bestest" author in the world.

Where do you go for inspiration?

Into the deepest recesses of my mind, which teems with endless stories and ideas, which might be original, or possibly regurgitated from all the movies I've seen, and the thousands of books that I have read. My imagination seems limitless, especially when it comes to dreaming up sex scenes and sexual fantasies. I attribute some of this to those tiresome years I spent in that convent boarding school when boys were *verboten*, and sex a dirty word. It's amazing how fascinating a subject becomes when it is forbidden!

I have occasionally taken a setting from places where I have been, but never the plots. I never, ever rely on real life or real people for inspiration. For me, that would be the kiss of death. Of course, one must try to make one's story *seem* like real life. And occasionally real life does bob up in a chapter or two. But on the whole, my stories are strictly works of my vivid imagination.

Where do your characters come from and do they ever surprise you as you write?

Once again, my characters are always creations of my mind. I do occasionally have a picture of a movie star or someone in a magazine to help with physical features, but that's all. I rarely base any of my characters on real people. My characters are created to fit the conflict I have chosen. I give them descriptions to suit (eg, a sheikh's heroine is always a blonde). Personalities and ages to suit. Backgrounds to suit. I also choose a name which suits. That is most crucial. I like soft sounding names for most heroines and strong, masculine names for my heroes. I would never have a heroine called Erica. Or a hero named Nigel. Do my characters ever surprise me? Occasionally, but not too often. My plotline sometimes surprises me, taking a twist I wasn't expecting. If something more exciting occurs to me along the way, I am quite happy to change courses, provided I end at the same place. I always know my ending before I start.

Do you have a favourite character that you've created and what is it that you like about that character?

Hard question. I try to temporarily wipe my mind clean of past plots and characters whenever I start a new book, so my favourite character is usually in the book I'm work-ing on. Unless I find I'm not liking the book I'm working on, which is a worry. I had to abandon a book recently after a few chapters because I just didn't like any of the characters. I deleted the whole thing in one press of a button. Yep, I'm a Scorpio. Scorpios can be like that. Ruthless!

One character which stands out for me, however, is the hero in *The Passion Price*. Another bad-boy-made-good, Jake Winters is a man who does everything right for the heroine in my eyes. It is the one story I've

'...Writing is a profession that is as difficult as brain surgery...'

written which still brings me to tears, especially in the scene when his son swims the last leg in a relay, and wins against all the odds. This is the theme of Jake's story. He wins, against all the odds. *The Passion Price* didn't sell all that well for some reason. I think the title didn't grab the readers. But if you haven't read it, I suggest you try to get a copy. It was a finalist in the Australian Romance Book of the Year.

When did you start writing?

In 1981. I sent off my first manuscript in 1982. I was finally accepted in December 1988, and that book came out in 1990.

What one piece of advice would you give a writer wanting to start a career?

Don't expect instant success, no matter how good a writer you think you are. Writing is a profession that is as difficult as brain surgery. You wouldn't expect to operate on a patient's brain after a few months' apprenticeship, would you? Put in the hard yards and you will succeed. Above all, never give up. My husband – who had a training in sales – always said to me (during my rejection years) that submitting a book is like knocking on a door in search of a sale. If you keep knocking, then one day, that door will open, and some-one will buy your book.

What are you currently working on?

The story of two characters whom you will meet if and when you read *Blackmailed into the Italian's Bed*, which will come out soon. The heroine is called Sharni, a rather tragic figure who lost her husband and baby in an acci-dent. The hero is called Adrian, a successful architect who just happens to be the exact physical double of her dead husband. It is called *The Millionaire's Inexperienced Love-Slave.*

A DAY IN THE LIFE

I don't have a typical day as I have lots of unexpected demands on my time with family and grandchildren and various other activities which I enjoy, such as bowls. If it is a day set aside for writing, however, I am usually at my computer by nine, work through till lunchtime, then back to work all afternoon till about four-thirty or five, when I knock off to have a glass of wine – or two – and watch game shows on television. Occasionally, if I am on a deadline, I might return to write into the wee small hours of the morning. To relax I enjoy going down to a local club for dinner and a flutter on the poker machines. I don't cook much as my darling husband does that. Lucky me!

"…If I am on a deadline, I might return to write into the wee small hours of the morning…"

Celebrating Our Authors

MIRANDA LEE'S FUTURE PROJECTS

I am going to write a trilogy next, set around wealthy marriages. I haven't explored the details as yet but I've always liked the theme of shattered marriages. The title of the first book is *The Billionaire's Bride of Vengeance*. I like revenge in stories too, though it is a difficult emotion to bring off with credibility in a romance.

If you enjoyed *The Guardian's Forbidden Mistress,* and like your romances hot, we know you'll enjoy these great reads!

The Markonos Bride by Michelle Reid

Still married – in the bedroom…

The Greek island of Aristos holds bittersweet memories for Louisa: here she met gorgeous Greek playboy Andreas Markonos – the man who changed her life. After a whirlwind romance they married, and Louisa gave Andreas a precious son. But when tragedy struck Louisa was compelled to leave her handsome husband, and the beautiful Aegean island she'd come to call home…

Now, five years later, Andreas can't believe that his runaway wife has dared show her face on Aristos again! But seeing Louisa once more makes him realise how much he desires her still. Their separation has lasted long enough! Andreas will reclaim his wife with the one thing that they continue to share…intense physical passion!

On sale from 2nd May 2008!

The Millionaire's Inexperienced Love-Slave by Miranda Lee

One wicked night with the Sydney millionaire…

Adrian Palmer's success as a millionaire architect was all-consuming – though he always made sure he had a beautiful female warming his bed. Perhaps he *was* the workaholic womaniser his last conquest had accused him of being…?

When he met Sharni Johnson he should have held back. The young widow was shy, pretty and unsophisticated – perfect for his wicked brand of seduction. And wicked it was; Adrian's mind was blown by the passion and intensity of their lovemaking. But Sharni was not the kind of girl to have a one-night stand…

When she fled back to her Blue Mountain home, he followed her. He had to have her, again and again, and without mercy. But this wasn't just a simple affair that would burn itself out – and Adrian just couldn't get over the fact that he was the spitting image of Sharni's late husband…

On sale from 6th June 2008!

0408/05a

100ᵗʰ Birthday Prize Draw!

£500 worth of prizes to be won every month. Now that's worth celebrating!

To enter, simply visit **www.millsandboon.co.uk**,
click through to the prize draw entry page and quote
promotional code **CEN080404**

Alternatively, complete the entry form below and send to:
Mills & Boon® 100ᵗʰ Birthday Prize Draw
PO Box 676, Richmond, Surrey, TW9 1WU

Mills & Boon® 100th Birthday Prize Draw (CEN080404)

Name: _____

Address: _____

Post Code: _____

Daytime Telephone No: _____

E-mail Address: _____

❏ I have read the terms and conditions (please tick this box before entering).

❏ Please tick here if you do not wish to receive special offers from
  Harlequin Mills & Boon Ltd.

Closing date for entries is 15ᵗʰ May 2008

Terms & Conditions

1. Draw open to UK and Eire residents aged 18 and over. No purchase necessary. One entry per household per prize draw only. 2. Prizes are non-transferable and no cash alternatives will be offered. 3. All prizes are subject to availability. Should any prize be unavailable, a prize of similar value will be substituted. 4. Employees and immediate family members of Harlequin Mills & Boon Ltd are not eligible to enter. 5. Prize winners will be randomly selected from the eligible entries received. No correspondence will be entered into and no entry returned. 6. To be eligible, all entries must be received by 15ᵗʰ May 2008. 7. Prize winner notification will be made by e-mail or letter no later than 15 days after the deadline for entry. 8. No responsibility can be accepted for entries that are lost, delayed or damaged. Proof of postage cannot be accepted as proof of delivery. 9. If any winner notification or prize is returned as undeliverable, an alternative winner will be drawn from eligible entries. 10. Names of competition winners are available on request. 11. See www.millsandboon.co.uk for full terms and conditions.

Celebrate 100 years of pure reading pleasure with Mills & Boon®

To mark our centenary, each month we're publishing a special 100th Birthday Edition. These celebratory editions are packed with extra features and include a FREE bonus story.

Plus, starting in February you'll have the chance to enter a fabulous monthly prize draw. See 100th Birthday Edition books for details.

Now that's worth celebrating!

15th February 2008

Raintree: Inferno by Linda Howard
Includes FREE bonus story Loving Evangeline
A double dose of Linda Howard's heady mix of passion and adventure

4th April 2008

The Guardian's Forbidden Mistress by Miranda Lee
Includes FREE bonus story The Magnate's Mistress
Two glamorous and sensual reads from favourite author Miranda Lee!

2nd May 2008

The Last Rake in London by Nicola Cornick
Includes FREE bonus story The Notorious Lord
Lose yourself in two tales of high society and rakish seduction!

Look for Mills & Boon 100th Birthday Editions at your favourite bookseller or visit www.millsandboon.co.uk

0108/CENTENARY_2-IN-1

4 FREE

BOOKS AND A SURPRISE GIFT!

We would like to take this opportunity to thank you for reading this Mills & Boon® book by offering you the chance to take FOUR more specially selected titles from the Modern™ series absolutely FREE! We're also making this offer to introduce you to the benefits of the Mills & Boon® Reader Service™—

- ★ **FREE home delivery**
- ★ **FREE gifts and competitions**
- ★ **FREE monthly Newsletter**
- ★ **Exclusive Reader Service offers**
- ★ **Books available before they're in the shops**

Accepting these FREE books and gift places you under no obligation to buy, you may cancel at any time, even after receiving your free shipment. Simply complete your details below and return the entire page to the address below. You don't even need a stamp!

YES! Please send me 4 free Modern books and a surprise gift. I understand that unless you hear from me, I will receive 6 superb new titles every month for just £2.99 each, postage and packing free. I am under no obligation to purchase any books and may cancel my subscription at any time. The free books and gift will be mine to keep in any case.

P8ZED

Ms/Mrs/Miss/Mr .... Initials ....

BLOCK CAPITALS PLEASE

Surname ....

Address ....

....

.... Postcode ....

Send this whole page to:
UK: FREEPOST CN81, Croydon, CR9 3WZ